NEWCOMER

BY KEIGO HIGASHINO

THE DETECTIVE GALILEO MYSTERIES

The Devotion of Suspect X

Salvation of a Saint

A Midsummer's Equation

THE KYOICHIRO KAGA MYSTERIES

Malice

Newcomer

Under the Midnight Sun

NEWCOMER

Keigo Higashino

Translated by Giles Murray

Minotaur Books

New York

This is a work of fiction. All of the characters, organizations, and events portrayed in this novel are either products of the author's imagination or are used fictitiously.

Published in the United States by Minotaur Books, an imprint of St. Martin's Publishing Group

www.minotaurbooks.com

Designed by Omar Chapa

The Library of Congress has cataloged the hardcover edition as follows:

Names: Higashino, Keigo, 1958– author. | Murray, Giles, translator.
Title: Newcomer : a mystery / Keigo Higashino ; translated by Giles Murray.
Other titles: Shinzanmono. English
Description: First U.S. edition. | New York : Minotaur Books, 2018.
Identifiers: LCCN 2018022774 | ISBN 9781250067869 (hardcover) | ISBN 9781466876538 (ebook)
Classification: LCC PL852.I3625 S5613 2018 | DDC 895.63/6—dc23
LC record available at https://lccn.loc.gov/2018022774

ISBN 978-1-250-23540-4 (trade paperback)

Originally published in Japan as *Shinzanmono* by Kodansha, Ltd.

First Minotaur Books Paperback Edition: November 2019

10 9 8 7 6 5 4 3 2 1

CONTENTS

CAST OF CHARACTERS

Mineko Mitsui — victim

Kyoichiro Kaga — detective, Nihonbashi Precinct

OMAKARA, THE RICE CRACKER SHOP

Satoko Kamikawa — grandmother

Naho Kamikawa — granddaughter

Fumitaka Kamikawa — son of Satoko and father of Naho

Shinichi Takura — insurance agent

MATSUYA, A TRADITIONAL JAPANESE RESTAURANT

Yoriko — manager and co-owner

Taiji — co-owner with his wife, Yoriko

Shuhei — apprentice

Katsuya — apprentice

YANAGISAWA'S CHINA SHOP

Naoya Yanagisawa — husband and son

Maki Yanagisawa — wife and daughter-in-law
Suzue Yanagisawa — mother and mother-in-law

TERADA'S CLOCK SHOP
Genichi Terada — owner of the shop
Shimako Terada — wife of Genichi
Kanae Terada — daughter of Genichi and Shimako
Akifumi Yoneoka — apprentice

QUATTRO, A PASTRY SHOP
Miyuki — clerk
Reiko Nakanishi — manager
Kenichi — Miyuki's partner

HOZUKIYA, A HANDICRAFTS SHOP
Masayo Fujiyama — owner
Misaki Sugawara — part-time worker

Koki Kiyose — son of the victim
Naohiro Kiyose — ex-husband of the victim
Tamiko Yoshioka — translator and friend of the victim
Yuri Miyamoto — new secretary to Naohiro Kiyose
Yosaku Kishida — accountant to Naohiro Kiyose
Hiroshi Uesugi — detective, Tokyo Metropolitan Police, Homicide Division

1

THE GIRL AT THE RICE CRACKER SHOP

1.

"Thank goodness it's finally a bit cooler. It's only June, for goodness' sake."

Emerging from the back of the shop, Satoko began rearranging the packets of rice crackers on the shelves.

"You just got out of the hospital, Grandma. You shouldn't be running around so much. Dad will give me a hard time if he sees you carrying on like this." Naho frowned.

"It's okay, really. I'm better now. That's why the hospital let me come home. It's back to business as usual. You know that old saying about how people who don't work have no right to eat? It won't be long before you'll have to stand on your own two feet."

"Oh God, not that again." Naho crammed a piece of mayonnaise-flavored rice cracker into her mouth.

Satoko peered into her granddaughter's face.

"But my, you do love your rice crackers. I know it's the family business and all that, but you've been eating those things since the day you were born. How you don't get sick of them I'll never know."

"This is a new flavor."

"New or not, a rice cracker's still just a rice cracker. I can't bear the things myself. They play havoc with my teeth."

"Then why did you spend fifty years running a rice cracker store?"

"Like I've told you before, Naho, we only started selling rice crackers thirty years ago. We used to sell Japanese sweets until your father decided to switch to rice crackers. Gosh, I still miss those sweet bean jellies."

"Miss them?" said Naho, pursing her lips. "How? You're always eating the things."

Just then, a plump man in a gray suit opened the glass door and entered the store.

"Hello, all," he sang out cheerfully, giving a little bow.

"Oh, Mr. Takura, thanks for dropping by," said Satoko. "I feel terrible making you go out of your way in this heat."

"That's not a problem. This is my job, after all. Besides, it's already cooled down a lot this afternoon. At noon, it was unbearable."

"You must be exhausted. Come in and I'll fix you a nice cool drink." Satoko motioned him toward the room behind the store. It was the family living room.

"Thank you, but I've just come to pick up that . . . you know." Using the tips of two fingers, Takura sketched a square in the air.

"My medical certificate, you mean? No problem. Naho and I went to the hospital today. I told her I'd be fine by myself, but she insisted on coming along."

Satoko kicked off her sandals.

"It's all right, Grandma. I'll get it." Naho gently edged her grandmother aside and disappeared into the back room.

"You know where it is?" Satoko called out.

"Of course. I'm the one who put it there. You're the one with no idea where anything is."

Her grandmother must have made some sort of comment as Naho heard the sound of laughter behind her.

"Don't forget the tea while you're at it," Satoko yelled.

"Yes, I know."

Naho clucked her tongue. What a nag her grandma was.

She poured out a glass of cold oolong tea, put it on a tray, and went back to the shop. Her grandmother and Mr. Takura were happily chatting away.

"I'm delighted to see you looking so well. When was I last here? Four days ago? You look so much better already." Takura shook his head in amazement.

"Being back home has helped. I feel much better. I get to be up and doing even though Naho's always telling me to take it easy. Such a pest."

"That's only because she's worried about you." Takura reached out and plucked the glass of oolong tea off the tray. "Ah, thank you. It looks delicious."

"Here you go, Grandma."

Naho handed an envelope to Satoko.

"Thanks, dear."

Satoko took a single sheet of paper out of the envelope, glanced over it, and held it out to Takura.

Takura took the document and looked it over.

"Good heavens, you were in the hospital for two whole months? That must have been tough."

"I wouldn't have minded if they'd actually taken care of what I was sent in for, but they didn't do anything about that. Instead, they found out I had something else wrong with me and then spent two whole months treating that. So frustrating."

"The certificate says you had an infection of the bile duct. Oh, what's this here? You also had tests for an aneurysm?"

"The aneurysm's the important thing. I went in to have it operated on, but the operation was postponed."

"But you will have the operation at some point?"

"Apparently, yes. But it's probably better for me just to keep going as long as I can. Operations can be risky at my age."

"I see what you mean. It's a difficult call to make." Takura was looking a little uncomfortable.

"Is the certificate in order?" Satoko asked.

"Yes, along with the documents you gave me the other day, I've got everything I need. I'll go back to the office and process it as fast as I can. Your hospitalization claim will be paid by next month at the latest."

"You're going to go back to the office now? That's terrible."

"Not at all, not at all. Now, if you'll excuse me." Takura put the certificate into his briefcase and smiled at Naho. "Thank you very much for the tea."

"No. Thank you," Naho replied.

Satoko walked Takura to the street and waved to him as he went on his way.

About two hours later, Fumitaka—Satoko's son and Naho's father—got back home. There was grime on the collar of his white polo shirt.

"I was at the rice cracker wholesaler," he said, slipping off his shoes. "On the way back, it looked like something big was going on over at Kodenmacho. There were loads of police cars around. No sign of a car crash or anything like that, though."

"Something serious?" Naho suggested.

"Why else would the cops be all over the place?"

"This area's not safe anymore," declared Satoko, who was in the kitchen tasting the miso soup. "There are just too many newcomers moving into those new apartment complexes."

Fumitaka said nothing. He turned the TV on to watch the baseball game while Naho busied herself with setting the table. The idea that new apartment buildings meant more people—including bad people—moving into the neighborhood was a theory Satoko never tired of expounding upon.

The rule in the Kamikawa family was to wait and have dinner once all three of them were home. Since Fumitaka had been out, they were eating later than usual this evening.

Naho had been doing all the cooking until a week ago, when Satoko came home from the hospital. Now everything was back to normal.

Naho had been in kindergarten when her mother was killed in a car crash. Although she'd been little more than a baby at the time, some of the shock and sorrow of those days stayed with Naho even now. That her father was around all day running the family store definitely softened the blow. Satoko's presence also helped. Although she hungered for a mother's love, she had Satoko to cherish her and feed her. In fact, the other kids were always jealous when they peeked into Naho's lunch box.

Back in April, Naho had paled with shock when she learned that Satoko was critically ill. The news caught her off guard, and she couldn't stop crying.

As Satoko had explained to the insurance salesman, she'd originally been hospitalized to have an aneurysm removed. Before she was operated on, however, she developed a raging fever. No one knew the cause, but it was severe enough for her to lose consciousness.

She was unconscious for three days. When Satoko came around on the fourth day, Naho burst into tears all over again.

The doctor told her that Satoko's fever was caused by cholangitis, an infection of the bile duct, and in that moment, Naho realized that the person she had most depended on her whole life was now an old woman ridden with disease.

When Satoko was discharged, Naho held her grandmother's hand and said to her: "You took care of me for many years. Now it's my turn to look after you."

Touched by her granddaughter's words, Satoko wept loudly.

However, their lovefest didn't last. At first Satoko was willing to overlook Naho's various domestic missteps, but gradually they started to get on her nerves. Nothing her granddaughter did was right. Satoko criticized her and sometimes barged in and took control of things. Stubborn and quick-tempered, she had no idea how to avoid hurting Naho's feelings. Unfortunately, Naho's temperament was similar. "If all you're going to do is complain, why don't you just do it yourself?" In no time at all, everything was back to how it had been before Satoko went into the hospital.

No one was more pleased about that than Fumitaka. He'd lost ten pounds while Naho was in charge of the cooking. Now that Satoko was back in the kitchen, he was starting to put the weight back on.

"By the way, you are going to your beauty school, aren't you?" Fumitaka asked Naho. "You're not cutting classes?"

"Of course not, Dad. Today's a school holiday. That's why I'm at home."

"That's all right, then."

"My little Naho, a hairdresser. I really hope you can make the grade."

"Of course I will." Naho glared at her grandmother. She could hardly come out and say that she'd had to skip several days of school because of her grandmother's condition.

"The important thing is for you to learn to stand on your own two feet, so you can earn money and take of yourself," said Fumitaka. "I know I've said this before, but—"

"Yeah, yeah, I know. If I've heard it once, I've heard it a million times. 'People who don't work have no right to eat.'"

2.

Naho had started beauty school in April. She'd completed her enrollment and had been looking forward to classes when Satoko was hospitalized. As a result, she'd fallen far behind and only recently caught up. She'd dreamed of becoming a hairdresser since elementary school. The idea of going to college never once crossed her mind.

The family business wasn't doing very well. They were just about scraping by. Satoko wasn't getting any younger, and Fumitaka's health would give out at some point too. Naho knew she would have to step into the breach one day; that was why she was eager to be financially independent as soon as possible.

Classes at the beauty school went on until four. As usual, Naho caught the subway home at 4:20. She got off at Hamacho Station, passed in front of the theater, crossed Kiyosubashi Boulevard, and headed home. On the way, she noticed several men walking in the opposite direction with their jackets slung over their shoulders. It was a scorcher of a day.

Omakara, the rice cracker shop that doubled as Naho's family home, was on Amazake Alley, a narrow shopping street.

No one could possibly accuse the street of being trendy. The clothes displayed in the shop windows were for middle-aged and elderly women, and at lunchtime the sidewalks were overrun by office workers dislodging food from between their teeth with toothpicks. The only thing to be said in the area's favor was that it retained something of the atmosphere of the Edo period—premodern Tokyo. It had taken Naho a while to realize that few other districts in the capital had shops that specialized in wicker suitcases or shamisen lutes.

Naho was walking past Hozukiya, a handicrafts shop

with wooden spinning tops and Japanese pellet drums displayed out front, when a figure in an apron shouted hello from inside. It was Misaki Sugawara, the part-time shop assistant at Hozukiya. She was a year older than Naho, and the two had recently become friends.

"How's things at the beauty school?"

"Not too bad."

"Great. You stick with it now."

"Thanks," said Naho, raising her hand to say goodbye.

Omakara was three shops farther down. As she approached, Naho noticed three men standing in the street right in front of the store. Two wore suits; one was more casually dressed in a short-sleeved checked shirt with a T-shirt underneath.

Nearly all of their customers were female, so Naho assumed the men weren't planning to go in, but just as she reached out to push open the store's glass door, the man in the short-sleeved shirt did the same thing. If he hadn't taken a step back, they would have collided.

"I'm sorry. After you." The man motioned for her to go in. He smiled broadly.

"No, you first. I work here."

The man nodded at her.

"Oh, do you? Well, that's good timing, then," he said as he stepped inside.

Inside the shop, Fumitaka looked at the two of them with a mildly puzzled expression on his face.

"Good afternoon, sir," he said. The man waved his hand deprecatingly and gave a slightly shamefaced grin.

"I'm afraid I'm not here to buy rice crackers. I'm actually from the local police station." He pulled out his badge wallet from the pocket of his pants, opened it, and showed them his ID.

To the best of Naho's knowledge, this was the first time the police had ever visited the store. She peered at the ID and read the name: Detective Kyoichiro Kaga.

She tried guessing the man's age. Definitely in his thirties, she reckoned, but she couldn't tell if he was above or below the halfway mark.

"Did a Mr. Takura visit yesterday? Let's see now. His full name is Mr. Shinichi Takura of New City Life Insurance."

The question startled Naho.

"Yes, he was here," she stammered back.

"Were you here at the time?"

"Yes, me and Grandma—I mean, my grandmother—were minding the store."

Kaga nodded.

"A couple of detectives from the Tokyo Metropolitan Police would like to talk to you about his visit. Would it be all right if I called them in?"

The words *Tokyo Metropolitan Police* evoked a twinge of fear. The Tokyo Metropolitan Police were the municipal police, and they were in charge of more serious crimes.

"I . . . uhm . . ." Naho glanced across at her father.

"Yes, of course. Has something happened?" asked Fumitaka.

"Just something we need to check up on. Won't take a moment."

"I see. Fine, go ahead. Shall I call my mother?"

"You mean this young woman's grandmother?" said Kaga, darting a look in Naho's direction. "That would be very helpful, yes."

"Got you," said Fumitaka, disappearing into the room at the back of the store.

Kaga gestured at the two men waiting outside. They had tough, weather-beaten faces. Naho had no idea what sort of age they were. If she had to classify them, she'd have to go with "geezer." They had geezer hair and geezer clothes, with big, fat faces and beer bellies to top it all off. They introduced themselves to Naho, but their names went in one ear and out the other.

The older-looking of the two detectives began asking questions as soon as Fumitaka reappeared with Satoko.

"We have been informed that this gentleman paid you a visit yesterday. Can you confirm that is correct?" asked the detective, holding out a photograph. It showed Takura with a meek expression on his face.

"Yes, that's correct," said Naho and Satoko in chorus.

"Around what time was that?" asked the detective.

"What time do you think it was?" asked Satoko, turning to Naho.

"Six or six thirty—something like that."

"You're sure it wasn't *before* six?" asked the detective.

"Oh, maybe you're right." Naho clapped her hand to her mouth. "I'm really not sure. It was still light outside, I think."

"It stays light until around seven at this time of year,"

the detective said. "Anyway, I take it you're not sure about the exact time?"

"Down to the exact minute and the hour . . . no," said Satoko dubiously.

"And what was Mr. Takura here for?"

"It was with regard to the paperwork necessary to file a claim for my recent hospitalization. He needed my medical certificate, apparently, so I gave it to him."

"And how long did he stay here?"

"Let's see." Satoko thought for a moment. "Ten minutes or so, I reckon."

Naho silently nodded her agreement. She was watching Kaga, who was inspecting the rice crackers in the glass display case and appeared to have no interest in the conversation.

"Did he say where he was going next?" the geezer detective went on.

"Back to the office. To take care of the paperwork for my claim, he said."

"That makes sense." The detective nodded. "How did he look?"

"What do you mean?"

"Did Mr. Takura look any different from normal?"

"He didn't, did he?" Satoko glanced at Naho for confirmation.

"He had on a different suit," Naho ventured. "The time before his suit was navy blue, but yesterday it was gray. It suited him better. That's why I remember it."

"I'm not talking about his clothes. Was he on edge? Did you get the impression he was in a hurry? Anything like that?"

"No, I don't think so."

Despite seeming a little disappointed at Naho's responses, the detective squeezed out a smile in an effort to keep things friendly.

"So to sum up, you don't recall the precise time when Mr. Takura was here. It could have been before six, and it could have been after six. Can I safely say, 'sometime between five thirty and six thirty'?"

"That sounds reasonable," replied Naho, looking at her grandmother.

"Good. Thank you very much for making time to talk to us."

"Excuse my asking, but is Mr. Takura all right?" Naho asked.

"Let's just say that this is an ongoing inquiry and leave it at that." The detective jerked his eyebrows at Kaga, who thanked the family and bowed at them.

The three men left the store.

"I hope this hasn't got anything to do with what happened at Kodenmacho," blurted out her father.

"What do you mean?" Naho asked.

"Haven't you seen the papers?" Fumitaka frowned. "A good barber should always read the papers."

"I'm not going to be a barber, Dad," protested Naho. She darted back into the living quarters and opened the newspaper.

The crime Fumitaka had referred to was featured on the local news page. The body of a forty-five-year-old woman who lived alone had been found in her apartment in the Kodenmacho area. She'd been strangled. The fact that the room showed no signs of a struggle suggested that she knew her attacker. The local police and Tokyo Metropolitan Police were treating the incident as a homicide.

"There's no way that Mr. Takura was involved in that. The man's a true-born Tokyoite with our natural dislike for anything underhand," Satoko said. She was standing next to Naho, reading the paper over her shoulder.

"From the questions the detective was asking just now, my guess is he was checking up on Mr. Takura's alibi. Doesn't that mean he's a suspect?"

"Oh, come off it. It doesn't matter what the police think. By testifying that Mr. Takura was here yesterday, we cleared him."

"But remember how insistent they were about the exact time he was here. That has to be important."

"Can you really not remember the precise time?" said Fumitaka, sticking his face through the door from the shop.

"We only know that it was sometime between half past five and half past six. We can't be any more precise than that."

"You're useless, you two."

"That's not fair. I mean, it's not like you know what you're doing every minute of every day either, Dad."

Eager to avoid a confrontation, Fumitaka pulled his head back out of the doorway.

"Well, I, for one, am very worried." Satoko knit her brows. "I just hope they can clear Mr. Takura very soon."

After dinner, Naho went to close the electric-operated roller shutter in the front of the store. It was about halfway down when she noticed a man standing on the other side of it. She automatically pressed the stop button.

The man bent down and peered up from under the shutter. It was Detective Kaga. Their eyes met, and he grinned and ducked under the shutter and into the store.

"Can you spare a minute?"

"Uh . . . yes. Shall I call my father?"

"No, just you is fine. There's one thing I need to double-check."

"What?"

"It's about what Mr. Takura was wearing—you said he had a suit on, right?"

"Yes. A gray suit. And the time before it was dark blue."

Kaga smiled sheepishly and waved her remark away.

"I don't care about the color. Do you remember if he had his suit jacket on when he was here?"

"He did, yes."

"Really? I thought as much from what you said about him looking good in it."

"What's that got to do with anything?"

"Not quite sure myself yet, but thanks anyway." Kaga plucked a packet of rice crackers off the shelf. "These look nice. I'll take them." He handed Naho 630 yen.

"Thanks."

"Right. Good night, then." Kaga ducked back under the shutter and out onto the street.

Naho just stood there blankly for a while, then walked over to the shutter switch. Before pressing it again, she squatted down and surveyed the street outside.

A handful of businessmen were strolling along the lamp-lit street. Work was over for the day, and they were probably heading out for a drink somewhere. Kaga was nowhere to be seen.

3.

The next day was freakishly hot from early morning. When Naho got off the train after class that afternoon, the short climb up the station stairs to the street level was enough to make her break into a sweat.

Fumitaka was outside the shop putting up the awning. "Oh, you're back," he murmured, noticing his daughter.

"Hi, Dad. Any more detectives come around today?"

"To our place, no," Fumitaka said in a quiet voice. "But it sounds like they're talking to everyone around here."

"I wonder why?"

"Rumor has it they're still checking up on Mr. Takura. They're asking every man and his dog if they saw him that day. Seems like the time that he was at our place is crucial."

"Our testimony alone isn't good enough for the police?"

"I guess not." Fumitaka went back into the shop.

Naho looked around. She wondered if the police were busy making inquiries nearby right now.

Her gaze wandered to a café diagonally across the road. She caught her breath: there was a face she recognized behind the big plate glass window. The other person, realizing he'd been spotted, grinned awkwardly back.

Naho crossed the street, went into café, and strode over to a table overlooking the street.

"Who are you spying on?" she asked Kaga, who was sitting there.

"I'm not spying on anyone. Why don't you sit down?" Kaga raised his hand to summon the waitress. "What'll you have?"

"I'm fine."

"No need to stand on ceremony." Kaga pushed the menu toward her.

"Okay then, I'll have the banana juice," Naho told the waitress as she sat herself down. "Are you keeping our store under surveillance?"

"Come off it. Like I said, I'm not watching anyone."

"What are you doing, then?"

"Nothing. Or if you insist, I'm just enjoying this iced coffee—slacking off, in other words." Ignoring the straw, Kaga tipped his ice coffee down his throat.

"Is Mr. Takura a suspect in the Kodenmacho murder case?"

Kaga's face tensed. He glanced around at the other tables.

"I'd be grateful if you could keep your voice down."

"Give me an answer or I'll turn the volume up to eleven."

Kaga sighed and ran his fingers through his shaggy hair.

"Mr. Takura's on our list of suspects, yes. He visited

the victim's apartment on the day of the crime, and we found his business card and an insurance pamphlet there. He, of course, claims that he was there on insurance-related business."

"Is that all you've got?"

"It's significant enough from a police point of view."

The waitress brought Naho her banana juice. She drank it all in one swallow through a fat straw.

"Does it really matter what time Mr. Takura came to see us?" she asked, after a brief silence.

Kaga thought for a moment, then nodded curtly.

"Mr. Takura claims to have left the victim's apartment at around five thirty p.m. The victim was still alive at that point. We know that for sure because we've confirmed that she went out shopping a little after that."

"Really? Shopping for what?"

Kaga blinked and peered at Naho. "What does that matter to you?"

"It doesn't. I'm just curious. I mean, it was right before she was killed, wasn't it?"

"She probably had no idea that someone was going to kill her. Why shouldn't she go shopping? She bought some kitchen scissors, if you really want to know. You may know the store, Kisamiya?"

"Oh yes."

"Anyway, enough about that. Let's get back to Mr. Takura. He claims that after leaving the victim's apartment, he dropped in to your place and then went back to his office, where he handed all the documentation for your grandmother's insurance claim to a female colleague and then went home for the day."

"What's the problem?"

"On his way home, he went out for a drink with a friend. Now, if we calculate backward from the time at which this friend told us they met, we end up with Takura leaving his office at six forty. Takura's female colleague, however, says that he left the office at six ten. That leaves us with a gap of roughly thirty minutes unaccounted for. Thirty minutes is enough time for him to run over from his office to the victim's apartment, commit the murder, and then set out for home. When we confronted Takura on this point, he stated that he did leave his office at six forty and did not stop off anywhere before meeting his friend. He thinks that his colleague at the office simply got her times wrong."

"Maybe he's right?"

"The trouble is, another witness came forward to say that they saw Takura returning to the office after six p.m. We cannot ignore that discrepancy. On the other hand, Mr. Takura's testimony and that of his female colleague do agree in one particular: both of them peg the time he spent in the office at just ten minutes. That's what makes the precise time he visited you so important. You can walk from here to New City Life Insurance's head office in under ten minutes. Takura claims to have gone straight from your store back to his office; if we knew what time he left your place, we'd be able to verify his entire account."

Kaga delivered this explanation at high speed, so Naho needed a little while to digest it all.

"Now I understand why you were so obsessed about the precise time."

"Exactly. Since neither you nor your grandmother can recall the precise time Takura was with you, I've been visiting all the other stores along this street, asking if they saw Mr. Takura that afternoon. Unfortunately, no one saw him going into your shop. I asked the staff at this café. Drew a blank here, too."

"What's your next step?"

"Not sure." Kaga stretched and leaned against the back of his seat. Naho noticed that his eyes were still focused on the street outside. "As we don't have any other plausible suspects right now, the Metropolitan Police guys have the hots for Takura."

"That's ridiculous. He wouldn't hurt a fly."

"That's what murderers' friends always say—even after they're convicted."

Naho didn't like the detective's tone.

"Come off it. Mr. Takura's got no motive."

"Hmm."

"What's 'hmmm' supposed to mean?"

"It means that we almost never know the motive until the perpetrator himself tells us. Maybe the Met guys will get it out of him any moment now."

"You sound like you're perfectly happy to leave everything up to them."

"I do?"

"Yeah, sounds to me like you couldn't care less."

Kaga had finished his iced coffee. He picked up his glass of water instead.

"The Tokyo Metropolitan Police are the lead investigators on this case. We precinct cops provide support and show them around the neighborhood. Basically, we just do what we're told."

Naho frowned as she looked at Kaga's lined face.

"What a letdown. There I was, thinking you were different from the normal run of cops. With your attitude, you'll stagnate at the local police level and never get anywhere."

"I'm not stagnating. The thing is, I just got transferred to this precinct and I honestly don't know much about it yet. I'm just easing myself in, familiarizing myself with the place. It's an interesting district. I was in the local watch store; they had this extraordinary clock. It was a prism with clock faces on all three sides and all three clocks moved together. I wonder what sort of mechanism it's got."

"You've got to be kidding. You weren't joking when you said you were goofing off, were you?" Naho put money on the table for her banana juice. She didn't want Kaga to pay for her.

"It's hot again today," murmured Kaga, looking out the window. "Look. All the businessmen walking up this way from the Ningyocho subway station—see how they've got their jackets off and their shirtsleeves rolled up?"

"What the heck do I care?" Naho said sharply. She could no longer bother to be polite.

"You see? Here comes another one. He's taken his jacket off and slung it over his shoulder. Poor chap."

"Why shouldn't he, in this heat?"

"It's cooler than it was earlier, though. See? Here's a guy who's kept his jacket on."

Sure enough, a rather stout man strolled by with his suit perfectly in place.

"Are you trying to tell me something?" Naho couldn't keep the note of irritation out her voice.

"Take a good look. What do you see? Most of the men walking from right to left—in other words, from the Ningyocho neighborhood to Hamacho, the next neighborhood over—have taken their jackets off. With the men walking from left to right, it's the opposite: they've all got their jackets on."

Naho swiveled around in her seat to inspect the street.

A gaggle of businessmen passed by, going from right to left. Naho's jaw dropped. Kaga was right: nearly all of them had their jackets off.

"It's true," she murmured under breath.

"Interesting, eh?" said Kaga.

"But why? Is it just a coincidence?"

"You shouldn't dismiss something like this as a coincidence. That's too easy. You should assume there's a reason for it."

"Do you know what that reason is, Detective Kaga?"

"Perhaps I do." Kaga smirked.

"What are you grinning for? Why are you so pleased with yourself?"

"I'm not being conceited. To be honest, once I've told you the reason, I doubt you'll be very impressed. A lot of office workers walk along this street, but most of them work for firms with offices in Hamacho. Okay, so here's my question. The time now is half past five. What sort of people would you expect to find walking from right to left, in other words from Ningyocho toward Hamacho, at this time of day?"

"Well, given what time it is . . . ," said Naho thoughtfully, as she stared at yet another businessman walking by in his shirtsleeves, "they must be on their way back to their offices."

"Right. In other words, these are the people who've been out of the office all day. They work outside, probably in sales or service, stuff like that. The people who are going from left to right are the opposite: they've been in the office all day. Because they've been in an air-conditioned office most of the day—in contrast to their colleagues who are all hot and bothered from running around outside—they're a little on the chilly side if anything. That's why they're wearing their jackets. Plus by this time in the afternoon, the temperature has gone down quite a lot. Take a closer look at the people coming from the direction of Hamacho. On the whole, they're on the older side. My guess is they're quite senior and their jobs don't involve much running around outside the office. That also helps explain why they get to leave at five thirty on the dot."

As she listened to Kaga's explanation, Naho inspected the men walking down the street. There was the occasional exception, but all in all she had to admit that the detective's theory was very plausible.

"Wow . . . I think you're right. I've lived here my whole life, but I never noticed that until you pointed it out."

"Well, it doesn't have much practical value."

Naho nodded, then suddenly looked at Kaga wide-eyed.

"Does this have any connection to the murder?"

Kaga picked up the check from the table.

"You remember me asking you what Mr. Takura was wearing?"

Naho blinked in acknowledgment.

"He looked smart and had his jacket on. . . ."

"But Mr. Takura is one of those people who are out and about all day. He told us that he went to visit you *after* going to the victim's apartment in Kodenmacho. That would have involved quite a lot of walking. Given the circumstances, he did well to have his jacket on and look so neat and tidy."

"I see what you mean . . . Of course, he could just have been toughing it out."

"That's a possibility, sure. Still, I think that's where we may find the answer to the riddle of the missing thirty minutes." Kagawa got up and walked over to the cash register to pay.

"Hang on. What are you implying?"

"I can't tell you any more yet. I need to unravel that riddle first," said Kaga, as they left the café.

4.

Over dinner, Naho relayed what Detective Kaga had told her. Getting Satoko to grasp the concept of the missing thirty minutes was quite a struggle. Naho had to write out a timeline of Takura's movements before her grandmother could understand.

"Huh," snorted Satoko, her head cocked to one side. "I don't think those thirty minutes matter much, one way or the other."

"Thirty minutes is long enough for someone to have committed the murder. That's why the police are taking it so seriously."

"Then the police are idiots. First of all, would Mr. Takura do something like that? Of course not. He'd never do anything so horrible. He's not that kind of person. He always keeps his promises, always does his best to understand other people's points of view. People as considerate as he are rare nowadays. I mean, he came around the minute I got out of hospital—"

Naho interrupted Satoko with a dismissive wave of the hand.

"We all know that Mr. Takura's a nice guy. There's no point going on about it. The important thing is to figure out a way to prove to the police that he didn't do it."

"That's exactly what I'm saying. We need to tell the police loud and clear. The only reason they could possibly suspect Mr. Takura is because they have no idea what kind of man he is."

"I'm wasting my time," muttered Naho under her breath. She looked over at Fumitaka, her father. He was sitting in silence, a solemn expression on his face.

"What are you thinking, Dad?"

"Huh? Oh, I was wondering if Mr. Takura really said those things."

"What things?"

"You know, about how he dropped in on you here after going to Kodenmacho and before going back to the head office, then heading home after that."

"That's what Detective Kaga told me he said."

"Hmm. I wonder . . ." murmured Fumitaka, deep in thought.

"What's wrong, Dad?"

"Oh, I don't know."

"That Detective Kaga is a handsome young fellow," declared Satoko, as she prepared a pot of tea. "He's got the perfect face for a samurai drama on TV. He's clever-looking, too."

"I think he is clever. He pointed out something very interesting to me." Naho then told Satoko about Kaga's observation regarding how the businessmen walking along Amazake Alley were dressed.

"Gosh, he's right!" exclaimed Satoko wonderingly. "That would never have occurred to me."

"Anyway, that set Detective Kaga wondering why Mr. Takura still had his jacket on when he came to see us on that day. He thought it might be connected to that thirty-minute gap."

"How?"

"He doesn't yet know."

"Well, he's got some eccentric ideas. Who knows, perhaps that makes him a better detective."

"Who knows?" said Naho, picking up her teacup. "I didn't get the impression that he was very fired up about the case. And then, him talking so openly about the investigation to me—that doesn't seem very professional."

"You were the one who asked him."

"Well, asking's one thing, and telling's another. I don't think it's quite normal, eh, Dad?" Naho looked at her father for his support.

"What? . . . Oh, yes, I guess not."

Fumitaka got to his feet.

"Time for me to have my bath. That was a very nice dinner."

Naho cocked her head. She was puzzled. Why was her father so distracted?

5.

In the late afternoon, Fumitaka went out front and closed the awning. He did this every day. It was cooler than it had been at lunchtime, but the sun was getting stronger by the day. He was thinking that before the summer got under way in earnest, he should change the shelf displays. Some rice crackers and snacks went better with beer than others.

A shadow floating across the sidewalk alerted him that there someone was behind him. He was about to greet the person as a customer, when he recognized him. It was someone who was on his mind.

"Another scorcher today, eh?" Kaga spoke first.

"Tell me about it. If it's my daughter you want, she's not back yet."

Kaga waved away the idea.

"It's you I want to talk to. Have you got a few minutes to spare?"

Startled, Fumitaka drew in his breath. He looked at Kaga. Kaga stared right back at him until Fumitaka had to look away.

"All right. Well, come on in, then," Fumitaka said, pushing the glass door.

"Where's your mother today?"

"She's here. Do you want me to call her?"

"No, if she's here, we'll need to go and talk somewhere else," Kaga said.

Although the detective was considerably younger than he was, Fumitaka still found him intimidating. The man definitely hadn't come just to double-check his facts this time.

Fumitaka sighed and nodded.

The two men went into the store. "Hey, Mom," Fumitaka yelled in the direction of the back room. "Are you awake?"

"Why, what's up?" came Satoko's voice from the living room.

"I have to go out for a minute. Will you mind the store?"

"Off to play pachinko again, are you? You're a lost cause." As Satoko shuffled into her sandals, she spotted Kaga behind her son. "Oh, if it isn't our local debonair detective. Is Mr. Takura still a suspect?"

"We're still looking into him."

"Well, I'm relying on you. He's a good man. Not murderer material. I guarantee that personally."

"Very good. I heard that you got out of the hospital quite recently. How are you feeling?"

"Fit as a fiddle from the minute I got home, thank you very much. Going into the hospital in the first place was probably a mistake." Satoko looked at Fumitaka. "Are you going to have a talk with Detective Kaga? You be sure to tell him what a good fellow Mr. Takura is."

"Yeah, yeah, Mom. I know." Fumitaka turned to Kaga. "Shall we get going?"

"Take good care of yourself," Kaga said to Satoko.

"It's great to see your mother looking so well," Kaga said as they emerged from the shop.

"She can still talk the hind legs off a donkey."

They walked over to the café on the far side of the street. Fumitaka remembered what Naho had told them about her conversation with Kaga there the night before. Both men ordered iced coffee. When Fumitaka pulled out a pack of cigarettes, Kaga pushed the ashtray across.

"I had a chat with your daughter here yesterday."

"I know."

"So she told you? No surprise, I suppose. Anyway, that should simplify things."

"She was telling us that you'd noticed something quite funny, if *funny*'s the right word for it. That business about the difference in the way the men walking in the street are dressed—I'd not noticed it, either."

"I notice details. That's the sort of person I am. I couldn't stop thinking about how Mr. Takura was dressed. What was he doing with his suit jacket on after pounding the streets all day?"

Their iced coffees arrived. Fumitaka lit a cigarette.

"Have you figured that out yet?"

"Pretty much, yes."

"Yes?"

"You don't sound surprised. Aren't you interested?"

"It's not that."

"Well, perhaps what I've got to say isn't something all that interesting to you. After all, I'll only be telling you something you already know, Mr. Kamikawa."

The glass of coffee Fumitaka was carrying to his lips stopped in midair. "What do you mean?"

"Why did Mr. Takura have his jacket on when he went to your store? The answer's simple enough. It's because he didn't drop in at your place after having been outside all day. No, before going to your place, he swung by his office, finished off all his work, and only then did he go to see your mother and daughter. That's why he wasn't hot and bothered and was quite comfortable keeping his jacket on."

Fumitaka was looking resolutely at the floor.

"Takura left Kodenmacho at five thirty and got back to his office before six," continued the detective. "He gave all the documents related to Satoko Kamikawa's hospitalization claim to a female colleague to process, then put on his jacket and headed back out. He dropped in at your place, then went to meet his friend for a drink and headed home for the day. In this account of things, his movements tally perfectly with all the different testimony we have. There are no missing thirty minutes. We can suppose that the missing half hour was taken up getting from his office to your place and then chatting with your mother, Satoko Kamikawa, and your daughter, Naho Kamikawa. However, this leaves us with just one discrepancy to explain: Mr. Takura needed to have a medical certificate in order to submit your mother's insurance claim. That means he couldn't have handed the paperwork over for processing unless he'd visited your family *before* returning to the head office. And that brings us to a second question: if this really is what Takura did that afternoon, why didn't he just come out and tell us?"

Fumitaka looked up to find the detective staring right at him.

"You . . . you know everything, then," said Fumitaka.

Kaga broke into a smile.

"I went to Shin-Ohashi Hospital and spoke to the doctor in charge. He told me everything, except for the nature of your mother's illness, that is."

Fumitaka sighed, took a sip of his iced coffee, and gave a slight shake of the head.

"It looks like the Nihonbashi Precinct has got a very smart new detective. . . ."

"The doctor admitted to issuing two different medical certificates, one listing your mother's actual condition, the other listing a false one. Why should he do that? According to him, it's because you asked him to."

"You're right. I made him do it. It was the only solution I could come up with. My mom's so pigheaded that she insisted on handling the insurance claim herself. You've got to have a medical certificate to submit a claim, but I was determined not to let my mom see what was on the certificate. I was in a jam."

"So you asked the doctor to give your mother a fake certificate when she went to the hospital to collect it."

Fumitaka nodded.

"At first the doctor told me that it was against the rules and he couldn't do it. But he's a nice guy, so he agreed to make an exception. The only condition was that I mustn't show the fake one to anyone other than my mom. After my mom was safely back home, I went to the hospital myself to pick up the real medical certificate."

"Which you gave to Mr. Takura—"

"A little before six o'clock that same day. I went over near his office and handed it to him in person. He processed it right away, he said."

"That left one more thing for Mr. Takura to take care of: he had to pick up the fake medical certificate from your mother. So he left his office and went around to your place."

Fumitaka frowned and scratched the side of his head.

"I really got Mr. Takura in trouble. He has a legitimate alibi, but he can't give it to you because he bent the rules for me. As far as I'm concerned, he's welcome to tell you everything. There's no other way out."

"Mr. Takura hasn't breathed a word about the fake medical certificate."

"That's because he's thinking about the consequences. When I gave him the real certificate, he promised not to mention it to anyone. 'I'm a trueborn Tokyoite. I'd rather die than break a promise.' Those are his exact words."

"How come you didn't say anything, either?"

This comment flummoxed Fumitaka. He was briefly at a loss for words.

"Apparently, she's got cancer of the bile duct."

"The bile duct . . . I see." The expression on Kaga's face was grave.

"She's too weak for an operation. They've discharged her—for now, at least. The idea is to keep an eye on her and treat her at home, but she's unlikely to get her old energy back." Fumitaka took a deep breath and went on, "She may only have six months left to live."

"I can only offer my deepest sympathies."

Fumitaka just smiled.

"It's nice of you to sympathize, but the important thing is for no one else to find out the truth. Not my mother, obviously, but not Naho, either."

"I understand completely," said Kaga.

"That girl loves my mom like her own mother. Her real mother died when she was little more than a baby, so her granny means everything to her. I don't want to tell her what's really going on until she has finished classes and has got her start as a hairdresser." A thought struck Fumitaka midflow, and he looked at Kaga. "I suppose I can't hide the truth any longer. We'll have to come clean about the fake medical certificate to provide Mr. Takura with a proper alibi."

Kaga shook his head slowly and deliberately.

"I discussed the matter with my superiors, and I've

arranged for someone from the local precinct to have a word with the homicide detectives at the Metropolitan Police. The only thing we'll need is a statement from you."

"I see. If I do that, everything will be okay."

"Sorry for the bother."

"No worries," said Fumitaka, shaking his head. "The woman who was murdered in Kodenmacho—she lived alone?"

"That's right."

"Does she have any family?"

Kaga briefly looked down, something between a grimace and a smile on his lips. Fumitaka sensed that the detective was reluctant to speak.

"I'm sorry. Of course, you can't talk about the investigation."

"No, those aren't really details that we need to keep secret. The woman was living by herself after separating from her husband. She had a son, but they seldom saw each other."

"That's interesting."

"We don't yet know why she decided to move to the Nihonbashi area. She's a bit of a mysterious newcomer."

Fumitaka looked startled.

"Just like you, then."

"I guess so."

The two men laughed.

"Ah, look. It's your daughter." Kaga motioned with his eyes toward the street.

Naho was standing outside the store, rearranging the rice crackers in the display cases. The glass door opened and

Satoko emerged onto the street. They exchanged some words. Naho face's was a sulky pout.

"If Naho finds out that we met, she's bound to ask all sorts of questions."

"Why not just tell her that Mr. Takura is no longer a suspect? That should do the trick."

Fumitaka nodded and stood up. "Do you expect to stay at the local precinct for a while?"

"Probably."

"Well, I'm delighted to hear it. Please come around for more rice crackers anytime."

"Will do."

Placing the money for his iced coffee on the table, Fumitaka went out onto the street. A businessman in shirtsleeves hurried past the café.

2

THE APPRENTICE AT THE JAPANESE RESTAURANT

1.

At four o'clock every day, Shuhei had to sprinkle the sidewalk outside the restaurant. Wearing a special white smock, he used a ladle to splash water from a bucket. It would have been easier to use a hose, but when he suggested this to Yoriko, the restaurant's co-owner and manager, she glared at him and called him a fool.

"You're not washing a car, you know. The point of sprinkling water is to keep the dust down. Soaking the whole sidewalk will only inconvenience our customers.

"People who choose to come to a restaurant like ours take atmosphere seriously. They love the sight of an apprentice sprinkling water from a bucket. Some kid in jeans squirting water from a hose—where's the poetry in that?"

Since their customers only started to arrive around six o'clock, objected Shuhei, none of them actually saw him sprinkling the sidewalk. So what did it matter?

Yoriko's response was a smack on the head. "Don't talk back. Debating isn't part of your job description."

That's not very nice, thought Shuhei. But he held his

tongue; despite Yoriko's occasional high-handedness, he respected her abilities as a manager.

A man came out of the restaurant just as Shuhei was ladling out the last of the water. It was Yoriko's husband, Taiji, the other owner of Matsuya, as the restaurant was called. He was decked out in a Hawaiian shirt and white chinos, with a pair of shades and a gold neck chain thrown in for good measure. Taiji was convinced that he was the last word in style, though Shuhei felt that his look needed work. Shuhei had half a mind to tell Taiji that he resembled a low-level gangster from a B movie.

"Hi there. Got my things for me today?" asked Taiji, looking around anxiously.

"Yeah, I got them."

"Where are they?"

"Safely out of sight."

"Good work, kid. Go fetch 'em, will you?"

Shuhei put the bucket down and ducked into the alleyway that ran down one side of the restaurant. He pulled out a white plastic bag from the basket of a parked bicycle and brought the bag back to Taiji. Taiji was looking at his watch and casting nervous glances in the direction of the restaurant's main entrance. He was clearly worried that Yoriko would come out and find him.

"Here you go." Shuhei held out the plastic bag.

"Thank you, thank you. I owe you." Taiji peered into the bag and gave a satisfied nod. "You got what I asked for?"

"Yes. Seven with bean paste, three without."

"Appreciate it. Appreciate it. Keep the change."

"Okay." Shuhei inclined his head slightly. The change was all of fifty yen.

"Remember, this is a secret. Not a word to anyone. You got that?" Taiji placed his index finger up against his lips.

"Yes, I know."

"Don't breathe a word to anyone. I'll never forgive you if you do."

"I said I wouldn't, didn't I?"

"Good. We're both on the same page, then." Clutching the plastic bag, Taiji walked off toward the main street. Shuhei sighed quietly as he watched him go.

Starting at six o'clock, the restaurant had a steady stream of customers. Shuhei was a server; he brought the food from the kitchen. The cooks provided him with a brief explanation of each dish, what the ingredients were and how it should be eaten. Nonetheless, he often found himself at a loss when customers asked him anything too finicky. When they did, he would have to make his way back to the kitchen and ask his fellow cooks or the owners for additional information. Nine times out of ten they reproached him for not having listened properly the first time around.

When regular customers came to dine, Yoriko would make a point of greeting them in person. She always wore a kimono. Shuhei knew that there were rules governing what kimono to wear in what season and that Yoriko followed those rules very scrupulously. That night, she was wearing a lilac kimono made of semitransparent fabric.

The sight of Yoriko chatting to the customers mesmerized Shuhei. Her face became animated and she appeared far younger and more beautiful than normal. Shuhei couldn't believe that she was almost the same age as his mother.

The restaurant's patrons were the only people to whom she displayed her captivating smile. The instant she turned away from their table, her eyes hardened.

"What are you standing around daydreaming for? Can't you see that the glass of that gentleman over by the window is empty?"

"Oh . . . uh . . . sorry."

Shuhei had to jump to it every time Yoriko made a sharp comment.

By ten o'clock, the customers started to go home. Shuhei couldn't help feeling pleased when they thanked him for the delicious dinner on their way out, despite his not having had a hand in the cooking.

Then it was time for tidying up. Shuhei was responsible for washing the dishes and scrubbing down the kitchen. Since he had only joined the restaurant in the spring, he hadn't yet learned even how to handle a carving knife. Katsuya, another apprentice who had started two years before him, had only just recently been permitted to help out with the cooking. Shuhei would have to put up with his present duties for a while yet.

He was only seventeen years old. He'd been in high school until last year, but somehow never settled into the rhythm of school. No, that was putting a gloss on the truth; the fact was that he wasn't able to keep up with his classmates and got frustrated. He'd never wanted to go to college, but his parents had begged him to at least complete high school, so reluctantly he'd tried. In the end, and to no one's great surprise, he simply couldn't hack it.

After he dropped out of high school, his parents started asking him what he planned to do with his life. His answer—that he wanted to become a chef—was off the top of his head. The reason for it was simple enough: there was a sushi restaurant near the family home, and Shuhei had always thought the chefs working there were the last word in cool. His father used his connections to get him the Matsuya job.

Having finished the cleaning and tidying, Shuhei was about to leave when Taiji wandered in, wearing the same outfit he'd had on in the afternoon. He must have been out all evening.

"How'd we do tonight?" Picking up one of the glasses that Shuhei had just washed, Taiji opened a nearby bottle of sake.

"Same old, same old. Oh, Professor Okabe was here."

"Oh yeah? The great self-styled gourmet who tragically lacks any sense of taste?" Taiji poured himself a glass of sake and took a sip. His face was already purple. *Must have been doing some serious boozing*, thought Shuhei.

Taiji drank the rest of the sake and put the empty glass down on the table. "Cheers, that was delicious," he said, and left the room.

What was that about? Are you just trying to make my job harder than it is already? thought Shuhei, sulking as he reached for Taiji's dirty glass.

2.

Matsuya offered a reasonably priced lunch that was popular with the better-heeled workers from nearby office buildings.

Shuhei was hard at work waiting tables when Katsuya, the senior apprentice, came up to him.

"The boss is asking for you. She wants you in the Cypress Room."

Shuhei wondered what it was all about. The Cypress Room was never used at lunchtime.

When he got there, Shuhei found Yoriko and a group of three men sitting on opposite sides of the table. Two of the men were in suits, while the third was more casually dressed in a short-sleeved checked shirt over a T-shirt.

"These gentlemen are from the police, Shuhei. Detectives, they tell me. They want to ask you a few questions," Yoriko explained.

"Sorry, I know this is a busy time of day," said the man in the short-sleeved shirt. He swung back around to Yoriko. "If you don't mind, ma'am, we'd like to talk to the young man alone."

"Be my guest," said Yoriko. For all her winning smile, there was a trace of uneasiness in her eyes. Shuhei was baffled. Why on earth did the police want to talk to him?

The three men filed out of the room and headed for the front door of the restaurant. Shuhei followed. They went outside, stopping when they got to Ningyocho Boulevard.

Ningyocho Boulevard was a broad, multilane one-way street lined with all sorts of restaurants and bars.

"God, it's hot today. Want a nice drink?" The detective in the checked shirt thrust a plastic carrier bag in Shuhei's direction. Inside were several cans of cold coffee.

"I'm good, thanks."

"Don't say that. If you don't have one, then neither can we."

"Really?" Shuhei peered into the bag and took out a can. The three detectives then did likewise.

"Do you have draught beer at Matsuya?"

Shuhei shook his head.

"No, only bottled, but it's a craft beer we get directly from a brewery in Hida, in Gifu Prefecture."

"Sounds good. Go on, drink up."

"Sure," replied Shuhei, pulling the tab on the can. It was only June, but the heat was already intense. The cool liquid seemed to seep into every pore of his body.

"Heard you bought a bunch of ningyo-yaki recently?" began the older-looking of the two men in suits, after taking a swig of his coffee. Ningyo-yaki were small snack cakes, baked in molds—a Tokyo specialty.

Shuhei almost choked. "What?" Blinking, he looked back at the detective.

"You bought a bunch of snack cakes at a shop on this street three days ago, didn't you?" reiterated the detective, staring into Shuhei's eyes.

Shuhei's heart started racing. He couldn't very well lie straight to a cop's face.

"Yes, I did."

"What time was that?"

"A little before four."

"Good. How many did you buy?"

"Ten. Seven with sweet bean paste filling, three without."

"Did the shop pack them in a wooden box?"

"No. Just a see-through plastic container."

"A present for someone?"

Shuhei shook his head and nervously licked his lips. His promise to Taiji flashed through his mind. "No, I bought them for myself."

"Really? Ten of the darn things?" the shorter of the two detectives wearing suits asked, his eyes widening in surprise.

"I ate some that afternoon and polished the rest off that night."

The other detective in a suit gave a sardonic smile. "You youngsters!"

"You really ate the whole lot yourself?" asked the shorter one.

"Ye . . . yes."

"What did you do with the plastic container?"

"I threw it away."

"Where?"

"Uhm . . ." Shuhei was getting flustered. He wasn't sure how to parry that question. "Don't remember. Some bin or other, I guess."

"The boss told us that you live above the restaurant. Was it in the bin in your room there?"

"Maybe . . . or, no, I think it was another bin somewhere else."

"Try to remember. We really need to find the thing."

"The plastic container?"

"That's right." The detective's eyes drilled into Shuhei.

Shuhei lowered his gaze. He was in trouble. The easy way out would be to come clean and tell the cops he'd bought the small cakes for the owner, but then he'd be hauled over the coals by Taiji. Who knows, he might even get fired.

A second later, he had a flash of inspiration. He looked up. "I put my trash out today."

The dismay in the detectives' faces was visible.

"What, this morning? With all the other garbage?" asked the shorter detective.

"That's right. Today's the day they come around."

That, at least, was the truth. Putting out the trash was one of Shuhei's responsibilities.

The two detectives in suits exchanged unhappy looks. By contrast, the third detective, the one in the short-sleeved shirt, was glancing up and down the street in an easygoing way. When he noticed Shuhei looking at him, he shot him a grin. "Go on. Drink your coffee."

"Oh, yeah." Shuhei drank the last of his coffee. He was surprised how thirsty he was.

"Okay, good. Thanks for your time," said the shorter detective.

"Yes, thanks for helping with the investigation."

The detective in the checked shirt was holding out the plastic bag to Shuhei. "I'll throw that away for you."

"Oh . . . uh . . . thanks." Shuhei dropped his empty can in the bag.

Yoriko was waiting just outside the main entrance when Shuhei got back to the restaurant.

"How did it go? What did they want to know?" she asked.

Shuhei hemmed and hawed, unable to improvise a convincing story off the cuff.

"Was it about the snack cakes?" she asked.

Taken aback, Shuhei nodded. The police must have told Yoriko what they planned to question him about.

"You bought some small cakes three days ago and they wanted to know what you'd done with them, right?"

"Yes, ma'am."

"What did you say?"

Shuhei repeated the story he had told the detectives. What else could he do?

He was expecting Yoriko to yell at him for ducking out to buy sweets during working hours, but instead she just inquired what else the police had asked him about.

"Nothing else."

"I see. Well, hurry up and get back to work."

"Yes, ma'am. What's this all about, though? I mean, what do the detectives want with me?"

Yoriko looked slightly uncomfortable.

"Three days ago, in the evening, there was a murder over in Kodenmacho. The police are looking into it."

"In Kodenmacho? What's that got to do with me?"

"Apparently, the police found some small cakes in the woman's apartment. They're looking for anyone who bought some that day."

Shuhei gasped. Suddenly the roof of his mouth felt dry and a wave of heat surged through him. He tried to conceal his shock.

"How did they find out that I'd bought some?" Shuhei muttered. His voice was hoarse.

"Goodness knows. They didn't go into detail with me. Anyway, you've got nothing to do with any murder, have you?"

Shuhei shook his head frantically. "I didn't even know that there'd been a murder."

"Well then, you've got nothing to worry about, have you? Go on, enough dawdling. Back to work. We mustn't inconvenience our customers." Yoriko's tone was stern.

"Sorry, ma'am," said Shuhei. With an apologetic duck of the head, he headed back to the kitchen.

After lunch was over, Shuhei had a short break. He discreetly went looking through the stack of old newspapers and found a story on the murder in the evening edition from the day before yesterday. The victim was a woman of forty-five living alone in Kodenmacho who'd been strangled in her apartment. Based on the crime scene, the police thought that she probably knew her killer. They also thought that it was highly likely that the crime had taken place sometime between late afternoon and early evening.

Snack cakes weren't mentioned in the article. The police were probably keeping that detail from the public.

A bead of sweat dribbled from his armpit as Shuhei pictured the faces of the detectives who had questioned him.

Shuhei was familiar with the rumors about Taiji, Yoriko's

husband, having a woman on the side. He'd heard his co-workers gossiping. They'd even said something about him having set her up in an apartment in Kodenmacho.

Three days ago was hardly the first time that Taiji had had Shuhei buy a batch of small sweet cakes for him. As soon as Shuhei gave him the cakes, Taiji would head out somewhere. Taiji didn't go toward the subway station; it was more in the opposite direction. If you walked in that direction for ten minutes or so, you'd end up in Kodenmacho.

Shuhei had always assumed that the cakes were a present for Taiji's girlfriend.

And now there'd been a murder in Kodenmacho. And they had found the same sort of cakes he'd bought that afternoon in the victim's apartment.

Shuhei prayed that the whole thing was nothing more than an unfortunate coincidence—but there were too many coincidences for comfort. And the detectives had come to talk to him specifically, when there had to be hundreds of customers who bought those cakes from that particular shop on any given day.

Was it Taiji's lover who'd been murdered? That would mean . . . Shuhei's imagination was running wild, but he had no one to confide in. Mistress Yoriko was out of the question, as were his coworkers. He wondered about talking to Taiji, but he quickly abandoned the idea. He'd only get yelled at: "How dare you accuse your own boss of being a murderer!"

All the worrying kept him from concentrating on his

work. He made countless small slipups that night and was subjected to repeated tongue-lashings from his coworkers and the head cook.

3.

The following evening, the detective in the checked shirt showed up at the restaurant. This time, he was wearing a charcoal gray jacket and was there as a customer. After leading him to his table, Shuhei went back to check the reservation list. The detective's name was Kaga.

"Hah, you look like you've seen a ghost," said Kaga merrily. "I suppose you think an underpaid cop like me has no business coming to a swanky joint like this?"

"Of course not, sir." Shuhei lowered his eyes.

"Think I'll start off with one of those Hida craft beers," said Kaga, without bothering to consult the drink menu. He obviously remembered their conversation from the day before.

In the evenings at Matsuya, they served from a prix fixe menu only. Shuhei first brought Kaga his beer, together with an amuse-bouche, then began to serve the appetizers. Kaga asked for the drink menu.

"The mistress's sake pairing menu looks interesting. Think I'll go for that."

"Yes, sir."

"Hey, have you got a sweet tooth?" Kaga asked as Shuhei was about to head to the kitchen.

Shaking his head vigorously, Shuhei was on the verge of

saying no, when he recalled his claim to have eaten an entire box of snack cakes by himself.

"Yes . . . uh . . . I quite like sweet things."

"Funny that you went for the no-sugar option, then."

"The no-sugar option?"

"The canned coffee." Kaga drank down the last of his beer. "You chose the can of sugar-free."

Shuhei gave a start. Kaga was right. Out of habit, he had gone for the sugar-free coffee.

"Coffee's different . . . I prefer it without sugar."

"Oh, do you?" Kaga put his empty glass down on the table. "All right, let's get started on the sake."

"On the double, sir," said Shuhei and went off.

What's that detective fellow on about now? Who cares about a stupid can of coffee?

Shuhei had broken out in a cold sweat. He knew that Kaga hadn't really come to the restaurant just to have dinner. The detective hadn't believed his story about eating all the snack cakes himself and was there to subject him to another round of questions.

There was no one he could turn to for help. He had no choice: he had to wait on the detective.

"This sake is from Akita Prefecture. It's called Rokushu," explained Shuhei, pouring a measure from a small earthenware bottle into a sake cup, which he had placed in front of Kaga. "It's a carbonated sake. The bubbles come from its being fermented twice."

"Delicious," said Kaga, after taking a sip. "It reminds me of champagne. Is it made the same way?"

"I . . . uhm . . . think so, yes. They put yeast in junmai-shu—that's sake made without any added alcohol or sugar—and then referment it."

"With champagne, they add a little sugar along with the yeast. How about with this sake?"

"Co . . . could you wait a moment, sir? I need to go and ask someone."

"It doesn't matter. You can tell me later. I wanted to ask if you'd heard about the murder in Kodenmacho?"

Despite his best efforts, Shuhei couldn't prevent his eyes widening at this unexpected and direct question. Kaga smiled smugly. "It seems that you have," he said.

"What about it?"

"Your boss probably told you that we found some snack cakes at the crime scene. Our guess is that the victim was enjoying them at the time of her murder. We found some of the same cake undigested in her stomach, as well as some in a plastic container on the table. The trouble is, we don't know who purchased them."

"It wasn't the victim?"

"No, unfortunately not. An insurance salesman visited the victim in her apartment prior to the murder. She offered him one, telling him that she'd just been given them. So we know that she got them from a third party."

"Oh." Shuhei couldn't come up with a coherent answer.

"It was easy enough to find out where the cakes came from. There was a slip of paper with the name of the shop attached to the container lid. That in itself wasn't particularly useful. I mean, tens, maybe even hundreds of people must buy those cakes from that shop every day. Luckily, though, there was something unusual about the snack cakes in the victim's apartment. It was a selection that included some cakes with and some without sweet bean paste filling. Usually they only sell this sort of mixed selection on request. Naturally enough, we asked them if anyone had requested a selection of cakes with and without filling on the day of the crime. The store clerk said that there had been several such orders. Unfortunately, she couldn't remember all the individual customers, but she did remember a certain young apprentice from Matsuya." Kaga pointed at Shuhei's chest. "She tells me you're around there all the time?"

Shuhei grunted ambiguously. Now he finally knew why this detective wanted to see him.

Shuhei was standing, rooted to the spot, when Katsuya, the other apprentice, stuck his head in. He was wondering what was keeping Shuhei.

"Sorry, sir. I'll be back later." Shuhei made his excuses and left Kaga's table.

"What the hell do you think you're doing?" asked Katsuya, eyeing Shuhei suspiciously.

"The customer was talking to me. . . ."

"You've got to learn to handle things better. You shouldn't allow any customer to monopolize your time like that."

"I know. I'm sorry."

Shuhei headed for the kitchen. Monopolizing him was probably exactly what Kaga was there for.

Shuhei went to serve Kaga several times after that, but

the detective didn't try to engage him in conversation again. He appeared to be enjoying his dinner.

That only had the effect of making Shuhei more nervous. What was the detective's plan? What exactly did he have up his sleeve? Why had he come tonight? No way was he there just to enjoy the food.

"This is Japanese mustard spinach. We mix it with stock to make a paste, which is then left to harden. This is a sprinkling of dried mullet roe powder on top."

As he slid the plate in front of Kaga, Shuhei examined the expression on his face. Kaga's only reaction was to comment on the exoticism of the dish and reach eagerly for his chopsticks. Shuhei turned away and started for the kitchen.

"We found three sets of fingerprints," Kaga said.

Shuhei stopped in his tracks and spun around in alarm. Kaga looked right at him, as he brought the chopsticks to his mouth.

"Very interesting. Despite being a paste, it still has that distinctive Japanese spinach taste. What else would you expect, I suppose?"

"What do you mean?" spluttered Shuhei. "About fingerprints?"

Not answering right away, Kaga lifted the sake cup to his lips with a self-important air.

"We found three sets of prints. On the plastic container with the cakes, I mean. One set belonged to the victim. We've established that the second set belonged to the store clerk in the cake shop. That leaves us with the third set. We think it likely that those prints belong to whoever brought the cakes to the victim's apartment. In the light of what happened, there's every chance that that person is the murderer."

The word *murderer* shocked Shuhei. He could feel the muscles in his face tightening, and he wasn't a good enough actor to hide his feelings.

"They're . . . they're not the cakes I bought." Shuhei's voice was quivering.

"No, because you ate all of yours, didn't you? You told us that."

Shuhei gave a series of frantic nods.

"You're a growing lad. No surprise that you occasionally have a snack in the middle of the working day. The owner said that at that time of the afternoon you have to water the sidewalk outside the restaurant. Where did you stash the cakes after you bought them? That white smock of yours doesn't have any pockets."

"That's why I . . . uhm . . . the bicycle basket."

"Bicycle?"

"I keep my bike parked in the alley beside the restaurant. I stuck the cakes in the bike's basket. After I'd finished watering the sidewalk, I brought them inside."

Kaga was silently gazing off into the middle distance. Shuhei wondered if he was drawing himself a mental picture. After a while, the detective looked at Shuhei and grinned.

"Of course you did. Polishing off a nice snack in secret is quite a challenge."

"Have we finished here?"

"Sure, I didn't mean to keep you," said Kaga, raising the

hand in which he held his chopsticks. "One last thing before you go. The last set of fingerprints on the container wasn't a match with yours."

Shuhei's eyes nearly popped out of his head. "*My* fingerprints? But how . . . when . . . ?"

"Oh, we have our little tricks."

Kaga's grin stretched from ear to ear.

That was when it hit Shuhei. He scowled. "The can of coffee!"

Now he realized why the police had been so insistent that he have a drink with them. It wasn't just about seeing whether he'd pick the sugarless coffee.

"Sneaky devils," he hissed before he could stop himself.

"That's how we cops operate, you know." Kaga drained his sake.

From then until Shuhei served the last of the dessert dishes, Kaga didn't say another word. Shuhei took care to avoid making eye contact.

After Kaga left, Yoriko called Shuhei over when he was carrying dirty dishes to the kitchen.

"That detective from the Nihonbashi precinct gave you the third degree, did he?"

"He's from Nihonbashi?"

"I asked around a bit. Seems he was transferred there quite recently. Anyway, what did he want to know?"

Although flustered, Shuhei decided to be frank. He figured he'd be fine as long as he didn't mention giving the cakes to Taiji.

"I can't believe it! Imagine coming here for dinner just to ask you about that!"

"What do you think I should do?"

"You've nothing to worry about. They didn't find your fingerprints, so you're okay. I shouldn't have called you over. Get on with the cleanup." Yoriko briskly turned her back on him.

4.

Shuhei was busy washing the dishes when Taiji stumped into the kitchen. Judging by his complexion, he'd hadn't yet had anything to drink that evening.

"Forget about this stupid job and come out with me for a while."

"Where to?"

"Who cares? Come and you'll find out soon enough. Chop-chop."

"I haven't finished cleaning up yet."

"I'm the boss, and this is an order. Shut up and do as you're told. Come on, get ready. I'll be waiting outside."

"Oh . . . uh . . . okay." Shuhei hastily dried his hands on a cloth and left the kitchen.

This was the first time Taiji had ever invited him out. As Shuhei went out into the street, he was feeling nervous. Where was Taiji going to take him?

"What the hell! Haven't you got any decent clothes?" Taiji scowled as he looked at what Shuhei was wearing.

"I'm sorry. Isn't this good enough?" He was wearing jeans and a T-shirt. "Should I go and change?"

"No, you're fine like that. Let's go."

They went out onto the main street, where Taiji hailed a cab. Shuhei was startled when he heard him ask the driver to take them to Ginza. Ginza was one of the most expensive, upscale shopping areas in Tokyo—in the world, in fact. Shuhei had never gone out there.

"What's wrong with you? Why get the wind up about Ginza?" Taiji grinned. "You want to be a successful chef, you need to get to know a little something about the grown-up world."

Shuhei spluttered something incoherent.

"Hey, be cool. It's not like I'm going to ask you to foot the bill or anything." Taiji bellowed with laughter, his mouth wide open.

The taxi came to a halt in a street packed with cars. The sidewalk was full of businessmen in suits and what Shuhei guessed were women from nightclubs and hostess bars. Shuhei had seen similar scenes in Ningyocho, but this was the first time he had been to a district devoted to nightlife.

"Get your head out of the clouds and follow me," snapped Taiji.

Shuhei hastily followed Taiji to a nightclub on the sixth floor of a building. It was spacious, but every single table was occupied. Everywhere there were flashing fairy lights, while the hostesses sitting with the male clientele exuded their own peculiar light and charm. Shuhei felt as though he'd landed on an alien planet.

A man in a black suit guided Taiji and Shuhei to a table. They sat down, and a woman came over a moment later. She was wearing a smart dress and had a petite face with her hair pulled back.

Taiji introduced Shuhei to her. The woman said that her name was Asami.

"You're seventeen? Wow! And planning to become a chef? That's just so cool. I guess you're too young to drink, then?" Asami was mixing Shuhei a whiskey and water when her hands came to a sudden stop.

"Beer will be fine for him. An aspiring chef who can't take a drink isn't worth his salt."

Shuhei felt tense and uncomfortable. He had no idea how one was supposed to behave in a place like this, nor could he think of anything to talk about.

Someone called Asami, and she left the table. Taiji beckoned to Shuhei.

"Come around here."

Shuhei slid around next to Taiji, who hissed into his ear.

"That Asami there, she's my woman. The cakes that you're always buying, I give 'em to her."

"Ah. . . ." gurgled Shuhei, staring at Taiji in surprise.

"The wife said something about a detective from Nihonbashi Precinct giving you grief about those cakes. There's no need to worry. They've nothing to do with the murder."

"I wasn't worried. . . ."

"No need to playact with me, kid. I know what you were thinking: that the murdered woman was my bit on the side?" Taiji held up his pinky finger in the Japanese sign for "girlfriend." "It was quite a coincidence, I grant you. Asami actually lives in the same apartment building where the murder happened."

"No?" gasped Shuhei.

"Yeah, that's the creepy thing. Like I said, though, I've got nothing to do with it, so you don't need to worry, either."

Shuhei nodded. He found it hard to believe that Taiji was lying.

"So why's the detective all over me?"

"Search me. Maybe cops just get off on hassling innocent people."

Asami came back to the table.

"What are you two whispering about?"

"Man talk. More importantly, how's my secret child? Eh?"

Shuhei's jaw dropped. Asami, catching his reaction from the corner of her eye, giggled.

"Oh, full of beans. Desperate to see Daddy."

"Jolly good, jolly good. Say hi to the little bugger from me."

Shuhei found their adult banter hard to follow.

A glass of beer was placed in front of him. He picked it up and took a swig.

Shuhei had drunk beer before, but this beer, which he was having in a Ginza nightclub, seemed to have a peculiarly bitter tang. *So this is what the adult world tastes like*, he thought.

5.

Yoriko heaved a heavy sigh. She was sitting at the far right end of the bar, the same place where she always sat. Her sigh expressed a mixture of emotions—relief that another week was safely over and done with, and pleasure at not having to wear her formal kimono here.

A waiter sidled up to her. "The usual, please," she said with a smile. The young man nodded and retreated. Coming by herself to this bar, hidden away in a hotel basement, was Yoriko's Saturday-night ritual. The neighborhood wasn't short of atmospheric old bars, but bumping into people she knew was the last thing Yoriko wanted on a weekend evening.

"Here you go, madam."

The waiter placed a small glass of gin and bitters in front of her. Yoriko disliked sweet cocktails.

She had just picked up her glass when someone slipped into the seat beside her.

"A drink with a kick—just what I'd expect from the manager of a famous old restaurant."

The voice was deep and memorable enough for her to recognize.

Sure enough, when she swiveled around, she saw whom she'd expected to see.

"Could I possibly take a minute or two of your time?" said Kaga with a smile.

"Be my guest," replied Yoriko, smiling back at him. Kaga was wearing the same charcoal gray jacket as earlier.

"Make mine a Guinness," he said to the waiter.

"I assume you're off duty, if you're drinking," remarked Yoriko.

"Absolutely. I've managed to solve one little mystery connected to the murder, so I'm planning to drink a toast to that."

"What, all on your lonesome? Where are your friends?"

Kaga swayed slightly from side to side.

"It's hardly worth holding a party about. I just managed to track down a dog I'd been looking for a while."

"A dog? Is a dog involved in the murder?"

"I don't know. All I can say for sure is that the dog isn't the murderer!"

Kaga's tone was grave. Yoriko scrutinized his face.

"The precinct commissioner dines at Matsuya from time to time. Why, he was there with someone just the other day."

"Oh, really? The commissioner at my last precinct was the same. Seems that precinct commissioners throughout Tokyo like nothing more than a good night out! If you want the lowdown on the best local restaurants, they're a much better source than the internet."

Yoriko laughed. "That was when the commissioner told me how he had brought in a rather 'interesting' new detective from another precinct. I asked him what exactly he meant by 'interesting.' He said that the detective in question was very sharp, very eccentric, and, to top it all off, very stubborn. I imagine he was talking about you, Detective Kaga?"

"Heaven only knows. . . ."

The waiter placed a glass of Guinness in front of Kaga. "Today's been another hard day," he said, lifting the glass to his lips.

"Cheers," said Yoriko, as she took a sip of her gin.

Kaga sighed contentedly.

"You look just as good in western clothes as you do in your kimono; either way, you're every inch the sophisticated, grown-up lady."

"Don't tease me."

"I'm not. All right, maybe I am being a touch ironic."

Yoriko put her glass down on the counter. "What do you mean?"

"What I'm trying to say, I guess, is that you seem to have a slightly childish aspect to your character—an immature side that takes pleasure in silly practical jokes."

"Detective Kaga." Yoriko swung around to face the detective full on. "If you've got something you want to say, then come out and say it. Patience isn't one of my virtues."

"I beg your pardon. Shall we get down to brass tacks? I'm talking about the Kodenmacho murder, of course."

"Are you're implying that we have something to do with it?"

"Let me go through this in the proper order. As I said the other day, we found some traditional small cakes at the crime scene, but we don't yet know who purchased them. There were three sets of fingerprints on the container: the victim's; the store clerk's; and a third, as yet unidentified, person's."

"Shuhei's already told me. They weren't his fingerprints either, were they?"

"No, they weren't."

"That's what puzzles me. If they're not his, then why come sniffing around our restaurant, Detective? Loads of people buy snack cakes from that shop. I bet Shuhei isn't the only one to have bought a mixed selection. Wouldn't it make more sense for you to start investigating other people?"

"That's precisely why I want to talk to you. As you say, Shuhei wasn't the only customer to order a mixed selection of cakes, nor were his prints on the container. That's why the guys from the Metropolitan Police were so quick to cross him off their list. In fact, I got the impression that they never really thought the person who bought the cakes was our murderer."

"What?" Yoriko's mouth was half open.

"Several places in the victim's apartment were wiped down," said Kaga in a jocular tone, before taking another swig of beer.

"Which means?"

"Which means that the murderer was careful to wipe down anything that he remembered touching. Which means that if the murderer and the purchaser of the snack cakes were one and the same person, he would definitely *not* have forgotten about the fingerprints on the plastic container. However, we could find no evidence of the plastic container having been wiped down."

"Aha, I see."

Yoriko looked into Kaga's swarthy face.

"In that case, Detective, why have you got such an almighty bee in your bonnet about the cakes? If they aren't connected to the crime, then what does it matter who bought the things?"

"That's not the how police investigations work. We have to sift through every little detail, asking ourselves why such and such a thing occurred. That will eventually lead us to the truth, even if all those individual things have no direct connection to one another."

Yoriko's glass was empty. She called the waiter and ordered a refill.

"Shuhei claims to have eaten all the cakes himself. It's not very professional of him, ducking out of work to stuff himself with sweets," Yoriko said.

"You really shouldn't give him a hard time. He didn't eat the cakes himself," declared Kaga emphatically.

"How can you be so sure? This isn't making any sense."

"I almost think you mean it. But I'll tell you what you really can't make sense of: the fact that the cakes Shuhei bought ended up in the murdered woman's apartment."

Yoriko felt slightly alarmed. How had Kaga guessed her thoughts? She quickly regained her composure.

"Like I said before, if there's something you want to say to me, then come right out and say it."

Kaga slowly pulled himself upright on his stool and looked straight at her.

"Fine. Let's start from the conclusion: the cakes at the crime scene *were* the ones Shuhei bought. How can I be so categorical about that? Because one of the cakes had something very distinctive about it. I think you know what I'm talking about?"

Yoriko swallowed and looked away.

Kaga giggled.

"It threw our forensics guys for a loop. They were like, what's this all about? I was pretty surprised when they told me that one of the cakes was spiked with wasabi. Unbelievable!"

A second gin and bitters was placed in front of Yoriko. She picked it up and turned toward Kaga.

"This sounds like a most amusing story. I promise not to interrupt. Go ahead and talk me through it nice and slowly."

"Would it be all right? For me to order another drink too, I mean?" Kaga plunked his empty glass down on the counter.

Yoriko took a cigarette and a lighter out of her handbag. This hotel bar was the only place she ever smoked. Since becoming the co-owner and manager of Matsuya, she was careful never to smoke in front of other people.

"One of the cakes at the crime scene was spiked with wasabi. Whoever did it didn't just cut a slit to inject the wasabi—they went so far as to conceal the slit by filling it with starch paste. It's hardly worth pointing out that wasabi-flavored cakes are not available at the store, meaning that someone must have tampered with it later. Was it the murder victim? Was it the person who gave the cakes to her? Or was it someone else entirely? We have some scientific data that should help us figure out the answer to that question. According to our forensics team's analysis, the cake with the wasabi was a little older than the others—it was a little drier and a little harder, to be precise. Forensics reckon that it was baked at least a day before all the others. What does that tell us? That the perpetrator—I'm referring here to the crime of 'wasabi spiking'—didn't add the wasabi to one of the freshly purchased snack cakes but prepared a doctored cake in advance, which they then swapped out for one of the newer ones. That means that cakes must have been purchased on two occasions on two successive days. I went to the shop to check up on this. When I inquired if any of the customers who'd bought the mixed snack cake selection on the day of the murder had also made a purchase on the previous day, the store clerk couldn't think of anyone who fit the bill . . . but she did tell me something else rather intriguing."

Another Guinness was placed in front of Kaga. He took a little sip, as if to wet the tip of his tongue. Wiping the foam from his lips with the back of his hand, he looked at Yoriko.

"She told me that the young apprentice from Matsuya came to the store only on the second day and that the owner had come the day before. As the owner of a famous old restaurant, everyone in the area knows and recognizes you."

Yoriko stubbed out her smoked-down cigarette in the ashtray.

This is one smart detective, she was thinking. *I don't know why he's wasting away as a precinct cop here in Nihonbashi, but I bet he's got an impressive record.*

Yoriko steeled herself. There was no longer any point in hiding anything.

"I see. So it wasn't Shuhei you were after, Detective Kaga, it was me."

"I needed to talk to Shuhei as well. I guessed that he had bought the cakes for your husband. I don't mean to be rude, but your husband is the only person at the restaurant with nothing to do at that time of the afternoon. I needed to talk to Shuhei to figure out when the wasabi-spiked cake was slipped in."

"Did you manage to figure that out?"

"I think I did." Kaga nodded. "Shuhei kept the cakes in his bicycle basket before giving them to your husband. Anyone who knew that could switch out a single cake easily enough, given that the back entrance of the restaurant's in the alley, too."

Kaga directed a searching stare at Yoriko. "You put the wasabi in, didn't you?"

"It's probably a waste of time for me to deny it this late in the game."

"If you did, we'd be forced to fingerprint you, so we could compare your prints to the third set on the plastic box."

Yoriko lit a second cigarette and sighed.

"I owe you an apology, Mr. Kaga. You're right on every count. But surely what I did doesn't constitute a crime?"

"Of course not," chimed in Kaga. "More like a practical joke. You wanted to surprise your husband's girlfriend, to make her nervous?"

Yoriko burst out laughing, and a cloud of white smoke billowed from her mouth. "The amount of research you've done, I imagine you know all about that woman, too."

"Oh, she was easy enough to track down. All I had to do was visit the clubs and bars your husband frequents. In that world, everyone's prepared to talk. What was the girl's name? Asami, I think. She works in Ginza and lives on the same floor of the same apartment building as the murder victim."

"She's a nasty little hussy. But that fool husband of mine has always had a weakness for women of that sort. Does she have any children?"

"Yes. One. About a year old."

"Apparently she's put the word out that my husband's the father. Any normal man would get in a funk about something like that, but not my idiot husband. No, he's tickled pink. Any free time and he's off to her place to coo over the baby. He even gives the girl an allowance. Oh, what a nice fellow he is."

"What are you getting at?"

"The whole thing's a lie. The baby's not his. A while back, I hired a detective to look into the matter. Before she leaves for work, she hands the kid over to a guy who lives in a cheap dive in Ueno. He's not a babysitter, he's the real father."

"Why don't they live together?"

"Because if they did, she'd no longer be able to squeeze any cash out of my husband. At some point the truth will come out: I'm guessing she's using the kid to scam as much as she can get out of him."

"So the wasabi-spiked cake was a sort of warning shot over the enemy's bow?"

Yoriko broke into a smile.

"You're a smart man, Detective Kaga, but you're wide of the mark there."

"I'm wrong?"

"Yes. It was that stupid husband of mine whom I wanted to eat the spiked snack cake. Remember, the box contained seven with bean paste and three without. He made a point of having Shuhei include some no-bean-paste cakes because my husband doesn't like the stuff; I knew he'd go for those ones."

"And you put the wasabi into one of the ones without sweet bean paste?"

Yoriko tapped the ash from her cigarette into the ashtray and nodded.

"The man really needs to wise up. To the fact that the kid's not his, I mean. Physiologically, he can't have children."

Kaga's hand gave a jerk, and he almost dropped his glass.

"Seriously?"

"Oh, for sure. He went to hospital for tests years ago. But our Taiji won't come out and tell the hussy what's what. It's partly about not wanting to cut ties with a woman who's grown to depend on him, but more than anything I think he enjoys the thrill of having a secret love child, even though he knows it's a lie. He likes to present himself as the great extramarital playboy, but in fact he's a rather timid little man. My guess is that he's only slept with that woman a couple of times."

Kaga exhaled loudly.

"And that rubbed you the wrong way?"

"I wasn't too happy about it. The fellow thought he was doing such a masterful job of pulling the wool over my eyes. That whole wasabi trick was me trying to punish him. . . .

Like you said, Detective Kaga, it was childish, a practical joke."

"The problem is that your husband doesn't even know he's been punished! He's oblivious to the existence of any wasabi-spiked cake. Nor does he know that the cakes he gave his girlfriend ended up in a crime scene."

"That's just it, though. How did the cakes get there? I can't figure it out."

Kaga gave a wry smile and stroked his stubbly chin.

"I asked Asami about that. She told me that *she* gave the box of cakes to the victim. Understandably enough, she didn't tell me who'd given them to her. She just described him as 'a good customer of the bar she works at.'"

"Why did she give them away?"

"That's because . . ." Kaga frowned as if unsure how to say it. "Because she doesn't actually like them."

"*What!*"

"Yes, apparently she dislikes Japanese sweets. The whole business of bean paste or no bean paste is neither here nor there—she never eats Japanese cakes of any kind. When she told your husband that she liked them, she was just trying to be diplomatic after he gave her a box of them. Now she's in trouble because he brings her the things all the damn time! She was getting so fed up with them that on that day she got rid of them by giving them to a woman in another apartment on the same floor almost immediately after your husband left. When Asami gave her the cakes, they were still in the original bag from the pastry shop; that's why we didn't find her fingerprints on the container, or your husband's prints, or Shuhei's."

"She's really playing my husband for a fool!" Yoriko pressed a hand to her temple. "You're telling me he hands over the cakes without her even letting him inside? Unbelievable. The thought of having to spend the rest of my life with such an idiot makes my head ache. Oh, and I must tell Shuhei not to buy any more cakes for him."

"That reminds me, I feel bad about Shuhei. Maybe I was a bit heavy-handed with the boy. Still, he's a good kid: he never admitted to buying the cakes at your husband's request."

"He's a useful person to have on the Matsuya team. Anybody can learn to cook, but the ability to keep secrets is a real asset in a people-centric business like ours."

"How about we drink a toast to the young cook in whose hands Matsuya's future looks secure?"

"Provided my fool of a husband doesn't bankrupt the business first!"

Yoriko raised a hand to summon the waiter.

3

THE DAUGHTER-IN-LAW OF THE CHINA SHOP

1.

"What's this Iga fish plate doing on the shelf here? The black Bizen ware is supposed to be displayed over here. You got it wrong again. Why do I have to tell you the same thing over and over again? I'm at my wit's end."

Suzue grumbled to herself as she rearranged the plates displayed on the store shelves. Naoya just raised his newspaper a little higher in front of his face and pretended not to hear. Having to absorb an earful of complaints after coming home from the office every day was not his idea of fun.

It was the ideal time of day for customers to wander in off the street, but none of the people walking by outside showed any sign of stopping. On a day this hot, popping into a nice, air-conditioned store for a bit of browsing was a natural impulse. Unfortunately, their shop was wide open, with only an old electric fan whirring away to cool the air.

"Getting air-conditioning is the least we can do—if we want any customers at all, that is," Maki had commented the other day. She and Naoya had married last fall, so this was her first summer at the family shop-cum-residence.

"What's the point? With an open-fronted shop like ours,

air-conditioning won't make a bit of difference," was Suzue's response. She was looking at Naoya as she spoke. Even when they were talking to each other, the two women barely looked at one another.

"Then we should close up the front of the store. If we got glass doors, people would be able to look in from outside, and the cold air would stay in," said Maki, looking at Naoya.

When Naoya made the mistake of emitting even a noncommittal grunt, Suzue felt that she had to argue the point.

"Closing up the front, even with sliding glass doors, will still make it that much harder for customers to come in. Anyway, what about the things we have on display out on the street? What are we supposed do with them? Bring them all back inside and slam the doors shut behind them? Everyone will think that Yanagisawa's gone out of business."

"It's like a sauna in here right now. Even the few people who've happily come in can't beat a retreat fast enough. No one spends any time browsing."

"That's just not true. Not everyone's in love with air-conditioning, you know. Some of the customers comment on our wind chime and how it makes them feel cooler."

"Only old-timers would say something like that."

"Those 'old-timers' are important customers for us."

The two of them went at it hammer and tongs. Naoya was stuck in the middle, unable to take sides. All he could do was waggle his head ambiguously and groan inside. But the womenfolk wouldn't let him off so lightly; in the end, both pressured him to express an opinion on the matter.

"Oh, golly," mumbled Naoya, scratching his head and smiling goofily at them both. "How about you let me think about it a while? Maybe we should have dinner now?"

The two women fell silent. Dinner was eaten in an atmosphere of subdued tension. That's the way things were in the Yanagisawa household.

Naoya wanted to improve things, but he was at a loss for ideas. He tried discussing the problem with an older colleague at work, but his colleague quickly diagnosed the situation as hopeless.

"When a wife and a mother-in-law are at loggerheads, the husband can't expect to sort things out. That's just naive. Here's what you should do: Hear both women out separately; shut up, listen, and never ever contradict them—that's just pouring oil on the flames. After you've heard what they each have to say, look like you agree, comment on how reasonable their point of view is, and promise to convey their opinion to the other party when the time is right. Then—this is the crucial part—never say a word about it to the other woman. Of course, they'll hound you, ask you how it went—but you'll just have to grin and bear it. Divert their anger toward yourself, that's the only viable solution."

"Doesn't sound like much fun," mumbled Naoya.

"Buck up," said his colleague, smacking him on the back. "You've got yourself a lovely young wife. I'm sure she's worth the hassle."

People tended to be more jealous of him for his young wife than sympathetic about the friction between her and his mother.

Naoya had met Maki at a sleazy hostess club. She'd been working there, and he'd come in with a friend.

That night she'd been wearing a pale blue dress that showed off her tanned skin to perfection. She wasn't classically good-looking, but she had unforgettably lovely eyes. A skilled conversationalist, she listened wide-eyed and with rapt attention to whatever Naoya had to say (which, frankly, wasn't all that interesting). She was cheerful, her features expressive, and her laugh sounded like cascading marbles.

When it came time to leave, Naoya was already head over heels in love with her. He went back to the club by himself the next day, and the day after. His salary was by no means lavish, but since he lived in the old family home, he had no living expenses and a good amount saved for a man of his age. He believed that Maki was someone well worth squandering money on.

When the friend with whom he had first gone to the club tried to warn him off, Naoya wasn't interested.

"You need to pull yourself together. What's a poor salaryman like you doing falling for a professional hostess? She's out of your league, man. You've got to put an end to this."

Guessing that everyone else would probably say the same thing, he decided to keep his mouth shut and keep going to see Maki discreetly.

Rather unexpectedly, the next warning had come from Maki herself.

"You'll run through all your savings if you keep coming here like this, Mr. Yanagisawa. You're coming alone, so I know you can't be charging it to your firm."

"Don't worry about it. I may not look like it, but I've got a pretty big nest egg."

"That may be, but keep this up and you'll be broke in no time."

"Coming here's the only way I get to see you, Maki-chan."

By Naoya's modest standards this was a bold declaration. And it worked like a charm.

"Why don't we go on a date one weekend?" Maki said.

At first, Naoya was sure she was pulling his leg, but then she emailed, asking him to pick a day.

On their first date they went to Tokyo Disneyland. In daylight, Maki looked healthier and less childlike than in the dark of the nightclub. She confessed that at the club she pretended to be three years younger than her real age. She was actually twenty-four. To Naoya, the difference seemed hardly worth lying about, but Maki insisted that, by pretending to be younger, she got better treatment from both the customers and the club's management.

Naoya couldn't have cared less one way or the other. He was in heaven just being able to date her.

As their dates became more frequent, Naoya didn't just want her to be his girlfriend, he wanted her to leave her job at the club.

"I wish you'd just quit," he came out and said once.

Maki looked uncomfortable.

"The thing is, I can't do any other kind of work. It's too late for me to get an office job, and even if I did, I'd definitely earn a whole lot less. I'd never be able to make my rent."

Naoya had been to her apartment a few times, and she was right—the average office worker would never be able to afford it.

"In that case . . ."

He paused, then launched into a speech he hadn't planned on delivering. "Why don't we get married and you can come and live with me?"

A look of surprise came over Maki's face; then she gave a shy smile, before bursting into tears and draping her arms around his neck.

Naoya introduced Maki to his mother, Suzue, a few days later. Things went okay. Suzue displayed a certain distaste when she heard about Maki's nightclub job, but not enough to veto the marriage. As for Maki, she didn't seem to dislike the idea of living with his mother and helping out at the family china shop. Naoya felt sure that everything was going to be fine.

At first, everything went swimmingly, and Maki enjoyed helping out at the shop. Things, however, took a serious turn for the worse for a most unexpected reason.

A cleaning rag was the cause of it all.

At the end of last year, Naoya got home from work one day to find Suzue sulking in the shop. "Where's Maki?" he asked.

"No idea," came the curt reply.

Sensing that something had happened, Naoya went upstairs to their bedroom. There he found Maki in a flood of tears, a cloth clutched in her hands. "What's wrong?" asked Naoya.

She spread the cloth in front of him.

"Look."

One glance was all Naoya needed to realize what had happened and to grasp the gravity of the situation.

The rag was made from several pieces of toweling chopped up and sewn together. Naoya immediately recognized the original white towel with the Hello Kitty pattern. Maki was a Hello Kitty fan and an avid collector of the branded merchandise. The towel had been part of her collection. She'd never have turned it into a cleaning rag; Suzue had to be the guilty party.

Naoya went back down to his mother and held the rag in front of her. "Why did you do this?" he demanded angrily.

"Why not? We'll be needing lots of rags for the big end-of-year cleanup."

"That's not what I mean. I'm asking you why you had to use *this* particular towel. It's not like we're short of towels here."

"Not just any old towel will do. Old, well-used towels make the best cloths. They're the ones I need."

"But, Mother, this was Maki's favorite towel. You know you shouldn't have used it."

"We just got some new towels as presents. A new one will be much better for her."

"That's not the point. Maki loved this Hello Kitty towel. It meant a lot to her."

"Oh, will you shut up! What is Hello Kitty anyway? Just some idiotic cartoon cat. What's an adult woman doing kicking up a fuss about something so infantile?"

Suzue didn't feel guilty and wasn't inclined to apologize. Had Maki decided to let bygones be bygones, things might have calmed down. But Maki had no intention of backing down. She told her husband that she wouldn't address another word to his mother until she apologized. When Naoya relayed this to Suzue, she stayed firm. "She's free to do whatever she likes," she declared.

Naoya's married life, which had been sailing along so smoothly, was suddenly buffeted by storm winds.

2.

Maki returned to the china shop with a bag from the supermarket. She was dressed in a T-shirt and ripped jeans. Although the rips were part of the design, Suzue had trouble grasping the concept of deliberately distressed clothing. A couple of weeks ago, the two women quarreled when Suzue criticized the jeans for being shabby.

"It's boiling outside." Maki was fanning her face with her hand as she came in. "I started sweating the minute I left the supermarket."

"You poor thing." Naoya aimed the electric fan directly at her.

"There's not a breath of wind," Maki said, turning her back to the fan and enjoying the play of air on her sweat-beaded neck. "Must be why the famous Yanagisawa wind-chime's so quiet today. Eh?"

"Oh . . . uh . . . yeah."

Did you really need to say that? Naoya thought. Maki's remark was aimed squarely at Suzue.

"I think I'll go sort out the payment slips," Suzue announced. "Having to rearrange everything on the shelves was a chore, especially when there's a meeting of the local shop owners' association tonight. Some people seem to enjoy making work for other people. I just don't know."

Maki scowled. Without so much as a glance in her direction, Suzue slipped off her sandals and vanished into the room behind the shop.

"What was that about redoing the shelves?" asked Maki.

"Mother was making a fuss about the sweet fish plates. Something about the white Iga ware being mixed in with the black Bizen ware."

Maki screwed up her face as if she had bitten into a lemon. "Who cares if they're white or black? I went to a lot of trouble to make an attractive display."

"There's no accounting for tastes."

"Except that *you* said I could redo the display in line with *my* taste."

"I know, but just for today, why don't we be nice and let Mom have her way." Naoya placed his hands together in a beseeching gesture.

Maki pouted back at him.

"That reminds me, what about the air-conditioning? We should get a unit installed before summer arrives in earnest."

Naoya flinched. *Not that again!*

"I'm thinking about it."

"What do you need to think about in this heat? Or have you sided with your mother?"

"No."

Unable to come up with a better riposte, Naoya was mentally squirming when a man called out, "Hello there." *A customer!* Naoya thanked his lucky stars.

"Good afternoon."

The man wore a pale blue shirt over a black T-shirt. He looked to be in his early thirties.

"You must be Mr. and Mrs. Yanagisawa?" the man said, looking first at Naoya, then at Maki.

"That's right," Naoya replied. "How can we help you?"

"Mrs. Maki Yanagisawa?"

"That's me."

The man smiled and pulled out a business card.

"This is me. I'd like you to help us."

Maki's eyes widened as she read the card. "You're from the police?"

"What!" exclaimed Naoya.

Maki handed him the card. Their visitor was a detective from Nihonbashi Precinct by the name of Kyoichiro Kaga.

"Do you know a woman named Mineko Mitsui?" Kaga inquired.

"Mitsui? No, never heard of her," answered Naoya, glancing over at Maki.

After thinking for a moment, Maki asked hesitantly:

"Does she live in Kodenmacho by any chance?"

"She does, she does." Kaga nodded his head several times. "So, you do know her?"

"She shops here from time to time. Has something happened?"

Kaga's face stiffened slightly. He looked at each of them in turn.

"I'm sorry to say she's dead. It happened two days ago."

Maki gave a shocked gasp. "How, why?" she murmured.

"She was strangled. We're treating it as murder."

"Murder!" Naoya exclaimed, then looked back at his wife. Her jaw had dropped and she gaped back at him.

"You said she came here 'from time to time.' Can you give me a clearer idea of what you mean? About once a week?"

Maki shook her head.

"More like once a month."

"When was the last time she was here?"

"Let me think." Maki consulted the desktop calendar beside the cash register. "Probably about a week ago."

"Do you remember how she looked?"

"I do. Completely normal."

"Did you talk to her?"

"I did. Only a little, though."

"What about? If you don't mind."

"What did we talk about?" Maki paused. "She'd come to buy some chopsticks. A present, she said. We didn't have the set she wanted in stock, so she left empty-handed."

"Do you know who she planned to give the chopsticks to?"

"It wasn't really my place to ask."

"The chopsticks she wanted—are you still out of stock?"

"I ordered them right away, but they haven't come in yet. I can show you the catalog page."

Kaga's eyes gleamed. "Could you?"

"Let's see now," said Maki. She pulled out a catalog that was squeezed up against the cash register, opened it, and showed the detective. "It's this set here."

Naoya peered over his wife's shoulder. It was a his-and-hers set for married couples. The chopsticks for the man were in black lacquer, and those of the woman, vermilion. Both were decorated with a cherry blossom motif in real mother-of-pearl.

"Very nice," said Kaga.

"It's one of our most popular items. It sells especially well in the marriage season."

Noticing how authoritative Maki sounded, Naoya reflected that she'd taken to the business like a duck to water. Suzue would have probably made some snarky comment if she'd been there. "Hah! She hasn't even worked here a year and already she's a know-it-all."

"Thank you," said Kaga, as he handed the catalog back to Maki.

"Detective, could I ask you something?" Naoya interjected. "Does her visiting our store have any connection to her murder?"

"Oh, no, no, no." Kaga smiled and waved his hand dismissively. "I'm going around to all the stores where Ms. Mitsui was a regular customer. Is there anything else you think I should know, Mrs. Yanagisawa?"

Maki cocked her head thoughtfully, then shook her head. Naoya wondered why the detective was being so persistent.

"Okay. Look, if you do remember anything, call me. My cell phone number's on the back of my card. No detail's too small," Kaga said, his eyes boring into Maki's face.

"We'll do that."

"Thank you very much. Sorry to trouble you." Kaga shot each of them a look and left the shop.

3.

Naoya immediately went out to fetch a newspaper and read up on the murder. Because Naoya only worked in the store on Saturdays, he'd never met Mineko Mitsui.

"She was a good-looking woman. The paper says she was forty-five, but she certainly didn't look it. I always thought she was in her thirties. To think that she was murdered, it's just too awful," said Maki gravely, as they were having dinner. "She was a nice person. She even brought me an ice cream once."

With Suzue out at the meeting of the local shop owners' association that night, it was just the two of them for dinner. Naoya was enjoying the uncharacteristically peaceful atmosphere, and his beer tasted better than it had in months.

"I don't really get why the detective came to our store." Naoya looked puzzled.

"He told us why. He's visiting all the stores that Ms. Mitsui went to regularly."

"I know. The point is, how did he know that she shopped here? Perhaps she mentioned to someone that she was here last week, although the article said that she lived alone."

"Maybe the police found a receipt from here."

"From when? You said she didn't actually buy anything last week."

Maki frowned, then shrugged her shoulders as if sloughing off the whole business.

"Then I don't know the answer. Anyway, what does it matter? It's nothing to do with us."

"I know, but still . . ." Naoya was chasing down a piece of pickled daikon radish with a slug of beer when a thought suddenly came to him. "That detective—he knew your name."

"What?"

"He asked for *Maki* Yanagisawa. I'm sure he did."

"Did he?"

"Yes, he did. Don't you think that's a bit odd? I mean, if he's just traipsing around a load of different stores, he'd have no reason to know your first name. It's definitely odd."

"Did he really say my name . . . ?" Maki began clearing the empty dishes off the table.

"I wonder how he knew? Do you think there was something with your name on it in the murdered woman's apartment?"

"You can ask keep asking till the cows come home. I've no idea."

Naoya had just crossed his arms over his chest, when a voice sang out, "It's me. I'm home." Suzue was back.

Discussing the murder was now off the menu. Maki vanished into the kitchen where she started busily washing the dishes.

"The meeting was a nightmare! The old boys were jabbering on, and I just couldn't get away." Suzue was massaging her shoulders as she came into the room. "They were talking about something called 'home pages.' Haven't the foggiest what that means! To be honest, I don't think the old boys had much of an idea themselves."

"You must be tired. Want some dinner?"

"I had something there," she said, sitting down at the table. "But maybe I'll have a little ochazuke rice." She glared disapprovingly at the pickled daikon radish. "What's this?"

"Maki made it. It's pretty good."

"Oh, *please*. She should know that I have problems with my teeth. The woman seems to go out of her way to make things like this, when she knows perfectly well that I can't cope with anything hard."

"Mother!"

Naoya glowered at Suzue, who was nonchalantly brewing some green tea.

Maki emerged from the kitchen and silently removed the dish of pickled radish. She put it in the refrigerator and left the room, still without saying a word. Hearing her charge noisily up the stairs, Naoya heaved a weary sigh.

Suzue picked up the newspaper from the table.

"What's this thing doing here? Honestly, that girl seems to think she's above doing any proper tidying up."

"You're talking nonsense, Mother. I went out and got the paper for a reason. There was something I wanted to find out about. Have you heard anything about what happened over in Kodenmacho?"

"Kodenmacho? No."

Suzue listened intently as Naoya gave her an account of the detective's visit. He was careful not to mention the fact that the detective knew Maki's name; that would only be asking for trouble.

"Now that you mention it, the proprietor of Kisamiya said that a detective had come around his place, too."

Kisamiya was a cutlery shop with a history stretching back to the Edo period. It sold such things as knives and shears, all handmade by in-house craftsmen. It also offered a knife-sharpening service.

"The woman went to Kisamiya not long before her murder. What was it he said she'd bought? Oh yes, kitchen scissors."

"Kitchen scissors, eh? Is that important?"

'Well, the proprietor said the detective wouldn't stop asking him questions. Was the woman a regular customer? Did she say why she needed the scissors? Stuff like that."

"Oh yeah? And what did he say?"

"That he couldn't remember having seen her before. As to why she bought the scissors, that's not something he would ever ask a customer."

"It's certainly an odd question."

"But the detective has a point. You can pick up a pair of cheap kitchen scissors anywhere. Normally the people who buy the handmade ones at Kisamiya have a very specific purpose in mind. According to the owner, she didn't seem to fit the mold."

"Interesting. . . ."

What was the significance of Mineko Mitsui buying a pair of kitchen scissors? Naoya couldn't see any link to the murder, but the police must have a reason for investigating the matter.

"You said the murdered woman was forty-five?" said Suzue, sipping her tea. "Poor thing. Still so young. Anything can happen at any time. You've just got to enjoy life while you can."

"You seem to be doing a good job in that department, Mother," Naoya said. "You're leaving next week on that trip with your pals from the ballad-singing group, right? You're going to Ise?"

"Yes, we're going to the Ise Grand Shrine and to Shima peninsula. It's the Shima peninsula part I'm looking forward to most. It's famous for its abalone."

"Great."

Suzue seemed to be far more eager to discuss her upcoming trip than the murder case. After she finished her tea, Naoya left the table. If he spent too much time with his mother, Maki would only give him a hard time when he got upstairs.

4.

Naoya worked for a large construction company. His main responsibility was providing after-sales service to residential home buyers. Having completed the ninety-day post-sale inspection of a detached house in Toyocho, he decided to swing by the family home, which was on his way back to the office.

Parking his little van on Ningyocho Boulevard, he peered into the shop. Suzue was on the phone, but there was no sign of Maki.

"Have you got a brochure? Could you mail me one? What sort of product line do you have? . . . What's that? Japanese spiny lobster? You've got some interesting things in stock. Anything else? Matsusaka beef? . . . What? Oh, I see. Yes, I'd buy that in a jiffy. You've been very helpful. Thank you."

Suzue didn't notice Naoya coming in, and she jumped when she hung up the phone and turned around.

"What are you doing here at this time of day?"

"I was passing by, so thought I'd drop in. Did that call have something to do with your trip?"

"In a way . . ."

"Uhm, what about . . . ?"

"She's at the hairdresser, if that's what you're about to ask. Heaven only knows what color she'll dye her hair this time."

Suzue's mouth turned down at the corners.

Naoya was mystified at how the two women managed to communicate when he was away. Given that they didn't actually *talk* to one other, how could Suzue have possibly known where Maki had gone?

"Oh, good afternoon." Suzue smiled warmly to someone behind Naoya.

Turning around, he saw the detective from the day before walking in to the shop. He was holding a small paper bag.

"Thanks for your help yesterday, Mr. Yanagisawa."

"Detective Kaga, was it?"

"That's right. Well remembered."

Suzue cast an inquiring glance at Naoya.

"This gentleman is the policeman who spoke to Maki and me yesterday," he explained.

"Oh, I heard you visited the folks at Kisamiya, too." Suzue looked at the detective.

"Word travels fast, eh. That should make my job easier. Did the people at Kisamiya tell you that the murder victim bought a pair of kitchen scissors there?"

"Yes, they did. Is that important?"

Kaga smiled broadly, paused a moment, then asked, "Do you have any kitchen scissors here?"

"What!" exclaimed Suzue and Naoya in unison.

"We have a pair, yes," Suzue said.

"Could you show them to me, if it's not too much trouble?"

"Certainly, but may I ask why?"

Kaga scratched his head sheepishly.

"A precinct detective like me has to do all sorts of little jobs involving things that may or may not have any significance. In this particular case, I'm looking into the question of kitchen scissors. I therefore need to get everybody even vaguely connected to the case to show me their scissors. I know it's a bore. Sorry."

Kaga had couched his request in such humble terms that he won Suzue over. "Just wait a minute." She disappeared into the back of the shop.

"Tough gig, huh?" ventured Naoya.

"Tell me about it." Kaga gave a rueful grin.

Suzue came back carrying a pair of kitchen scissors.

"They're completely plain, ordinary scissors. Nothing like the handcrafted ones they sell at Kisamiya," Suzue said, holding them out to the detective.

"They're on the new side. Did you get them recently?"

"A couple of years ago, I think. They don't get a whole lot of wear and tear."

"Thanks," said Kaga, returning the scissors to Suzue. "And your wife?"

"She's out," replied Naoya. "At the hairdresser's."

"I see. Oh yes, one more thing. Do you like rice crackers?" Kaga pulled a packet of rice crackers out of the bag in his hand and proffered them to Suzue. "Here, take these. I actually bought them a couple of days ago, I'm afraid."

"Are they from the shop over in Amazake Alley? I used to love their crackers, but my teeth have been acting up recently. . . ." Suzue looked at Naoya. "However, I'm sure the younger generation will be happy to step into the breach. Thank you very much."

"Yes, you've got to be careful with your teeth. Thank you for your help, and I'll be on my way."

Kaga nodded at the two, then turned and left the store. Naoya went after him.

"Excuse me, Detective, but something's been bugging me since yesterday."

"Oh yes?" Kaga stroked his chin. "Shall we go and get something cold to drink?"

The two men went to a local coffee shop and settled themselves at a table on the second floor that overlooked the street.

Without beating about the bush, Naoya asked Kaga how he knew his wife's first name. Kaga thumped the table in exasperation, though his expression remained cheerful.

"You're right. I did use your wife's first name. I didn't think she was involved. I was careless."

"What do you mean?" Naoya leaned in toward Kaga. "Is Maki involved somehow? Now you come around, asking to see our kitchen scissors—there's something off about this. Tell me what's going on."

As Naoya became increasingly excited, Kaga made soothing gestures with his hands.

"It's all right. It's nothing important. I can understand your concern, so let me explain. It all goes back to a pair of kitchen scissors we found in the victim's apartment."

"What, more kitchen scissors?"

"Yes, but hers were brand-new and still wrapped in Kisamiya paper. That was what made us curious. The victim already had another pair of kitchen scissors in her apartment, which weren't that old. So why buy a new pair? For a present, perhaps? The fact that the price tag was left on suggests otherwise. Normally, when you're giving someone something, you take the tag off.

"At the same time, we found something interesting in the email folder on the victim's computer. Examining the time stamps on her emails, we discovered she'd sent one just before she was killed." Kaga pulled out his notebook. "I can tell you the exact words. 'I bought them. They cost me 6,300 yen. I'll bring them around to the store soon.' I didn't make the connection with the kitchen scissors right away. I mean, you wouldn't normally think of scissors costing so much! But when I went to Kisamiya, I saw that was what their kitchen scissors cost: 6,300 yen. I took another look to see whom the mail was addressed to, and it was—"

"Maki Yanagisawa."

"Precisely," Kaga confirmed. "We also found a receipt from Yanagisawa's in the victim's apartment, so it was reasonable to assume that your wife or your mother was the intended recipient. I should point out that the mail never actually reached your wife. It looks as though her cell phone isn't set up to receive email, only texts. My guess is that this was the first time the victim had tried emailing your wife. I think the two of them only got to know each other recently."

"You think that my Maki asked this Mitsui woman to buy her a pair of scissors?"

"That was what I thought when I came to see you yesterday. Your wife, however, didn't mention it at all. That's what I meant when I said I didn't think she was involved."

"Maybe you'd be better off asking her directly."

Kaga chuckled meaningfully and took a sip of his iced coffee.

"A policeman never likes to show his hand. If we think someone's concealing something, we hang back to see how things play out. It's quite possible your wife had a valid reason for not saying anything—a family issue or something."

At the words "family issue," a light went on in Naoya's head. "Ah!" he exclaimed.

"What is it?"

"Oh, nothing," said Naoya, sucking up his iced tea through a straw.

"What I can't quite figure out is why your wife needed to ask Ms. Mitsui to buy the scissors for her. Kisamiya is close to your shop, so she can swing by herself easily enough. There's something else: why did she even need new kitchen scissors in the first place? Your mother showed me the ones you have now, and they look fine. I was hoping your wife would provide me with an explanation. But maybe that explanation involved something she felt uncomfortable with you hearing."

"Perhaps you're right."

"Got any ideas?"

Kaga's eyes bored into Naoya. Naoya sighed.

"Something occurred to me just now. I'm going to have to air some of the family's dirty laundry, but I guess that's better than leaving you with your suspicions. It's a bit squalid, but there's some family drama going on right now."

Naoya proceeded to tell a rather startled-looking Kaga about the feud between his wife and his mother. He was relieved to have someone to confide in.

"The wife and the mother-in-law at loggerheads. That's a bit of a cliché. What do you think it's got to do with the kitchen scissors?"

"Maybe you're lucky enough not to have firsthand experience, Detective, but women can be stubborn creatures.

My wife and my mother both cook, but they don't want to use the same utensils. The long and the short of it is that we have two of almost everything in the kitchen—one for my missus and one for my mother."

"I see." Kaga nodded sagely. "That would explain why your wife was planning to get another pair of kitchen scissors for her exclusive use."

"That's my interpretation. I guess she asked a third party to get them for her so that my mother and I wouldn't know what she was up to. The staff at Kisamiya all know Maki, so she was probably worried that they would let it slip to my mother."

"Thanks for letting me know. They're really at each other's throats, are they?"

"It's a nightmare," said Naoya, his lips twisting in distaste. "My mother will be away next week, so I'm looking forward to a little peace and quiet."

"She's going away? Where to?"

"Ise and the Shima peninsula. She's excited about the abalone she'll be able to eat there. Of course, that just made Maki fly off the handle. 'How come no one's taking me anywhere?'"

"Oh yes, the abalone . . . ," murmured Kaga, gazing into the middle distance.

5.

Two days later, Naoya returned from work in the evening to find a battle under way.

The two women weren't going at it like in the old days.

Suzue was sitting stony-faced at the low dining table in the living room watching TV, while Maki was upstairs crying in the bedroom.

"What on earth's going on?" Naoya asked his wife.

"I don't know what I did wrong this time. I just wanted to tidy up," Maki sniveled. "I found this letter, and your mother flew completely off the handle."

Maki explained that she was tidying up the sewing basket when she discovered a letter addressed to a Mrs. Suzue Yanagisawa. She had only looked at the envelope when Suzue started yelling at her about reading other people's mail.

"You didn't open the letter?"

"No. Why would I do that?"

God, what a mess! thought Naoya, as he went back downstairs. Suzue was looking as crotchety as ever.

"Mother, why get so worked up about Maki touching a letter addressed to you? It's ridiculous."

Suzue glared at him.

"It's straightforward enough: we may be family, but that doesn't mean privacy has to go out the window."

"Maki didn't read the letter or even open it."

"That's not the point. She should just keep her silly hands off."

"She didn't mean any harm. She just came across it in the sewing basket. That's all."

"That's exactly what I don't like. Besides, she never does any sewing anyway."

"She was going to sew my shirt buttons back on."

"You've got to be kidding. She can't sew worth a damn."

"She's been practicing, and she's pretty good now. The whole thing's your fault. I mean, what are you doing sticking letters in a place like that anyway?"

Naoya's eye was caught by a gray envelope on the table.

"Is that what all the fuss is about?"

Naoya was reaching for the letter when Suzue snatched it away.

"You may be my son, but that doesn't give you the right. Like I said, there is such a thing as privacy."

"If you're so desperate to keep your letters secret, you should find a better hiding place for them."

"Don't try and make out that I've got anything to be ashamed of. That's not what this is about. It's not me who's in the wrong."

Suzue got up, scuttled into her bedroom, and pulled the door shut with a bang.

Naoya sighed. Although he was hungry, now was hardly the time to start asking anyone to make him dinner. He scratched his head. *Maybe a simple bowl of ochazuke rice will do,* he thought.

6.

Suzue was due to leave on her trip the next day. When Naoya came out of the subway station that evening, he heard someone calling his name. He turned to see Detective Kaga hurrying after him.

"This is a stroke of luck. I was about to come around to see you."

"Now? Again?"

"It's nothing serious; just something I thought might put your mind at rest. Do you have a moment?"

"Right now?"

"We could pop in there, seeing as it's close by. It'll be easy enough." Kaga strode off without giving Naoya the time to reply.

Kaga led Naoya to Kisamiya. The shop's glass doors were shut, but the lights were still on. The gray-haired owner, who was standing behind a low glass display case, broke into a warm smile when Kaga pushed his way through the door.

"Hard at it as usual, eh, Detective? Oh, hello there, Naoya."

"Evening," Naoya replied. He had known the old man his whole life.

Kisamiya was a small store. An L-shaped glass display case took up most of the space. Inside it was row upon row of sharp-looking cutlery gleaming like precious artifacts.

There were more glass-fronted display cases around the walls. These contained traditional cutlery from the Edo period rather than regular products for sale. The shop was like a miniature knife museum.

"Hi, boss," said Kaga. "Got that thing for me?"

The storeowner grinned and extracted a pair of scissors from a case immediately behind him. They were a little under ten centimeters long, with blades that had blunt, rounded ends.

"What are those?" Naoya asked.

"The scissors your wife wanted to get. They're not actually kitchen scissors. Ms. Mitsui, the murdered woman, made a mistake and bought the wrong kind."

"What do you mean?" Naoya frowned.

"What kind of scissors are these, boss?"

The Kisamiya proprietor crossed his arms self-importantly over his chest.

"They don't really have a specific name. We usually refer to them as food scissors."

"Food scissors?" Naoya cocked his head to one side.

"That's what your wife probably asked for. My guess is that Ms. Mitsui mistakenly assumed that food scissors and kitchen scissors were the same thing." Kaga said.

"Plenty of people make that mistake." The old store-owner beamed.

"So what are these scissors for?" Naoya looked at him inquiringly.

"You use them at meals to deal with hard and chewy food. Squid, octopus—things like that."

"Don't forget abalone," interjected Kaga.

Naoya gasped.

"That's right." Kaga nodded and smiled. "Your mother has problems with her teeth, doesn't she? But she's still looking forward to eating lots of abalone on her upcoming trip. That's why your wife wanted to give her these food scissors."

"I can't believe it. . . ."

"A woman came in here yesterday to buy a pair of these food scissors. I had asked the boss here to call me if any of his customers tried to buy a pair, so I rushed right over. Luckily, I got here in time to have a word with that particular customer," Kaga explained.

"The customer—as I'd expected—was a friend of your wife's. Your wife had asked her to buy the food scissors for her. Your mother's trip is tomorrow, so your wife must have been panicking. I imagine her friend has given your wife the scissors by now."

"Maki . . . for my mother . . . ?"

"Women are complicated creatures, Mr. Yanagisawa. They can appear to be at each other's throats, when their real feelings are quite the opposite. Or vice versa. For me as a detective, sometimes I think that understanding the psychology of people is my hardest challenge."

"Did you bring me here to share that pearl of wisdom?"

"Sorry, I've overstepped my boundaries."

Naoya shook his head.

"No, I'm happy to find out what was going on. It's a relief. What should I say to Maki?"

"My advice would be to pretend not to know anything about it. As for the abalone . . ." Kaga waggled his index finger. "I bet that what your mother's most looking forward to is abalone *steak*, which is a local delicacy. Unlike raw abalone, it's extremely soft. Okay even for people with bad teeth."

"Oh, really."

"Best to keep that a secret from your wife, too," said Kaga, touching a finger to his lips.

The family store was already closed by the time Naoya got home. Maki was busy in the kitchen putting the final touches to dinner, while Suzue was sitting at the low table, sorting through a bunch of payment slips.

"I'm back," Naoya sang out.

"Evening," replied Suzue. Maki didn't even bother to turn around. Had they had yet another quarrel? Naoya was worried. That would only make it harder for Maki to give the food scissors to his mother.

As he headed for the stairs, to go up and change out of his suit, he noticed an overnight bag in the hallway. *Probably Suzue's luggage*, he thought.

Curious to see if Maki had presented the scissors to his mother, Naoya discreetly unzipped the bag. It contained a toiletry bag and clothes. There wasn't, however, any sign of food scissors. Maki hadn't yet given them to her, then.

As Naoya was zipping the bag shut, he noticed an envelope in one of its inside pockets. It had to be the letter Suzue had originally hidden in the sewing basket. Curiosity got the better of him, and he pulled it out.

The envelope contained a brochure from an Iseshima gift shop. As he flicked through it, Naoya couldn't suppress a smile when he came across a page entitled "Limited Edition Iseshima Hello Kitty Products." Among the goods pictured were an Iseshima Hello Kitty mascot and a Hello Kitty–themed Matsusaka black-haired cow mobile phone strap.

That detective fellow was right, Naoya thought. Perhaps he didn't need to worry. In their own peculiar way, the two women were already on the same wavelength.

4

THE CLOCK SHOP'S DOG

1.

Despite the air-conditioning, his armpits were damp. He always sweated heavily when all his concentration was focused in his fingertips. That was why Akifumi Yoneoka liked to keep a spare T-shirt on the premises. *I think I'll change into a new one when I'm done with this,* he thought, as he delicately moved the tweezers.

He breathed a sigh of relief when he succeeded in fitting the screw, which was little more than a millimeter long, into its destined hole. The door to the shop swung open. *Thank goodness that at least some of our customers are blessed with a sense of timing,* he thought to himself. Customers who barged in when he was in the middle of a delicate job didn't just disrupt his concentration, sometimes they even made him drop components on the floor.

The customer was a man in a short-sleeved shirt worn loosely over a T-shirt. He was carrying a small briefcase. Akifumi put him in his late thirties, a little older than himself. He was fit and muscular, with no trace of fat around the face. He was smiling. That was a relief. There was something about his eyes that suggested he'd be frightening if he got angry.

"Good afternoon," said Akifumi.

The man grinned amiably, waved, then handed him his business card.

"I'm not actually here to buy a watch, I'm afraid."

Akifumi tensed as he examined the business card. It said he was a Detective Kaga from the Nihonbashi precinct.

"Has something happened?" Akifumi asked.

"Sort of," replied the detective, obviously not keen to go into detail. "Is there a Mr. Genichi Terada here?"

"Yes. He's the owner."

The store was called Terada's Clock Shop.

"So I gathered. Is he in?"

"He's in the back. Shall I get him?"

"If you don't mind." Kaga flashed a smile.

In the back of the store was a small workshop, and behind that was the Terada family's living room. Genichi was standing in the workshop, his arms crossed, contemplating a half-disassembled wall clock. His mouth was turned down at the corners.

"Boss?" Akifumi ventured.

"It's one of the gears."

"What?"

"Missing teeth. Two of the darn things." Genichi pointed to the little gear wheel.

Akifumi looked and nodded. Sure enough, one of the gear wheels in the complex interlocking mass of machinery was broken.

"Shouldn't be much of a problem for you."

Genichi looked up at Akifumi, rolling his eyes. "Oh, why not?"

"Why not? It's not an especially small gear wheel; all you need to do is solder on a couple of new teeth. I can do it, if you want."

"Are you a complete fool?" Genichi hissed. "Attaching the missing teeth isn't the problem; the problem is why the teeth fell off in the first place."

"Wasn't it just wear and tear?"

"And you think that's not serious? These two teeth broke off. I can replace them, sure, but that doesn't guarantee that more teeth won't snap off later. Then what do you propose? That I just solder on more new ones, and everything will be hunky-dory? Seriously?"

"So are you going to put in a whole new gear wheel?"

"That's the least I can do." Genichi focused his attention back on the clock.

Akifumi knew why his boss was looking so stern. The clock was an antique, so it was impossible to find replacement parts. Genichi would have to craft the new gear wheel himself.

The customer who'd brought it in for repair said something about not wanting to spend too much money. Making a new gear wheel would make it more expensive, and from what Genichi was saying, it sounded like he was concerned about the other gear wheels, too. It was probably the thought of a run-in with yet another customer that was weighing on Genichi's mind.

"Oh, boss, I forgot. There's a guy from the police outside. Says he wants to speak to you." Akifumi showed him Kaga's card.

"The police. What the hell for?"

"Search me." Akifumi tilted his head to one side.

"Bet it's that punk kid. Probably went and got in trouble with the law." Genichi pulled himself slowly and awkwardly to his feet.

Akifumi followed Genichi back out into the store. Kaga was inspecting a table clock that was sitting on the work surface. It was the piece that Akifumi had been working on when Kaga came in.

"I'm Genichi Terada," said Genichi.

"Sorry to bother you, Mr. Terada. I know you're busy, but there's something I need to ask you."

"What?"

"Do you know a woman by the name of Mineko Mitsui?"

"Mitsui, you said? Could be a customer, I s'pose." Genichi scratched the corner of one of his eyebrows.

Akifumi couldn't recall any customer of that name.

Kaga shook his head. "I think you know her. This is what she looks like." Kaga pulled a photograph out of his briefcase.

Genichi put on his reading glasses and looked at the picture.

"I've certainly seen her. Can't put my finger on where, though," he muttered.

"Where were you at six o'clock in the evening on June the tenth?" inquired Kaga.

"June the tenth?" Genichi glanced at a calendar on the wall. "The day before yesterday?"

"Hey, boss," Akifumi volunteered. "At six, you were probably walking Donkichi."

"What? Yeah, you're right. I was out walking the dog. We always head out at about half past five."

Kaga's eyes were warm and smiling.

"Maybe you bumped into someone in the course of your walk?"

"Bumped into someone . . . ?" said Genichi. His jaw dropped and he looked down at the photograph.

"I bumped into her."

"You remember?"

"Yes. I saw her from time to time when I was out walking the dog. Come to think of it, she may even have told me her name."

"Her full name's Mineko Mitsui. You're quite sure that you've met her?"

"Yes, we've met. Or, rather, we've said hello to each other quite a few times." Genichi handed the photograph back to Kaga.

"Where did you meet her?"

"That would be—"

Genichi cut himself short and directed a penetrating look at the detective. "First of all, though, I need to know what sort of investigation this is for. Is my having met this woman a problem of some kind?"

"Not at all. I'm just checking something. Could you tell me where you encountered Ms. Mitsui?"

"Happy to. I've got nothing to hide. It was in the park."

"The park? Which park?"

"Hamacho Park. It has a special area for people with dogs. The park's a little way past the theater—"

A wry smile on his face, Kaga stopped Genichi mid-sentence.

"That's fine. I know the place. Was Ms. Mitsui on her own that evening?"

"She was. She generally was."

"What did you talk about?" Kaga pulled a notebook out of his pocket.

"Talk about? Like I said, we just said hello. We didn't stop for a chat or anything."

"Do you know if Ms. Mitsui was going somewhere? Did she mention anything like that?"

Genichi gave a thoughtful grunt, folded his arms, and tilted his head to one side. "I didn't ask her. Looked to me like she was just out for a walk."

"What was she wearing? Was she carrying any bags?"

"I don't remember how she was dressed." Genichi frowned. "I don't think she was carrying any bags—though I'm not a hundred percent certain."

Akifumi had trouble suppressing a laugh. Genichi was the last person in the world to notice how a woman was dressed. Even when his wife went out decked out in her smartest outfit, he'd assume that she just popped out to pick up something at the local supermarket.

"How did Ms. Mitsui look?"

"Look?"

"Did you notice anything about her? Could be anything."

"Nothing special, no. She seemed to be in quite high spirits."

"In high spirits?" For the first time, a look of suspicion crossed Kaga's face.

"Maybe 'high spirits' isn't the right word. Let's say she looked like she was having fun, like she was enjoying her walk. That's what I'm trying to say."

"Good," said Kaga encouragingly, returning his notebook to his pocket. "Sorry to have interrupted your work."

"Are we done?"

"Yes, we're done. However—" Kaga glanced at the clock on the workbench. "That's an unusual clock. With those three faces like that."

"That one? Yes, it's rather extraordinary."

The clock was a columnar prism with a face on each of its three sides.

"Do all three dials display the same time?"

"Yes. The hands of all three dials move together."

"Together?"

"So when one face starts going wrong, all three dials go wrong together. The same when it stops."

"Wow, that's amazing." Taking a last look at the clock, Kaga bowed first to Genichi and then to Akifumi. "Thank you for your help," he said and left the store.

"What the heck was that about? Seems a funny sort of detective to me." Genichi was bursting with curiosity.

2.

Shimako came back a minute or two after the detective had left the shop. She had a cloth bag in one hand and a white plastic one in the other. Tall and broad at the best of times, she looked even more strapping than usual. Akifumi's secret nickname for his employers was "the gigantic duo."

"I bought some daifuku rice cakes. Let's all have a nice cup of tea," she said, as she disappeared into the back.

A few minutes later, she called Akifumi into the workshop behind the shop. On a small table next to the workbench sat the soft, sweet-filled rice cakes and three glasses of barley tea. Three in the afternoon was official teatime at Terada's Clock Shop.

"Come to think of it, I heard that there was something in the papers about a nasty incident in Kodenmacho. I wonder if the detective has anything to do with that," commented Shimako when the men told her about the detective's visit.

"Heard about something in the papers? You didn't read it yourself?" Genichi.

"No, I overheard some ladies at the supermarket talking about it."

"Huh. That figures."

"What's that supposed to mean? I'm quite capable of reading a newspaper for myself, you know."

Akifumi, ignoring the sour looks the couple were exchanging, began leafing through the newspapers of the last couple of days until he found the article. There had been a murder in Kodenmacho. The victim was a forty-five-year-old woman who lived alone. When he saw her name, Akifumi gasped: Mineko Mitsui.

He showed the article to Genichi. The older man scowled savagely and stuck his lower lip out.

"Can't believe it. Her, of all people. Too awful."

"What was she like?" Shimako asked.

"Don't know much about her. We just fell into the habit of saying hello because we were always bumping into each other."

"Forty-five and living alone. It's a little unusual not to be married at that age."

"I remember her saying something about having a kid."

"Had her husband passed on, then?"

"Search me. She didn't say anything, and I didn't ask."

"I wonder if she had a job?"

"Put a lid on it, woman. I don't know. How many times do I have to say that?"

"I wasn't asking you. I was just thinking aloud, asking myself 'Did she have a job?' The poor thing. She was forty-five; more or less the same age as me." Shimako shook her head from side to side as she read the article.

"You're well north of fifty, woman. The same age? *I don't think so!*"

"Fifty-five, forty-five, it's all the same. I wonder how old this child of hers is? Probably a bit younger than our Kanae."

When he heard the name Kanae, Akifumi began wolfing down his daifuku.

"What's she got to do with anything?" Sure enough, Genichi sounded even more cantankerous than before.

"Nothing in particular. I was just wondering about the age of this woman's child."

"Well, it's got damn all to do with our own daughter. She ran off. I don't want you talking about her."

"I can say her name if I want to."

"Shut it, woman. I said don't want to hear it."

As Akifumi had anticipated, the atmosphere in the room was now heavy and threatening. He hastily crammed the last of the cake into his mouth and gulped down his tea, before he got sucked into the maelstrom.

Kaga paid them a second visit a little after seven in the evening the next day. Genichi had just got back from walking Donkichi, the store was closed, and Akifumi was getting ready to head home.

"You told me that you bumped into Mineko Mitsui in Hamacho Park. Are you quite sure of that?" The detective's expression was somewhat sterner than on the day before.

"Quite sure," insisted Genichi.

"I need you to think hard. Memory plays tricks on all of us. Cast your mind back to the last time you saw her: you're quite sure that it was in Hamacho Park."

"You're as bad as my wife, Detective. I know what I know."

"Indeed?" Kaga looked skeptical.

"I want to know how *you* know that I ran into Ms. Mitsui on that day. That's what's bugging me."

"Didn't I tell you? We found a half-written email in the

drafts file on her computer. In it she said she'd bumped into the clock shop man from Kobunacho."

"Email!" Genichi snorted contemptuously.

"Last time we spoke, you said that Ms. Mitsui was alone. Are you quite certain about that? Think very carefully."

"She was alone. If there was anyone with her, then I didn't see them."

"And the place was Hamacho Park?" Kaga directed a piercing look at Genichi.

"Hamacho Park. Correct." Genichi glared at the detective.

"Around what time did you get back from your walk that day?"

"Seven-ish, probably."

Kaga thanked him and went on his way.

"That cop's an odd one," muttered Genichi under his breath, as he headed into the back of the store.

3.

When the glass door opened, Akifumi looked up and was startled. It was Kaga—yet again. That made three days in a row. This time, however, he was dressed smartly in a dark gray jacket.

"You again?"

"I know. I'm sorry. There's something I just can't get my head around."

"If it's the boss you're looking for, he's out and won't be back until later," Akifumi said. Genichi had gone to a memorial service for a friend.

"Oh, really? That's a pity." The detective didn't seem particularly disappointed. He looked at Akifumi. "It's almost five thirty. Doesn't that mean it's time for the dog's walk? Or will Mrs. Terada be walking Donkichi today?"

"Mrs. Terada is doing the shopping, so I'm going."

"What about the store, then?"

"I'll shut up shop before I go. We don't get many customers in the late afternoon. Besides, we usually close around six—the Teradas told me we could close at five thirty today."

"Interesting. I have a little favor to ask: could I accompany you on your walk?"

"With the dog, you mean? No problem. Though I'm just going to take the same old route we always take."

"It's your everyday route that I'm interested in. So, if you don't mind . . ."

Kaga politely inclined his head. Akifumi responded with an ambiguous half sigh, half grunt.

At five thirty on the dot, after lowering the rolling security gate, Akifumi left through a side door and walked around to the front where Kaga was waiting. The detective smiled when he saw the dog.

"I didn't realize your dog was a Shiba Inu. How old is he?"

"Eight, I think."

Donkichi glanced up at Kaga, then looked off to one side as though he'd lost all interest. Genichi was always bellyaching about the dog's utter lack of charm, despite doting on him more than anyone else in the family.

Donkichi set off and Akifumi followed, hanging on to the lead. The dog seemed to know which way to go.

"It's an interesting name for a dog, Donkichi. Did your boss come up with it?" asked Kaga, walking side by side with Akifumi.

"No, it was the Teradas' daughter. She was the one who insisted on getting a dog in the first place."

"They've got a daughter?"

Me and my big mouth, thought Akifumi. Still, he was dealing with a detective. The man could find out anything he wanted, so trying to conceal things was a waste of time.

"She got married and moved out recently. Lives in Ryogoku now."

"She did, huh? And she's the one who named 'baby'?"

"She actually christened him Donkey, but her mother and father said that an English name wasn't their family style. The two of them started calling him Donkichi, and that's the name that stuck. For my part, I think he looks like more of a Donkichi than a Donkey."

Donkichi himself was straining at the leash and sniffing at all the street smells. His tongue was dangling from his open mouth. He was clearly hot.

They took a left after the elementary school and passed a well-known chicken restaurant. The route would take them over Ningyocho Boulevard and into Amazake Alley, which led right to Hamacho Park.

Donkichi, however, came to an abrupt halt after they crossed Ningyocho Boulevard. Turning his head this way and that, he appeared a little lost.

"What's got into him today?" Akifumi muttered.

"Maybe we're going the wrong way?"

"No, this is the right way."

Akifumi gave the lead a tug and headed down Amazake Alley. Donkichi followed obediently, then raced ahead, just as before.

After a short distance, they reached a narrow patch of greenery that doubled as a traffic median. At the entrance stood a statue of Benkei, the warrior monk from a kabuki play. Donkichi tried to cock his leg on the statue's base, but Akifumi pulled him away.

"That triangular clock was very interesting," said Kaga, a propos of nothing in particular. "Especially the way the three dials malfunction together and stop together. You'd expect for each clock face to have its own movement. How come all three move together like that?"

Akifumi laughed. "Isn't it amazing? When I disassembled it, the thing just blew my mind. The guys in the old days had so much imagination."

"Any chance of you explaining the mechanism to me?"

"Well . . ." Akifumi grunted noncommittally.

They could see the theater just up ahead. From there, it wasn't far to Hamacho Park.

"How long has Terada's Clock Shop been going?" asked Kaga, changing the subject.

"It was founded by the father of the present boss. The original store was a bit closer to Kayabacho, but they moved to where they are now after the original shop burned down."

"So it's a long-established business?"

Akifumi gave a sardonic smile.

"The boss isn't keen on stressing our heritage. Nihonbashi is awash with specialty stores that have been around for centuries. Unlike them, we're not famous for making our own products. All we do is sell things we get from various manufacturers. Also, most of the store's income is actually from repairs."

"I've heard that Terada's is famous for its know-how. People say you're in a league of your own when it comes to mending old clocks."

"The boss has an incredible level of skill. He can mend anything. Despite being such a hulk of a man, his fingers can perform the most delicate and intricate tasks. I'll never get to be as good as him."

"Why did you choose to work there?"

"It's not an extraordinary story. As a boy, I liked watches. I'm not talking the ordinary quartz and battery watches—I mean proper mechanical timepieces driven by coil springs and pendulums. I still remember the first time someone showed me the insides of an old watch; the intricacy of it had a powerful effect on me. I was like, *This is what I want to do with my life.*"

"That's wonderful." Kaga nodded. "The Teradas must be very happy to have someone who can carry on the business for them."

"I'm not ready for that yet. I want to get better, especially as these days there are fewer and fewer people capable of mending mechanical watches. Then again, with people buying fewer mechanical watches, who knows what the future holds?"

"Quality never goes out of style," declared Kaga forcefully.

They walked into Hamacho Park. After crossing a little plaza of patterned mosaic, they headed toward a patch of grass where groups of people, all with dogs, were standing around chatting.

"This is where the dog owners get together every evening," Akifumi explained, lowering his voice.

"It certainly looks that way. I heard it was a kind of forum where dog lovers exchange tips," Kaga replied. He'd obviously made some preliminary inquiries.

A gray-haired old lady with a poodle wished them a good evening. "Good evening," responded Akifumi. It was all very civilized.

The old lady then turned her attention to Kaga. She looked him up and down. "Oh, it's you!" Her eyes widened behind her glasses.

"Thanks for your help yesterday." Kaga slightly inclined his head.

"Did you find what you were looking for?"

"Unfortunately not. I'm having a hard time."

"Poor old you. Not an easy life being a detective."

The old lady walked off.

"What didn't you find yesterday?"

"Her." Kaga whipped out a photograph. It was the same picture of Mineko Mitsui that he had shown them in the store the other day. "Or, rather, anyone who saw her."

"What do you mean?"

"When I spoke to Mr. Terada the day before yesterday, he claimed to have seen Mineko Mitsui here in this park at six o'clock on the evening of June tenth."

"Right . . ."

"Yesterday evening I came here to speak to the dog-walking brigade. *Had any of them seen her?* Not one of them had. They all remembered Mr. Terada being here with Donkichi, though. Donkichi's quite a celebrity around here.

"While I was talking to them, Mr. Terada showed up with Donkichi in tow. I didn't want him to see me, so I had to leave. That's when I came around the store."

"Oh, so that's why you showed up last night."

"The thing that puzzles me is why no one except your boss should recall having seen Ms. Mitsui."

Akifumi now understood why Kaga had been so persistent in asking Genichi if he remembered things correctly.

"Did Ms. Mitsui have a dog herself?"

"No, she didn't."

"Perhaps that explains why the boss was the only person to see her. Maybe she wasn't near the area where all the dog people congregate."

"That just raises another question."

Kaga pulled a folded sheet of paper out of his pocket. He opened it up and showed to Akifumi.

It looked like a computer printout.

I just got back. I went to the same old plaza as always. I stroked the puppy on the head and bumped into the clock shop man from Kobunacho. We had a good laugh about the way we always seem to go for our walks at the same time.

"You see that bit about stroking a puppy? I don't think she's referring to a stray dog or anything. She must have run into someone with a puppy before she bumped into your boss."

"I see what you mean." Akifumi looked over at the clusters of dog owners. "Perhaps the person with the puppy was here on the tenth, but didn't come yesterday or today."

"I thought the same thing, but so far I haven't found anyone who fits the bill. The other dog owners can't think of anyone with a puppy. According to the old lady we just spoke to, they know all the dogs who are walked in this park, even if they're not friends with the owners."

I can believe that, thought Akifumi. He didn't walk Donkichi all that often, but when he did, he always felt that he was being watched.

"That's a tough job, Detective. Having to check out fiddly stuff like that."

"There's no such a thing as an easy job. Investigative work can be fun sometimes."

"It can?"

"For example." Kaga paused rather self-importantly. "Questions like, Why was there wasabi in the ningyo-yaki?"

"*Wasabi?*"

"I'm off to a very fancy Japanese restaurant to get to the

bottom of that mystery tonight. Hence the nice jacket I'm wearing."

"Oh, I see," Akifumi said. However, in reality, he had no idea what Kaga was going on about.

After a single circuit of the park, they headed back to the shop.

"Who's the 'punk kid'?" asked Kaga, out of the blue.

"Huh?"

"It was something Mr. Terada said in his workroom when I was there the day before yesterday. Remember? 'Bet it's that punk kid. Probably went and got in trouble with the law.'"

"Oh yeah," grunted Akifumi. He remembered now. Genichi had said it when Akifumi told him that a policeman wanted to see him. "So you could hear us?"

"Just that bit. Mr. Terada raised his voice. Anyway, who is it?"

Akifumi thought better of trying to mislead Kaga. He'd probably just end up digging himself into a hole.

"He was talking about their daughter's partner."

"Their son-in-law?"

"The boss would go ballistic if he heard you say that." Akifumi gave a twisted smile. "They ran off and got married without permission."

"They eloped?"

"Don't tell anyone I told you."

"Don't worry, I won't." Kaga's eyes were shining with curiosity.

4.

Kanae, the Teradas' only daughter, had graduated from high school that spring. But she didn't return home after the graduation ceremony. Instead, she sent a text to her mother's cell phone. "I'm sorry. I'm going to go and live with the man I love," it said.

Genichi Terada got into a towering rage and went charging over to the Sawamuras' house. Hideyuki, the Sawamuras' eldest son was Kanae's boyfriend.

Hideyuki was two years older than Kanae. They'd attended the same elementary and junior high schools and had continued to see a lot of each other after Kanae went to high school, eventually falling in love.

Genichi, however, had no time for Hideyuki. That was mainly because the young man had dropped out of college without any kind of full-time job to fall back on. Worse still, while he was going through a motorbike phase back in his high school days, he'd hit someone. Genichi insisted on referring to him as "that Hells Angels fellow."

"I don't care who you date—just so long as it's not him," Genichi had told his daughter.

Of course, these days a girl doesn't pay much attention to a demand like that. Kanae continued meeting Hideyuki in secret until they decided to move in together after she graduated.

Seizo, the head of the Sawamura family, was unfazed by Genichi's ranting and raving. "What's wrong with two people who love each other getting together?" he responded coolly. Quite beside himself with anger, Genichi threw a punch. Things, however, didn't go as planned. A tough customer with a black belt in judo, Seizo deployed a sweeping leg throw that sent Genichi sprawling.

Genichi was back home getting patched up when another text arrived from Kanae. Short and to the point, it urged him to "try not to behave disgracefully." Infuriated, Genichi smashed his cell phone to smithereens.

"I disown her," he bellowed at Shimako and Akifumi. "That girl is no longer my daughter. I don't want to hear her name in this house again. Never. Got it?"

Kaga seemed to be enjoying Akifumi's storytelling. At the part about Genichi being knocked down, he laughed out loud.

"The upshot is that we're not allowed to talk about Kanae anymore. Her name is taboo."

"But you know that she lives in Ryogoku?"

"Mrs. Terada heard that via the Sawamuras."

"Your boss could always go and try to bring her home by force."

"Except that he's always ranting about how he won't be the one to go to her. 'If she wants me to accept her, then she needs to come here and beg my forgiveness. And she'll have to leave that man.'"

"He's pretty stubborn, then."

"Stubborn doesn't do him justice. He's the most pigheaded dad in the world. He's incapable of compromise. That probably explains why he's so good at his job."

Akifumi and Kaga went back by the same route they'd

come. They walked side by side, with Akifumi holding Donkichi's lead. They were about halfway home, waiting for the lights to change on Ningyocho Boulevard, when Kaga began staring at something off to the left. He had a grave expression on his face.

They continued on when the light turned green and were almost back at the shop, when they happened to stroll past a taxi waiting at an intersection. A single female passenger was seated in the backseat on the right. "Oh!" exclaimed Akifumi, when he saw her profile. "It's Mrs. Terada."

"What?" Kaga turned to look.

The taxi sped off, before coming to a halt forty or fifty meters down the road.

Shimako had only just stepped out of the taxi by the time Akifumi and Kaga reached the shop.

"Hi, Mrs. Terada," said Akifumi.

"Oh hi, Aki," she said. "You've been walking Donkichi?" She cast a suspicious look at Kaga and made a small bow.

"This is the detective I told you about," Akifumi said. "He wanted to see where we walk the dog, so I took him along with me."

"Oh, did you now?"

From the expression on Shimako's face, it was clear that she was wondering what possible purpose that could serve.

"You went shopping in Ginza?" Kaga was looking at the bag Shimako was holding. It was decorated with the logo of one of the major department stores.

"Yes. I went to order a batch of midyear gifts."

"By yourself?"

"Yes, by myself. Why?"

"Nothing. Do you normally take a cab back from Ginza?"

"Not always. I normally take the subway, but today I was feeling a bit worn out." Shimako shot Akifumi a glance. "Don't tell the old man. He'll just grouse about me wasting money."

"Tell me about it," murmured Akifumi.

"I'd better be off." Kaga consulted his watch. "It's already six thirty. Apologies for taking up so much of your time. It was highly informative. Thank you very much." Kaga bowed to Akifumi.

"What did you tell him that he found so informative?" Shimako asked Akifumi, as soon as Kaga was out of sight.

"Goodness knows. I don't think I told him anything very significant." Akifumi cocked his head thoughtfully.

He went around to the back of the store and put Donkichi back in his kennel. When he went into the house, Shimako was on the phone.

"Oh no, did he? Oh, the man's always putting his foot in it. . . . You're sure? No one's angry at him? Well, I'm relieved to hear it, if it's true. . . . I'm truly sorry. . . . Thanks for letting me know. . . . Yes, goodbye."

She replaced the receiver with a thoroughly miserable expression on her face. "He went and lost it again."

"Lost it? You mean the boss? At the memorial service?"

Shimako pulled a face.

"Somebody said something that rubbed him the wrong way. 'They're in love, let them do as they please' or 'Only a bully would oppose a marriage out of spite,' something like that."

"That would set him off, all right."

"He threw beer on the guy, and next thing anyone knew, they were wrestling on the ground. At his age, for goodness' sake!"

Plastering a rueful "such is life" smile on his lips, Akifumi hastily started packing up to go home. Genichi would be back soon, and Akifumi wanted to be long gone when he got there.

5.

Sure enough, when Akifumi got to the store the next morning, Genichi was in a foul mood.

"How's the repair of this watch coming along? Didn't you promise the customer to get it back to them today?" Genichi asked in a threateningly loud voice, picking a watch out of the "Awaiting Repair" box.

"I'm waiting on a component. I called the customer to let them know it wouldn't be ready till next week."

"You did? As usual, nobody bothered to tell me."

Actually, Akifumi had informed Genichi, but there was no point in contradicting him when he was like this. "Sorry," Akifumi mumbled, with an apologetic tilt of the head.

"Honestly, is there no one I can rely on around here?" Genichi stalked off toward the back of the shop. A moment later, there was a mighty thump. "Ouch! Goddamn it! Why must people always put stuff in such stupid places! I hit my damn knee."

Akifumi was tempted to go back and point out that it was Genichi himself who had put the "thing" there, but thought better of it in time.

By the time closing time came around, Genichi's mood seemed to have improved considerably.

"Righty-ho, think I'll take Donkichi for his walk," said Genichi, stretching luxuriantly as he came out of the workroom. "Will you take care of things here?"

"No problem, boss. Have a nice walk."

About ten minutes after Genichi had left, someone pushed open the front door. Akifumi frowned when he saw who it was: it was Kaga—yet again—wearing the same charcoal gray jacket as yesterday.

"Are you here to ask even more questions?"

Kaga waved his hand in front of his face.

"Not tonight. I've actually got something to tell you."

"Really? I'm afraid the boss is out walking the dog."

"I know. I waited until he'd left. Now, where's Mrs. Terada?"

"She's here. Shall I get her for you?"

"Could you?" Kaga smiled.

Shimako was busy making dinner. When Akifumi called her, she came into the shop, an expression of incredulity on her face.

"I'm sorry to be such a pest." Kaga grinned. "Don't worry, though. This really is the last time."

"What on earth is it now?" Shimako asked him.

Kaga turned to Akifumi. "Did you tell Mr. and Mrs. Terada what we discussed in the park yesterday?"

"No, I didn't. The boss has been in a foul mood all day."

"You didn't? That's good. It's probably best not to mention it to him."

"What did you two discuss yesterday?" Shimako looked from one man to the other.

Kaga then repeated to Shimako what he had told Akifumi about no one else seeing Mineko Mitsui in Hamacho Park.

She looked puzzled. "That's strange. Do you think the old man is lying?"

"It certainly looks that way." Kaga turned toward Akifumi and went on: "According to Mr. Terada, he left here at about five thirty and got back at around seven on that day. In other words, his walk lasted roughly an hour and a half."

"Oh!" Akifumi's jaw dropped in astonishment. He had been there when the boss told Kaga about his walk and hadn't thought twice about it. When you did the math, though, Genichi's account made no sense.

"Yesterday, I did the identical walk with you. Even the slowest walker could do it in less than an hour. Obviously everyone has their own pace, but an extra thirty minutes? That's too much to overlook."

"You think the boss took a different route from the one we took?"

"That's the logical interpretation. I think he may be making a detour somewhere along the way—and that he bumped into Ms. Mitsui there. He's claiming that they met in Hamacho Park to keep that other place secret. That's my guess."

"Where can he be going?" Shimako looked questioningly at Akifumi.

"No idea." Akifumi cocked his head.

"I've actually found out where your husband has been going. I can also hazard a guess as to why he doesn't want anyone else to know. One thing I want to be crystal clear about: this has *absolutely no connection to the murder.* If I'm right, the best thing will be to let sleeping dogs lie. For my part, I have to confirm the facts so that I can report them to my superiors. That's the reason I've been dropping in here so often. I thought about confronting your husband directly, but given the sort of person he is, I was pretty sure that he wouldn't tell the truth. Pressuring him by ambushing him during one of his walks would be taking things too far. Secret hopes can be a source of great happiness. I don't want to do anything to wreck that."

Akifumi and Shimako exchanged looks. What was this verbose speech supposed to mean?

"Stop beating around the bush and just tell us where my husband's been going!"

"Let me ask you a question first. It's about your daughter. She's married and living in Ryogoku?"

"Has something happened to her?" Shimako's face clouded with anxiety.

Akifumi stared at Kaga in bewilderment. Why had the detective brought up Kanae?

"In a way, yes. Your daughter's pregnant."

Akifumi gasped—and his surprise was only deepened by Shimako's reaction.

"How do you know?"

Kaga grinned merrily. "So I'm right."

"Is it true?" Akifumi asked Shimako.

"Yes, but don't tell the old man."

"Are you still in touch with Kanae?" asked Akifumi.

"I see her from time to time. I was never against those two getting married in the first place. Hideyuki has a job—for now he's only a contract worker, but it's with a good company. Everything's on track for him, except that pigheaded father of hers—" Shimako clapped a hand to her mouth, suddenly remembering that Kaga was there. "I'm sorry, Detective. I shouldn't be washing the family's dirty laundry in front of you."

Kaga waved a deprecating hand. "Not to worry. You saw your daughter yesterday. The two of you went shopping together. Am I right?"

Shimako's eyes widened.

"How did you know?"

"After bumping into you here, I went and made a few inquiries in the baby goods section of the department store you'd been to. A store clerk confirmed that two women who matched the description of you and your daughter had been in earlier. That's how I know Kanae's pregnant."

"Did I tell you I'd been with my daughter?"

"You didn't, no. It was just something that came to me when I saw you in the taxi."

"The taxi—?"

"Yes, you were in the right-hand passenger seat in the back. Normally when people take taxis by themselves, they sit on the left, because that's the side you get in. It's the side with the automatic door. The fact that you were sitting on the right suggested that someone else had been sitting on the left. Someone you dropped off, before returning home. I'd already heard from Akifumi about the family's problem, so it was easy enough to guess who that secret someone was."

Akifumi looked at Kaga admiringly. *That's one smart detective.*

"Okay, so you figured out that I'd been shopping with my daughter. How did get from there to the baby goods department?"

"That was simple. I already had reason to suspect that your daughter was pregnant."

"What!" Akifumi hollered. "I'd only told you about Kanae a few minutes before. How could you possibly figure out she was pregnant from what I told you?"

"Well, I wasn't a hundred percent certain. It was more of a hunch."

Akifumi folded his arms on his chest and groaned.

"I just don't get this. I mean, I work here, and I had no idea whatsoever that Kanae was pregnant. How did you get this hunch, Detective? Are you clairvoyant?"

"No such luck. Unlikely as it sounds, it was Donkichi who gave me the idea."

"The dog?"

"About halfway through our walk yesterday evening, Donkichi got confused about which way to go. Do you remember?"

"Now that you mention it, yes."

"It was at the intersection on Ningyocho Boulevard. When you pulled on the lead, he followed you obediently into Amazake Alley and toward the park. Why did he seem lost and confused for a moment or two before that?"

"You tell me."

"That set me thinking. What if your husband was in the habit of turning off at that point rather than going straight ahead? Going left would bring you back here. What about if you take a right? Where does that take you?

"Hah!" Shimako cried. "To the Suitengu Shrine!"

"Precisely." Kaga nodded. "There was an email on the murdered woman's computer. She said that she'd 'stroked the puppy on the head' at the same old plaza and 'bumped into the clock shop man from Kobunacho.' When I saw the word 'plaza,' I thought she was talking about the park. Then I thought, hang on a minute, what if she's talking about a shrine or temple? And there is a puppy at the Suitengu Shrine, you know."

Kaga pulled out his cell phone, rapidly pressed a few buttons, then turned the phone so Shimako and Akifumi could see the screen. Akifumi's jaw dropped when he saw the picture.

It was a bronze statue of a seated dog with a playful puppy off to one side.

"The statue's called the Dog of the Beloved Children. You see these symbols around the base? They're from the Chinese zodiac. Touching your star sign is supposed to bring you luck. Plenty of people pat the puppy's head for the same reason. So many people touch it, that it's gone all shiny."

"I know. I've stroked it myself." Shimako smiled.

"I thought, what if Mineko Mitsui had been stroking the head of a bronze puppy, rather than a real one? Assuming she had, that invites the question: what was your husband doing at the shrine? Since Suitengu is the shrine of conception and safe childbirth, there was only one possible answer."

"I see. That's most impressive," declared Shimako.

She did a sudden double take. "But doesn't that mean that my husband knows Kanae's pregnant?"

"Yes, he must. My guess is that he was worried about her—she is his daughter, after all—and that he made some inquiries of his own. He probably discovered she was pregnant that way."

"He must have made up his mind to forgive them for running off together. Why doesn't he just say so instead of slipping off to shrines on the q.t.?"

"That's never going to happen," Akifumi said.

A rueful smile replaced the frown on Shimako's face.

"I guess you're right. That's not how the man operates."

"He knows the young couple will come here to show you their newborn. My guess is that he will use that opportunity to end the standoff and 'accept the marriage out of compassion for the little one.'"

"But Akifumi's right. My husband hates to admit that he's wrong."

"It's not my place to stick my nose into your family affairs, but I'd be grateful if we could all pretend that this little conversation never took place," Kaga said. "Like I said earlier, I don't want to take your husband's precious secret away from him."

Shimako looked hard at the detective.

"You're a man of compassion, Detective."

"Me? Oh, hardly." Kaga laughed shyly.

"I see where you're coming from. You didn't tell us anything. Akifumi, are you okay with that?"

"Absolutely," replied Akifumi.

Kaga consulted his watch.

"I've said everything I came to say. Your husband may be back any minute, so I'd best be going. Thanks for your help."

"Thank you very much."

"Good-bye."

Shimako and Akifumi bowed.

After Kaga had left, Shimako sighed long and loud.

"I guess there are all sorts in the police."

"You're right about that," said Akifumi.

"Anyway, time to get dinner ready, I suppose."

Shimako passed Akifumi as she made her way toward the door at the back of the shop. Noticing the moistness in her eyes, he felt a warm surge roil through his chest.

A few minutes later, he heard raised voices from the back of the house.

"What the hell's going on here? What are you doing, woman? Where's my damn dinner?"

Genichi was back. Judging from his tone, he hadn't noticed the tear tracks on Shimako's cheeks.

"Grab yourself a slice of bread if you're starving to death.

Believe it or not, I'm sometimes busy, too." Shimako's voice was loud and angry.

"Busy? You? Busy gabbing away on your idiot cell phone, you mean? I'm dying of hunger here. Get a move on."

"Okay, okay. Will you please shut up?"

Smiling to himself, Akifumi returned to the workbench and pulled the prism-shaped clock toward him. The repairs were almost done.

He remembered how curious Detective Kaga had been about how the thing worked. The mechanism that moved the hands on all three dials in synchrony was actually quite simple. In most clocks, the mechanism sits immediately behind the dial; in this one, however, it lay flat upon the prism's base, with the spring-driven axis rising vertically from the middle. Gears were then used to transmit the motion of the axis to all the three dials.

I'll make a point of explaining it to Kaga next time I see him, Akifumi thought. It occurred to him that the three-sided clock had a lot in common with the Terada family: three people, all seemingly facing in different directions, all of whom in fact were joined by a single axis.

5

THE CLERK AT THE PASTRY SHOP

1.

"Three cherry and fig tarts—that comes to one thousand, seven hundred and twenty-five yen," said Miyuki, handing the box to the woman at the counter.

The woman, who appeared to be in her early thirties, placed two thousand-yen notes on the money tray. Miyuki picked them up and put them in the cash register, then handed the woman the change along with the receipt. "Thank you very much."

After the woman had left the store, Miyuki checked the time on her cell phone. *Just fifteen minutes until seven o'clock.* Seven was when the Quattro pastry shop closed.

Miyuki was bending down to rearrange the few unsold cakes still in the display case when the front door of the store opened. "Good evening," Miyuki said, as she stood back up, before her lips creased into a spontaneous smile. This customer was a regular.

The woman who had just come in smiled back at her. She had her usual sweet expression and her eyes brimmed with tenderness as they contemplated Miyuki. In the course of one of their chats, she had told Miyuki that she was past forty, but her figure and her glowing complexion were those of a much younger woman.

"Hello. Are you still open?" the woman asked.

"Very much so."

"One of my neighbors gave me some snack cakes today, so there's no excuse for me being here. I happened to be passing by and—surprise, surprise!—I simply couldn't resist." The woman examined the contents of the display case. Perhaps it was because she wore her hair short, but her movements all seemed light and graceful. "I've got nothing against traditional Japanese sweets, but when I've completed a big job, I like to celebrate with a nice piece of cake. It's what motivates me."

"What is your job?"

"What do you think it is?"

"I wonder. . . ."

Miyuki cocked her head thoughtfully to one side. The woman winked at her mischievously. "It's something I can do at home, almost like a side job."

Miyuki could only um and ah in response.

"Seems I'm out of luck. I was after one of your jellies. You've got some lovely passion fruit and almond jellies, haven't you?" said the woman, looking into the case.

"I'm sorry. We're all sold out."

"It's been so hot. Everyone wants to have something nice and cool to eat. What shall I go for instead?"

Just then, the ring tone of a cell phone came from inside her handbag. With a slight frown, she pulled out the phone and consulted the screen. She looked a little puzzled as she answered the call.

"Hello, yes? . . . Oh, it's you. But why are you using a pay phone? . . . Oh, poor you. Okay, just hang on a second." Clutching the phone in one hand, the woman looked at Miyuki and held up the other in a gesture of apology. "Sorry. Afraid I'm going to have to take a rain check. I'll be back tomorrow."

"Lovely."

With a final "sorry about that," the woman exited the shop. Through the plate glass window, Miyuki could see her talking on the phone as she walked off.

Miyuki sighed just as Reiko Nakanishi, the manager, came over from the café area at the back.

"It's been a busy day, Miyuki. I'll handle the rest of the cleaning up."

"Don't worry. I'm fine. I'll do it."

"We don't want you overdoing things. I bet you're tired."

"Not at all, actually. I'm feeling stronger recently."

"That's good to hear." Reiko Nakanishi smiled a tight smile, then went back to looking serious. "The lady just now left without buying anything?"

"The thing she wanted was sold out."

"I see. She was a bit late today. She usually shows up around six. Listen, Miyuki, you just clean up this display case, then you can go home."

"All right."

Squatting down behind the case, Miyuki couldn't help

smiling when she noticed a handful of unsold cream puffs. Kenichi didn't usually like sweet things, but cream puffs were the exception. The staff at Quattro were allowed to take home any leftover pastries, although giving them to anyone other than immediate family was strictly forbidden. After all, people who got sweets for free were unlikely to become paying customers.

The woman who'd just dropped in was also a cream puff fan. She normally came by at around six, as Reiko Nakanishi had said, picked out something she liked from the display, then settled down to enjoy it with a cup of tea in the café area. When there was a lull, Miyuki would sometimes look in her direction. Their eyes always seemed to meet, and the woman would give her a nice smile—a warm, kind, big-hearted smile.

Miyuki knew next to nothing about the woman. She'd come into the store for the first time about two months ago and now dropped in every couple of days or so. The staff had her pegged as a serious fan of Quattro's pastries.

I wonder what her job is, Miyuki thought. *Next time she comes, I'll just ask her.*

2.

He was sweating, and the sweat dribbled into his eyes when he leaned down to tighten the bolt. His T-shirt was soaked through. Wiping his face with the towel that was draped around his neck, Koki Kiyose reapplied himself to his task. The sooner they finished preparing the set, the sooner they could start rehearsing seriously. Around him, the other members of the company were busy finishing off the stage sets and adjusting the costumes. It was a small company, so the actors had to do everything themselves.

Koki was feeling around for another bolt when the cell phone in his back pocket started to ring. With an irritated sigh, he pulled it out. When he saw the name of the caller, his face wrinkled in distaste. He thought about not picking up; the call was from someone he really didn't want to talk to.

The other person probably didn't want to talk to him either, so if they'd gone to the trouble of calling, there must be a very good reason. Koki reluctantly answered.

"Yeah, it's me," he said in a hostile tone.

"It's me." Naohiro's voice was the same as ever.

"I know. What do you want? I'm kinda busy here."

"Just thought I'd let you know. The police will probably be contacting you."

"The police? Why? I haven't done anything."

"It's not you. It's Mineko."

The name took a fraction of a second to register. He hadn't heard anyone say it for a while.

"What? Has something happened to Mom?"

Naohiro didn't respond.

"Dad?" Koki insisted.

"They tell me she's dead."

"*What!*"

"Some detectives came around to see me this morning. Mineko was found dead last night, they said."

Koki took a deep breath. He couldn't get a word out.

Mineko's face flashed before his mind's eye. In his memory, at least, she was still smiling, young, full of life.

"Are you listening?" Naohiro asked.

"What do you mean?" said Koki. "Mom? I mean, what . . . ? Was there some sort of accident?"

"The police think she was murdered."

Koki's heart missed a beat. Then the blood surged through his veins, and he grew hot all over.

"Who did it?" he asked.

"They don't know. The investigation's just getting started. That's why the detectives came to see me."

"Where did it happen? Where was she?"

"In her apartment."

"Her apartment? Where?"

"The Nihonbashi district."

"Nihonbashi!"

"Kodenmacho, to be specific. The detectives said she was renting a studio apartment there."

That was pretty close to where Koki lived. His place was in Asakusabashi, and Kodenmacho was about half a mile away.

Why was she living there, of all places? The idea that his own mother had been murdered was too shocking; he couldn't yet accept it as real.

"Do you know anything?"

"Anything about what?"

"About why something like this should happen to your mom?"

"How could I? We weren't in touch."

At the other end of the phone, Naohiro sighed. "I didn't think so."

"What do you want me to do?"

"I'm not asking you to do anything. The police will probably want to talk to you, so I thought I'd let you know. They asked for your contact details."

"Got it."

"That's all I wanted to say."

"Dad?"

"Yeah, what?"

"What about the funeral?"

Naohiro lapsed briefly into silence, then said, "That's not my responsibility."

"I guess not."

"I plan to keep my distance. If they contact me, I'll do what I can."

Naohiro presumably meant he would be willing to help with the funeral expenses if Mineko's family asked him to do so. *That's the least you can damn well do*, Koki thought.

After the call ended, Koki just stood there, dazed and rooted to the spot. His head was a welter of confused thoughts. He had no idea what to do with himself.

"Hey, Koki, what's wrong?"

He finally snapped back to reality when someone spoke to him. It was Shinozuka, the head of the theater company.

"My mom. She was . . . murdered."

Shinozuka reeled back in stunned horror. "What did you say?"

"My mom . . . she was murdered . . . in her apartment,"

said Koki, before going into a crouch and burying his face in his knees.

About an hour later the police got in touch. Koki was working with intense concentration. His colleagues had all urged him to go home, but he'd insisted on staying. He didn't want their preparations to fall behind schedule because of his personal problems. Besides, there was nothing useful he could do, even if he did go home early. Staying busy at least kept him from having to think.

The call was from a Detective Uesugi of the Tokyo Metropolitan Police Department. Uesugi wanted a face-to-face meeting as soon as possible and proposed meeting at a diner near the theater.

When he got there, Koki found two men in suits waiting for him. Both were detectives from the Homicide Division of the Metropolitan Police. Uesugi was the older of the two.

After expressing his condolences, Uesugi asked Koki when he'd last seen his mother.

"Around the end of the year before last," answered Koki.

"The year before last!" Uesugi's eyes widened. "You hadn't seen each other for that long?"

"Didn't my dad tell you?"

"He said you'd dropped out of college and left home."

"Yeah, that was at the end of the year before last. I haven't seen my mom since."

"And you didn't bother to phone?" Uesugi looked at Koki with disdain.

Koki fixed him with a fierce stare. Who the hell did this geezer think he was?

"I just upped and left home. Go figure."

"What about your mother? Didn't she try to call you?"

"I got myself a new phone with a new number after I moved out. I didn't give the new number to my mom or dad."

"But your father knew the number."

"He hired someone to track me down. They must've worked their way through every single small theater company in Tokyo before they found me. About six months ago, this guy turns up out of the blue and is like, 'Contact your dad. He's got some important news.' So *I* called *him*."

"What was the important news?"

Koki sighed and looked the detective in the eye.

"That my parents were getting divorced. I was a bit surprised, but, hey, plenty of people get divorced, even after they've been married for years. I was like, 'If that's what you want, go for it. I've no right to kick up a fuss about it.' Guess they didn't want to finalize the divorce without keeping their son in the loop."

"Did he tell you why they were getting divorced?"

Koki cocked his head.

"No one told me jack. My father was never very into his own family, and my mom was going stir-crazy, stuck at home with nothing to do. Seemed like good news for both of them."

"Interesting. So your mom didn't like being stuck at home . . . right?"

Koki glared at the detective, who was nodding solemnly.

"Why are you even asking me this stuff? Does her divorcing my dad have something to do with the case?"

Alarmed, the detective said, "I have no idea. Right now, we know nothing about anything. Now, as regards where your mother was living . . ."

"I only heard about that today, from my dad. I can't believe how close by she lived."

"That's what we were wondering. Was it a coincidence, or something more than that? Mineko Mitsui moved to an apartment in this area a couple of months ago. Isn't it possible that she elected to live here after finding out where you lived?"

"That seems out of the question. There's no way Dad would have told her where I live. It had to be a coincidence, pure and simple."

"You think so?" Uesugi looked unconvinced.

The detective went on to ask Koki some questions about his mother's friends and her interests. Koki answered as best he could. He found it hard to believe that he was contributing much to the investigation; indeed, the detectives looked rather bored by his responses.

Koki tried to get some information about the circumstances of the crime from the detectives, but they told him very little. It was early days, and they knew almost nothing, they insisted. From their manner, though, Koki was convinced it wasn't a simple robbery that turned into murder.

"I have a final question." Uesugi raised a finger. "Can you tell us where you were last night between six and eight p.m.?"

Koki could feel the scowl forming on his face.

"You asking me for an alibi?"

"It's just routine. We have to ask everyone connected to the case. If you'd rather not answer, you're free not to."

Koki bit his lip, then said:

"I was in the performance space. You can ask any of the other actors."

"That's fine, then," replied the detective carelessly.

Koki got home a little after eight. Normally, he'd have stayed and worked on the set, but tonight he had no choice: Shinozuka had all but ordered him to leave.

There was a light in the apartment window. *Ami must be back already.* When he pushed the front door open, his girlfriend turned toward him, her face bright and cheerful. "Koki? You're early." She was watching TV.

Her face crumpled when Koki told her about his mother.

"God, come to think of it, my boss said something about it at work today." Ami frowned.

"Said something about what?"

"That there'd been a ton of police cars. Our shop's quite close to Kodenmacho. I just can't believe it, though. I mean, why on earth . . . ?" Ami blinked back her tears.

"I dunno. The detectives just told me she'd been killed. That and nothing else."

"What are you going to do? You'll have to go to the funeral."

Koki had no idea what his mother's life had been like since the divorce. In fact, he hadn't wanted to know. He had left home and was living his life the way he wanted, and she had every right to do the same. Not only that, he was just too darn busy to think about anyone else.

He lay down on his futon, but sleep wouldn't come. Ami, who was tossing and turning next to him, seemed to have the same problem. As Koki's eyes became accustomed to the dark, he could make out the vague outlines of the stains on the ceiling above his head.

Koki had met Ami Aoyama at a musical. She was in the seat next to him, and they got talking. Originally from Fukushima, she was a year older than he and had moved to Tokyo to study design. She was studying at technical school while working part-time.

The apartment they shared was originally Ami's. Koki had moved in with her.

Koki discovered acting during his first year at college. Wandering into a little local theater, he had caught a performance by Shinozuka's company. He'd made up his mind about his future on the spot. He stopped going to class and joined the company instead.

After some soul-searching, Koki made up his mind to drop out of college. Naohiro, his father, was violently opposed to this. That was no surprise. But Mineko, his mother, didn't support him, either.

"If you really want to drop out, then go ahead and do it. Just don't expect any help from me. You're on your own now," were his father's parting words.

"That's exactly how I want it," spat back Koki. He got up from the dinner table, went up to his room, and started to pack.

Mineko followed him as he was leaving the house. "Let me know when you've found a place of your own," she whispered.

He shook his head.

"I won't be calling you. And I'm going to get a new phone."

"But—"

"Mineko!" A shout from the dining room. "Just forget about that loser."

The expression on her face was a mixture of sadness and perplexity. Averting his eyes, Koki stalked out of the house.

Now his mother had been murdered. She was no longer among the living. Although Koki knew it was true, he still couldn't bring himself to believe it. It still felt like something from a soap opera.

3.

The next morning Koki left the apartment with Ami when she went to work. Her job was in a café in Horidomecho, the neighborhood next to Kodenmacho.

Koki mounted Ami's bicycle and got her to perch behind him. They'd often ridden the same bicycle back when he was working in the basement of Tokyo Station at a place that sold ready-made lunches. With the first night of the play getting closer, he was taking a temporary break from the job.

They got to the main Kodenmacho intersection in under ten minutes. Koki dismounted, and Ami took the handlebars.

"I've got school tonight," she said before pedaling off. That meant she would be back late.

"Got it," replied Koki, with a nod.

When Ami was out of sight, Koki took a look around. Spotting a convenience store, he headed for it.

There were no other customers. The clerk, a young man with dyed brown hair, was restocking the shelves with sandwiches and rice balls.

"Sorry to bother you," said Koki. "You know the murder that happened near here the night before last? Do you know where it took place?"

The shop clerk shook his head impatiently.

"Sorry, I don't have that shift."

"Oh . . . right. Well, thanks anyway."

Koki nodded at the clerk and left. Koki tried his luck at several other nearby stores, but nobody seemed to know anything about the recent murder. Their attitudes changed the instant they realized he wasn't going to buy anything; as far as they were concerned, he was just wasting their time.

After drawing a series of blanks, he finally hit pay dirt in a stationery shop.

"The woman who was killed, you mean? It happened in that block of apartments right there." The proprietor, a bald man, pointed a little way down the street. "A policeman came over to ask us if we'd seen anything suspicious. It must have happened about nine p.m. the night before. I told him that we'd closed several hours earlier, so could hardly have seen anything."

"Do you happen to know the apartment number?"

"I'm not that well informed, no. Why are you so interested?"

"I . . . sort of knew the victim. . . ."

"Gosh. I'm very sorry to hear that." The storeowner looked grave.

Quickly saying his goodbyes, Koki left the shop and walked over to the apartment building. It was a long, narrow, cream-colored building and appeared quite new.

Why was his mother living here, of all places? Her parents' house was in Yokohama. He'd assumed that she'd moved back in with them after the divorce. He had never imagined that she was living alone somewhere.

Still, given Mineko's character, it made sense. She'd always wanted to escape the drudgery of housekeeping and engage with the "real world."

She'd majored in English literature in college and had dreams of becoming a translator. Koki knew that she'd even planned to study in the UK after graduation.

Getting pregnant put paid to all that. Naturally, she knew who the father was: Naohiro Kiyose. Naohiro was a successful entrepreneur who'd launched his own business in his early thirties.

When she told Naohiro, he decided to marry her. Mineko accepted his proposal, and her family had no objections. Weddings based on accidental pregnancy were common enough back then.

Koki, though, had his own reasons for thinking that Mineko was less than happy with the marriage.

One day, when he was still in junior high school, he happened to overhear his mother talking to one of her old college friends on the phone.

"I want to try my luck in the real world. You understand, don't you? I'm still only thirty-seven. The thought of continuing to live as I do now is too depressing. God, I'm jealous of you and your job. Things wouldn't be like this if I hadn't gotten pregnant. Naohiro and I—we probably wouldn't have gotten married. Getting pregnant was my biggest mistake. It was already too late for an abortion when I found out. Besides, I wanted the experience of raising a child. That's not enough, though. I wasn't put on this earth just to be a mother. I spend every waking minute taking care of my son and my husband—but what about *me* and *my life*?"

Getting pregnant was my biggest mistake. The words were like a dagger in Koki's heart.

Koki had sensed that his father wasn't particularly interested in his family, but he'd never questioned his mother's love—until that moment. She cooked him his meals, looked after his every need, and if she lost her temper with him from time to time, that was only because she wanted the best for him.

Or so he thought. It turned out that she was just playing the part of a mother while resenting him all along. And it wasn't like it started yesterday: those negative feelings went back to the moment of his conception.

From that day on, Koki did all he could to avoid any sort of obligation to his mother. He hated the idea that she saw him as the reason her life had come to nothing.

Now, Koki saw things very differently. He no longer believed that Mineko didn't love him, her only son. The comment she'd made on the phone was the sort of thing anyone might say when they were feeling fed up. Still, she'd been sincere about her desire to start over. That explained why she'd moved to her own place in central Tokyo instead of returning to her parents' house after the divorce.

But why here specifically? Koki contemplated the building. He knew very little about his mother's life, but he couldn't imagine why she'd choose Nihonbashi.

He was still standing in the street when three men came out of the building. Koki was startled to see that Naohiro was one of them.

Naohiro stopped in his tracks.

"What the hell! What do you think you're doing here?"

"No, what are *you* doing here, Dad?"

"I'm helping the police. We've just been in Mineko's apartment."

"Are you the son of the victim?" a man in a suit asked him. "Who gave you the address?"

"I asked around. A couple of detectives came to see me yesterday, but they wouldn't tell me."

"Okay." The man nodded and glanced at Naohiro. "Should we let your son have a look at the apartment?"

"There's no need. He hasn't spoken to his mother in two years."

"Okay then, scratch that. Could you come down to the station with us, Mr. Kiyose?"

"Sure."

Ignoring Koki, the detectives stalked off. It was obvious that they had no interest in anyone they couldn't pump for information. Naohiro, who was about to follow them, spun around.

"If you hang around here, you'll only get in the way and screw up the investigation. Run along and go back to your actor chums."

Koki glared at his father. "Don't tell me what to do."

Naohiro went after the detectives without condescending to reply. Koki snorted derisively.

At that moment, he heard a voice behind him. "Excuse me a minute." He turned. A man in a blue shirt worn over a black T-shirt emerged from the apartment building. His face was dark and lined.

"I was standing in the lobby there and couldn't help overhearing. Are you Ms. Mitsui's son?"

"Yes. Who are you?"

The man pulled a police ID out of his back pocket and introduced himself as Detective Kaga of Nihonbashi Precinct.

"I guess you wanted to see where it happened?"

"That's right. I live quite nearby."

"Nearby? Sorry, where exactly?"

"Asakusabashi."

"That's certainly close. Did you walk?"

"No. My girlfriend works near here. We came over together on her bike."

"I see." Kaga pondered a moment, then looked into Koki's face. "Do you want to see the crime scene?"

Koki blinked in surprise. "Is that allowed?"

"As I'm the person in charge of preserving the crime scene, yes it is," said Kaga, whipping a key out of his pocket.

Mineko's apartment was on the fourth floor. About two hundred square feet, it was furnished with a single bed, a computer desk, a bookshelf, a table, and an armchair. It was spotlessly clean, yet it felt cramped. Koki was impressed that his mother managed to exist in such a tiny studio after years of living in a large house.

"How did it happen?" asked Koki, standing on the low concrete step in the entranceway.

"A friend of your mother's found her. They were supposed to have dinner together. The friend rang the doorbell, and when no one answered, she opened the door and discovered Mineko facedown on the floor. Initially, she thought it was a fit or a stroke, but when she noticed the marks on her throat, she called the police." Kaga rattled off the details without consulting his notes. Koki was taken aback: why was Kaga being so open with him? It was the complete opposite of the detectives of the day before.

"Who was the friend?" Koki mumbled.

"They'd been friends in college. She was working as a translator, and Mineko had been helping her out since the divorce."

"That's interesting. . . ."

So Mom was doing what she'd always dreamed of doing. The realization that her divorce hadn't left her lonely and embittered gave Koki some comfort.

This, then, was the place where she'd taken the first

steps in her journey as a translator. As Koki scanned the apartment, something caught his eye. There was a magazine rack in one corner of the room; one of the magazines in it had no business being in his mother's place. It was about baby care.

"Something wrong?" Kaga inquired.

"I don't know. It's that baby magazine over there. I was wondering what it's doing here." Koki pointed to the magazine rack.

Slipping on a pair of latex gloves, Kaga went over and picked up the magazine.

"You've got a point."

"No way my mom was pregnant, right?"

"If she was, I've yet to hear about it," answered Kaga gravely, as he replaced the magazine in the rack. "Did you know that your mother moved here about two months ago? Before that she was renting an apartment from a friend of hers over in Kamata, about ten miles from here."

"Really?"

"The friend who found the body told us that your mother's decision to move here was very sudden. When the friend asked why Kodenmacho specifically, your mother said something about 'inspiration.'"

"Inspiration . . . ?"

"Any idea what she might have meant? Why do you think your mother chose this neighborhood?"

Koki cocked his head to one side and sighed pensively. "I'm as surprised as anyone else. I never imagined that she was living so close by."

"You live in Asakusabashi. Do you think it had anything to do with that?"

"The detective I spoke to yesterday asked me the same thing. I can't imagine there's any connection, though." Koki's rejection of the idea was emphatic. "She had no way of knowing that I was living in Asakusabashi. It had to be pure coincidence."

"Is that so?"

"Do you think that there's any link between my mother moving here and her murder?"

"It's too early to say. The fact that none of the victim's friends or family has any idea why she chose this area does bother me."

"Did you go see her parents in Yokohama?"

"Someone else went. They didn't get any helpful answers out of them."

Koki could only cock his head in silence.

"Seen enough?" Kaga inquired.

"Yes."

Koki stepped back out into the hallway. Kaga followed him out, locking the door behind him.

"Could I ask you something, Detective?"

Kaga turned his lined face to Koki. "Sure, what?"

"My mother is the last person in the world to have any enemies. I suppose that's something the victim's family always says, but in my mom's case, it really is true."

Kaga smiled, but there was a piercing gleam in his eyes that made Koki flinch.

"Except, of course, that you have no idea what your

mother's been up to for the last two years. Or am I wrong?"

"Yes, that's true, but . . ."

Kaga's expression softened as Koki's voice trailed off.

"What you said just now will help with the investigation. Sadly, even people without enemies sometimes get murdered. We'll catch the killer. I promise you that."

Koki wasn't sure why Kaga was so confident, but he took comfort from his words nonetheless. Koki bowed his head, as though to say, *Please do that, Detective. I'm counting on you.*

4.

Five days had passed since the murder. Koki had no idea what sort of headway the police were making. He hadn't been contacted either by the police or by his father.

The only person who did get in touch was his mother's elder brother. This uncle called him to tell him that since the police had released the body, the family could finally hold the funeral. When it came to the investigation, however, his uncle was also in the dark.

"None of us knew what Mineko was doing with her life. She was always talking about wanting to make a fresh start, so we all thought it would be better if we stayed out of her hair."

His uncle's tone gave Koki the impression that he was trying to justify failing to stand by his divorced, lonely sister.

That same day, Detective Kaga dropped in to the theater company's performance space. They'd just finished a run-through of several scenes and were taking a break.

Koki and Kaga went out into the lobby and sat down on an old bench.

"You actors are extraordinary: look at you, buckling down to rehearsals, despite what happened to your mother."

"What else can I do? I'm going to my grandparents' place in Yokohama to help with the wake and the funeral tomorrow." Koki looked hard at the detective. "How is the investigation going? Have you found anything yet?"

"A certain amount. We now have a pretty good idea of what your mother did on the day she died," said Kaga calmly. "One odd thing. Just before she was killed, your mother was writing an email that she never finished."

Kaga flipped open his notebook.

"Here's what it said: '*I just got back. I went to the same old plaza as always. I stroked the puppy on the head and bumped into the clock shop man from Kobunacho. We had a good laugh about the way we always seem to go for our walks at the same time.*'"

"What's it mean?"

"I made a few inquiries and discovered something interesting: the puppy your mother says she stroked was a statue, not a real dog."

"A statue?"

"Do you know Suitengu Shrine? It's dedicated to conception and safe childbirth."

"I've certainly heard of it."

"There's a statue of a mother dog and her puppy there. People believe that stroking the puppy's head brings you good luck. This email suggests that Mineko Mitsui was a regular visitor to the shrine."

"What would my mom be doing there . . . ?"

"Remember that baby care magazine you spotted in her apartment? I think we're justified in assuming that someone your mother knew is pregnant and that the two of them were probably very close. She wouldn't have visited the shrine daily otherwise. The only problem is, I've looked everywhere, and I can't find a woman who fits the bill. I asked your father, and he had no idea, either."

"Well, can't help you with that," Koki said. "As I said, I hadn't seen—or spoken to—my mother for two years."

Kaga nodded despondently.

"Wouldn't the person the email was addressed to be the best person to ask?"

"I did that, of course. It was addressed to the lawyer your mother used for her divorce. While the lawyer was aware of your mother's habit of going for a daily walk, she didn't know that she was going to the Suitengu Shrine. For some reason, your mother was deliberately vague, saying things like the 'same old plaza as always.' So, no, the lawyer didn't know anything about a pregnant friend of Ms. Mitsui's."

"It's all a bit . . . weird."

What had Mineko been doing with her life? What had she been thinking? Koki again reproached himself for the indifference he'd shown to his own mother.

"I'll try and dig up more some information. Sorry to bother you." Kaga stood up off the bench.

The next day, Koki went out to his grandparents' to help with the wake. When he peered into the coffin, Mineko looked normal, despite everything. There was a white scarf wrapped around her neck to conceal the strangulation marks.

Koki felt ashamed of himself in front of his mother's family. He had failed to reach out to his mother when she had embarked on her new, independent life.

None of Mineko's relations gave Koki a hard time, though. Instead they offered words of comfort for his loss. However, they seemed rather less charitably disposed toward his father.

Koki mentioned to several people that Mineko had some sort of association with a woman who was pregnant. Nobody had the faintest idea what he was talking about.

Somebody had to stay with the body overnight at the funeral hall, and Koki volunteered. His most important job was to ensure that the incense didn't go out. Since it was a series of concentric rings, it would probably burn all night without his having to do anything.

After everyone left, Koki was alone in the funeral hall. He sat down on a folding metal chair and gazed up at the photograph of his mother on the altar. Mineko was smiling and looking straight at him. The photo, apparently, was from a vacation she'd gone on with a friend.

Suddenly, Koki felt something welling up inside him. There was a burning sensation behind his eyes. It was strange. The sight of his mother's body hadn't brought home the reality of her death, but now, looking at her photograph, he realized she was gone forever.

His cell phone rang in his pocket. Before answering, he tried to get his breathing under control. It was Ami.

"Nice timing. I was just about to ring you."

Koki explained that he would be spending the night at the funeral home.

"Okay. Try not to wear yourself out."

"I'll be fine. Everything okay your end?"

"Something odd happened. This detective guy showed up at work today. Said his name was Kaga."

Koki tightened his grip on the phone.

"At Kurochaya?"

Kurochaya was the café where Ami worked part-time.

"Yes, and he asked me something weird."

"What?"

"He asked me if your mother . . . if your mother ever came by."

"My mom?" Koki repeated incredulously. "Why would my mom go to your café? She didn't know where I live, and she certainly didn't know that I was living with you."

"He was pushy. He even showed me a photograph. Got the owner to have a look at it, too."

"What did the owner say?"

"He said he'd never seen her before. The detective must have believed us, because he left—eventually. What was that all about?"

"Search me. I'll ask him the next time I see him, if there is a next time. Anything else?"

"No, nothing."

"Okay. I'll be back tomorrow after the funeral."

After hanging up, Koki became pensive. His eyes were drawn again to the photograph of his mother.

For some reason, Mineko's smile seemed to be tinged with mystery now.

5.

Thanks to the efficiency of Koki's uncle, the funeral went smoothly. The number of people who came was roughly what they had expected, so the ceremony ran without a hitch.

The coffin was carried out. Koki, together with the rest of the family, moved from the funeral hall to the nearby crematorium. He found an unexpected person waiting for him there: Kaga. As a concession to social niceties, the detective was wearing a black tie.

"I'm sorry to intrude at a time like this, but there's something I thought you should know as soon as possible," Kaga said, with a bow.

The cremation was going to take some time. Koki wondered if Kaga had timed his visit to coincide with that stage. Whatever it was the detective wanted to tell him, it had to be pretty important.

The two of them went outside. Nearby was a well-tended park dotted with benches. They sat down on one of them.

"We've discovered why your mother moved to Kodenmacho," Kaga began. "I'm pretty confident we're right about this."

"Why, then?"

"Do you know a Mrs. Machiko Fujiwara?"

"I think I've heard the name. . . ."

"Mrs. Fujiwara was a college friend of your mother. She

says she occasionally dropped by to see your mother while she was married and living with your father."

"Oh, okay," said Koki. "I know the lady you mean. Yeah, she came by from time to time. My mom called her 'Machi.'"

"That's her." Kaga nodded. "We went through your mother's computer and we contacted everyone in the address book, but had trouble locating Mrs. Fujiwara. The reason was that she'd moved to the US—Seattle, specifically, something to do with her husband's job. We finally managed to get through to her by phone this morning. Unsurprisingly, she didn't know about the murder, let alone have any idea who might be responsible. What she could tell is why Ms. Mitsui moved to Kodenmacho."

"Why?"

"Because of you."

"Me?"

"Mrs. Fujiwara moved from Tokyo to Seattle this past March. Not long before she left the country, she was strolling through Nihonbashi when, quite by chance, she saw someone she recognized: it was you." Kaga directed a piercing look at Koki. "You were on a bicycle with a girl perched on the back. You stopped and dropped the girl off, then rode away. Since Mrs. Fujiwara wouldn't be able to keep up with you, she decided to follow the girl instead. The girl went into a café that wasn't yet open. Mrs. Fujiwara lost no time in passing this information along to Ms. Mitsui. She knew your mother was eager to find you. Since your mother moved to Kodenmacho very soon after that, I think it's reasonable to assume that she moved there to look for you."

Koki listened to Kaga with bemusement. Until now, it never crossed his mind that his mother might be trying to find him. Now, though, it seemed the most obvious thing in the world: after splitting up with her husband, he was the only family she had left.

"How come she never got in touch with me, then? She knew where Ami worked; all she had to do was to ask her."

"I'm sure that was your mother's original intention. I suspect she changed her mind after seeing your girlfriend in the flesh."

"What do you mean?"

"Even after moving to the US, Mrs. Fujiwara stayed in regular contact with your mother. That's how she knew your mother moved to Kodenmacho. She assumed that you and your mother would soon be reunited; instead, she got an email from your mother saying she'd decided to hang back and keep an eye on things for a while. Sensing that things might have gotten complicated, Mrs. Fujiwara thought it better not to pry."

Koki pushed his hand through his bangs. "Why?"

"According to Mrs. Fujiwara, although your mother dropped in to Ami Aoyama's workplace often, she never revealed her identity to her. She was worried about creeping the girl out by going there so frequently."

"So you decided to go to Kurochaya yourself. Ami told me on the phone last night. The whole thing's so weird. I mean, Ami told you that she never saw my mother at Kurochaya?"

"Exactly. So how should we interpret your mother's

emails? Was your mother making it all up when she wrote to Mrs. Fujiwara?"

"Why would she lie about something like that?" Koki grimaced. The whole thing was too bewildering.

At the sight of Koki's face, Kaga broke into a big grin.

"Don't worry, she wasn't lying to anybody. Ms. Mitsui made repeated visits to the place your girlfriend works. That's an incontestable matter of fact."

"But Ami was convinced that she never—"

"Perhaps I should phrase that more precisely," Kaga continued. "She made repeated visits to the place where she *thought* your girlfriend was working."

When Koki looked nonplussed, Kaga pulled out a piece of paper from the inside pocket of his jacket. He'd sketched a simple map. Koki recognized it as the area around the main Kodenmacho intersection.

"What's that for?"

"After Mrs. Fujiwara saw the two of you on the bicycle, she emailed your mother to tell her where your girlfriend was working. She explained how to get there like this: 'From the Kodenmacho intersection, head in the direction of Ningyocho until you get to an intersection with a Sankyo Bank on the left-hand corner. Turn left, and the café is right next door to the bank.' What do you think of her directions?"

"I don't know. . . . No, I mean, it sounds good to me." Koki called up a mental image of the neighborhood. There didn't seem to be anything wrong with those directions.

"There was nothing wrong with it. . . . Not, at least, at that point in time."

"What are you saying?"

"It was early March when Mrs. Fujiwara spotted the two of you in the street. Your mother went to Kodenmacho for the first time around two weeks later. Following her friend's instructions, she walked from the main Kodenmacho intersection toward Ningyocho. At which point she made a serious mistake. The Sankyo Bank in Mrs. Fujiwara's email is located three streets away. But two streets before that, there's a bank with a very similar name: the Sankyo-Daito Bank. Sankyo Bank and Daito Bank merged; the merger took place immediately after Mrs. Fujiwara saw you. Do you see where this is going? When Mrs. Fujiwara was there, the bank at the first intersection was still named the Daito Bank. By the time your mother went, due to the merger, it had changed to the *Sankyo-Daito Bank*. So your mother turned left there—and who can blame her?"

"But why didn't she realize she'd made a mistake? When there was no café next to the bank. . . ." Noticing the grimace on Kaga's face, Koki flinched. "Oh no. You've got to be joking?"

"I'm afraid not," Kaga said. "There is a café next door to that bank, too. To be pedantic, it's more of a pastry shop than a café, but it has a small café area at the back for tea and coffee. I completely understand why your mother thought she was at the right place."

"And that was the place my mother was going to regularly?"

"I went to check. The pastry shop's called Quattro. When I showed the girl who works there Ms. Mitsui's photograph, she confirmed that she'd been there on multiple occasions. In other words, your mother mistakenly believed the girl at Quattro was your girlfriend."

Koki shook his head.

"What was she thinking? She had more than two months. She only needed to talk to the girl to realize her mistake."

"Remember, though, that she'd decided to 'hang back and keep an eye on things.' When she saw the girl, alarming her was probably the last thing she wanted to do. I imagine she planned to make herself known to her once things had settled down."

"I wonder why she felt like that?"

"If you go to the pastry shop, you'll see why. See the girl, I mean. Personally, I think that your mother enjoyed every minute of her new life in Kodenmacho. The pleasure of silently watching over someone, anticipating the future, probably meant a lot to her."

What was Kaga talking about? Koki was utterly mystified. "Go there, and you'll see what I mean," said the detective.

6.

It was about fifteen minutes before closing time when Kenichi came in. He was wearing a suit.

"The office of one of my biggest customers is near here, and I just got out of a meeting with them. I called my boss and got permission to head home, so I thought we could travel together?"

"That's nice of you. Why don't you have a coffee while you're waiting?" Miyuki said.

Kenichi strolled over to the café area in the back of the store. Reiko Nakanishi took Kenichi's order. Naturally, she'd met Kenichi before.

Kenichi always took good care of Miyuki, but lately he was even sweeter than usual, thought Reiko.

Miyuki placed a hand on her belly. She was in her sixth month of pregnancy and had a noticeable baby bump.

She glanced at her cell phone beside the cash register. It was accessorized with a strap decorated with a little plastic dog. That lady who came in almost every day, the one with the kind eyes, had given it to her.

"I bought it at Suitengu Shine. It's so you can have a healthy, happy baby," she'd said when she gave it to her.

Miyuki couldn't figure out why the lady was always so nice to her—and now she'd never know. The lady was dead. The detective who'd come by the day before had told her so.

The detective had started by showing her a photograph and asking her if she recognized the woman in it. Miyuki was taken aback: she'd recognize that lovely smile anywhere, she said. At her response, for some reason the detective looked desperately sad. He then launched into a whole series of questions: What did she and the lady talk about when she came into the store? When was she last there?

Feeling increasingly uneasy, Miyuki decided to ask a question of her own. What was going on? Was the lady okay?

The detective seemed reluctant to answer. Miyuki's

worst fears were realized. The lady with the kind eyes was dead; worse still, she'd been murdered.

Although Miyuki never even knew the lady's name, deep sadness billowed through her like a wave. Tears welled up in her eyes and slid down her cheeks.

Miyuki did her best to answer all of the detective's questions properly. She couldn't tell him anything useful, but she tried to dredge up all her memories nonetheless.

"I'll probably be back," said the detective as he left. The man had radiated sympathy and compassion. Miyuki couldn't understand why he was so emotionally involved.

She noticed someone outside the shop. The glass door opened, and in walked a young couple. Probably in their early twenties, Miyuki reckoned.

"Good afternoon," said Miyuki out of reflex.

There was something a bit stiff about the pair. The girl was looking down at the floor while the boy was staring straight at Miyuki. *Odd*, she thought.

Miyuki gave them a welcoming smile. That was when she got a shock: the young man's eyes . . . She had never seen him before, but those eyes—she knew she'd seen them somewhere.

She looked down at the cash register where her phone with the dangling strap caught her eye. She raised her head and looked at the young man again.

He's got the same eyes as that nice lady, she thought.

6

THE FRIEND OF THE TRANSLATOR

1.

Mineko Mitsui was holding a teacup and smiling. She was dressed casually in a T-shirt and jeans, and her wavy hair was pulled back and tied loosely.

"Thank goodness," Tamiko said. "I really thought you were dead."

Mineko smiled and said nothing.

A chime sounded. That was the sound of the doorbell. Tamiko swiveled around to look at the door of her apartment. It was wide open, and someone was just slipping out.

It's Mineko, she thought. *She was right there just a moment ago, and now she's gone. I must go after her.* Tamiko was in a panic, but her body refused to move. Although she tried to get up, her legs were frozen.

The chime sounded a second time. *Must help Mineko,* thought Tamiko. *Mustn't let her leave like this. Got to bring her back.*

Tamiko could feel something heavy pressing on her ankles. That was what was immobilizing her. She looked down. There was someone lying on her feet. It was Mineko, facedown on the floor. Her head began to turn. Her face would be visible any second now—

Tamiko woke up with a violent start. She was sitting in front of her computer. On the screen was a half-written email, of which the last paragraph was a meaningless jumble of random letters.

She must have dozed off. She was drenched in cold sweat, and her heart was pounding.

The door chime sounded for a third time. That, at least, seemed to be real. Tamiko got to her feet, tottered over to the intercom on the wall.

"Yes?" she said.

The response was instantaneous. "I'm from Nihonbashi Precinct. Could I come up for a quick word?"

It took Tamiko a second or two to figure out that the man was from the police. Mineko's murder was being investigated out of Nihonbashi Police Station.

"Ms. Yoshioka? Tamiko Yoshioka?" The policeman was calling her name.

"Sorry . . . uh . . . yes. Come on up."

Tamiko pressed the button to release the downstairs door autolock and replaced the handset on the wall.

Going back to her computer, she plunked herself into the chair. A mug about one-third full of milk tea sat on the desk. She'd been drinking it before she fell asleep. She raised the mug to her lips. It was stone cold.

She sighed as she thought back to her dream. What remained with her was a vague image of Mineko smiling. Was it fanciful to think that her friend was trying to tell her something? Although Tamiko enjoyed discussing the spirit world, in her heart of hearts she didn't really believe in ghosts.

She put her elbows on the desk and pressed her forehead into her palms. She had a dull headache that had persisted for days. She was sure it was due to lack of sleep. She hadn't had a good night's sleep since the murder. The best she'd managed was a brief catnap. If she tried to sleep properly, the ghastly memories would come crowding in, making sleep impossible.

The apartment doorbell rang. Tamiko dragged herself over to the entrance and peered through the peephole.

A man stood in the passageway outside. He was wearing a short-sleeved shirt over a T-shirt and carrying a shopping bag in one hand. Although he didn't look like anyone's idea of a proper policeman, Tamiko wasn't suspicious. They'd met before, though she couldn't recall his name. She was pretty sure he'd given her his business card, but she'd mislaid the thing.

She unlocked the door and opened up. The detective smiled and gave a little bow.

"Sorry to disturb you again."

Tamiko looked at him quizzically.

"What do you want? A whole series of detectives have already questioned me."

When Tamiko had called the police, this detective had been first on the scene.

He made a gesture of apology.

"I know this is uncomfortable. New facts have come to light in the investigation. When we learn something new, we have to re-interview everyone associated with the case. You're helping us solve the crime, and we really appreciate your cooperation."

Tamiko sighed.

"What do you want to ask me?"

The detective's name suddenly came back to Tamiko. It was Kaga. He had a gentle way of speaking that she had found reassuring.

"This could take a while, so perhaps it would be better if we went somewhere we can sit down. . . . Oh, I brought you these. They're supposed to be very nice." Kaga held out the paper bag. It looked like some sort of sweet.

"That's for me?"

"Yes. It's a passion fruit and sweet almond pastry . . . or I think that's what it is. Don't you like sweet things?"

"No, I do. . . ."

"Well, go ahead and take it. If you put it in the refrigerator, it will keep for a while."

"Well, thank you." Tamiko took the bag from him. Cold was seeping out of the box at the bottom of it. They must have used dry ice.

I might be able to eat something like this, she thought. Since the murder, she hadn't eaten properly. Her appetite was simply gone.

"You know that café on the far side of the street?" said Kaga. "I'll wait for you there. This won't take long, I promise."

Tamiko shook her head and pushed the door wide open.

"If we're just going to talk, here's as good as anywhere."

"I don't want to impose."

"And I don't want to get changed. Plus, if we go out, I'll have to put on makeup."

Tamiko was wearing a terry-cloth bathrobe. Because she worked from home, she always dressed like that. "I'm too old to worry about being alone with a strange man. Come on in. Sorry about the mess."

Kaga looked uncertain. "All right, then," he said and stepped in.

The apartment consisted of a living room, a kitchen area, and a separate bedroom. The living room contained a couple of armchairs and a coffee table, with the computer desk right at the far end. Tamiko didn't have a dining table.

After showing Kaga to one of the armchairs, Tamiko went over to the kitchen. She poured a couple of glasses of barley tea and brought them over to the table.

"Thank you." Kaga inclined his head slightly.

"Are you starting to come to terms with what happened?" he asked, sipping his tea. His gaze traveled between Tamiko and the computer.

"I still can't get my head around it. Sometimes I hope it's all just a bad dream. It's real, though, isn't it? Every time I realize that, I get depressed all over again. I've got to learn to accept it. . . . Maybe that is what I'm doing. I mean, I'm certainly not doing anything else." Tamiko gave a wan smile.

"The funeral was yesterday. Did you go?"

Tamiko nodded feebly.

"Yes, I went to offer incense. I almost didn't, though. I felt ashamed in front of her family, but even worse, I didn't know how to apologize to Mineko herself. I couldn't even bring myself to look at her portrait up on the altar."

Kaga frowned.

"You've no reason to feel like that. What happened isn't your fault. The only guilty party is the perpetrator: the person who killed Mineko Mitsui."

"Yes, but—" Tamiko broke off and lowered her eyes. She could feel emotion welling up again.

"I know it's a bother, but I'd like to run through the details again," Kaga said. "You originally arranged to go to Ms. Mitsui's apartment at seven p.m. At about half past six, you called her and postponed the appointment until eight. Correct so far?"

Tamiko sighed heavily. *Detectives really don't know when enough's enough*, she thought. *How many times have they already made me go through this?*

"That's right. I needed to see someone else at seven, so I postponed."

Kaga flipped open his notebook.

"The person you were meeting was a certain Mr. Koji Tachibana, an Englishman of Japanese origin. The two of you met at Cortesia, a jewelry store in Ginza. You then left the store at seven thirty, went straight to Ms. Mitsui's building, and discovered her body in her apartment. Is there anything you need to correct so far?"

"No. That's exactly what happened."

Tamiko knew that the police were asking around, trying to corroborate her statement. Koji had been visited by a detective from the Tokyo Metropolitan Police.

"I didn't tell them why we got together, but they looked like they were just bursting to ask," Koji had declared with a hint of conspiratorial enjoyment on the phone. When Tamiko said nothing, he realized how tactless he'd been and apologized. Koji had been born in Japan and spoke fluent Japanese. He had later acquired English citizenship after his father moved to the UK for work.

"Did anybody know that you and Ms. Mitsui had arranged to see each other that evening?" asked Kaga.

"The only person I told was Mr. Tachibana."

Kaga nodded and let his eyes wander around the room.

"That's your cell phone there?"

"That's right."

"Could I have a look?"

"If you must."

Tamiko picked up the cell phone and handed it to Kaga.

Kaga thanked her. Tamiko noticed that he had slipped on a pair of white gloves before he took it from her.

The cell phone was red and accessorized with a cherry-blossom-pattern strap. It was a couple of years old, and Tamiko had been thinking about switching to a newer model.

Kaga thanked her and returned the phone.

"Uhm, what are you . . . ?"

"This may seem an odd question, but do you know if any of Ms. Mitsui's friends or acquaintances recently mislaid their cell phone? It could be a man or a woman. Doesn't matter."

"Someone losing a cell phone? I didn't hear anything about it."

"I see," murmured Kaga, a thoughtful expression on his face.

"Why does it matter? What's the big deal about someone mislaying a cell phone?"

Sunk in thought, Kaga did not immediately reply. *Must be a secret he's not at liberty to reveal to ordinary members of the public,* Tamiko was thinking, when the detective finally spoke up.

"Someone called her from a pay phone."

"Huh?"

"Somebody called Ms. Mitsui from a pay phone. The call was made at six forty-five. That's only a short time before the murder occurred. Initially, we had absolutely no idea who the caller was, but recent evidence suggests that it was someone quite close to Ms. Mitsui. Someone overheard Ms. Mitsui's end of the conversation, and she was speaking in a very informal, friendly manner. From what Ms. Mitsui said on the phone, we think it's reasonable to assume that the other party had lost or mislaid their cell phone."

Kaga fixed his eyes on Tamiko. "So . . . any idea who it could be?"

"No, I don't. Besides, what does it matter?"

"We think it highly likely that the person who mislaid their cell phone is the murderer. The crime scene strongly suggests that Ms. Mitsui knew the murderer and thus let the murderer into her apartment. It is likely that the murderer contacted her to let her know they were coming. Your original appointment with Ms. Mitsui was set for seven o'clock. If that appointment hadn't changed, Ms. Mitsui might have told the murderer not to come over that evening. That's not what she did: she let the murderer into her apartment. She must have done so only after you pushed your appointment back one hour."

Having delivered this speech in a single, rapid burst, Kaga waved his hand in a deprecating gesture when he saw Tamiko's reaction to it. "I'm in no way criticizing you. Please don't get the wrong idea."

"I'm all too aware of the role that my postponing our appointment played in her murder." Tamiko could feel the muscles of her face stiffening. "Go on."

Kaga cleared his throat.

"That means that the murderer telephoned Ms. Mitsui *after* you called her. When we examined the record of incoming calls, the only call after yours was the one from the pay phone."

Tamiko finally saw where Kaga was going with this.

"I understand your theory, but I can't think of anyone."

"Think very carefully. We have grounds for believing that this person was very close to Ms. Mitsui. There's a good chance that she mentioned his or her name to you on multiple occasions."

Kaga's tone was forceful.

"How can you be so sure?" said Tamiko, looking at the detective. "Sometimes I don't use the proper forms of polite Japanese, even when I'm talking to someone I hardly know."

"We've got more evidence than just Ms. Mitsui's tone on the telephone," countered Kaga. "As I said, the call was made at six forty-five p.m. Let's assume that the person who made the call—the owner of the mislaid cell phone—asked Ms. Mitsui if they could drop in on her that evening. Given that Ms. Mitsui was due to meet you at eight, you'd expect her to turn them down due to lack of time. But she didn't. Why do you think that was?"

Tamiko cocked her head and exhaled through her teeth.

"I can think of one possibility: that the person who made that call did so from somewhere very close to Ms. Mitsui's building. You can probably guess where I'm going with this?"

Kaga's habit of throwing out sudden questions kept Tamiko off balance, but it was clear enough what he was hinting at.

"The owner of the cell phone knew where she lived?"

"Precisely," Kaga agreed, with a satisfied look on his face. "Not even Ms. Mitsui's ex-husband or son knew where she lived. You yourself told me that you didn't know why she'd moved to Kodenmacho."

"She didn't tell me. Just said something vague about 'inspiration.'"

"So Ms. Mitsui had no special connection with the Kodenmacho area. It's difficult to believe that the murderer just happened to be in the neighborhood. No, we're justified in assuming that the murderer knew that she lived there. That leaves us with a person who knows the address of Ms. Mitsui's apartment and whom she is happy to have drop in on extremely short notice. Surely that suggests that victim and murderer knew each other very well indeed?"

The detective's argument made good sense.

"I understand your theory and why you should want to

talk to me. Off the top of my head, though, I can't think of anyone. Can you give me some time to think about it?"

"Of course I can. Take all the time you need. Do you still have my card?"

Noticing the uncomfortable expression on Tamiko's face, Kaga pulled out another card and placed it on the coffee table.

"Give me a call if you think of anything," he said, getting to his feet.

Tamiko saw Kaga to the front door. He had his hand on the doorknob, when he turned to face her.

"As I said, you mustn't blame yourself for what happened. It's thanks to you that the crime was discovered so soon and that we're already developing a time line for the murder."

Tamiko knew that Kaga was being sincere and wasn't just trying to be nice. Nonetheless, she struggled to take his comments at face value. Averting her eyes, she gently shook her head.

"Thanks for all your help," said the detective and went on his way.

2.

Mineko Mitsui was one of a small band of friends from Tamiko's college days. There used to be more of them, but whenever one of them got married or had children, they tended to drift away. Tamiko sometimes wondered if her married friends stayed in touch with one another while excluding her because she was single.

Mineko was one of the first to get married. She and Tamiko fell out of touch when Mineko's every waking minute was taken up with caring for her son, but the fact that she'd become a mother at such a young age meant that she was over and done with child-rearing that much earlier. By the time her son was in the final years of elementary school, Tamiko was the recipient of frequent phone calls from Mineko. Mostly she just wanted to grumble about how her life wasn't much fun. Once, when Tamiko told Mineko she had it easy compared to most people, Mineko flew off the handle. "You can't begin to know how I feel," she'd protested. On another occasion, she burst into tears, complaining that life didn't seem worth living anymore. Her husband was indifferent to his family, apparently, and the two of them had fallen thoroughly out of love.

Mineko was deeply jealous of Tamiko. Not only did she have a job, but she was a translator. At college Mineko had dreamed of working as a translator of folktales and fairy stories.

Tamiko suggested to Mineko that she give it a whirl. She had explained that translation was the sort of job you could fit around your housework, whenever you had a minute or two to spare.

Mineko was convinced that it wasn't that simple. Her husband didn't like the idea of his wife working, and she was afraid that he wouldn't let her even do the occasional odd job.

Tamiko knew better than to get in the middle of a dispute between a married couple. The best she could do, she decided, was give Mineko a shoulder to cry on.

Recently, though, circumstances had changed. When her only son left home, Mineko had started thinking seriously about leaving her husband. The only problem was how to support herself.

"How about you helping me out?" Tamiko had proposed spontaneously. She needed someone to help out after her excellent assistant quit.

Mineko lacked self-confidence but acquitted herself well on the translations that Tamiko gave her as a test.

Armed with a newfound belief in her ability to earn a living, Mineko made up her mind and asked her husband for a divorce. Somewhat to her surprise, he readily agreed. The settlement he offered Mineko was very modest, in light of his high net worth. Tamiko told her to stick to her guns and demand more, but Mineko only laughed. "I don't care," she said. "Getting my freedom is way more important than getting his money."

Tamiko started sending translation jobs to Mineko almost as soon as she moved out. Tamiko planned to keep an eye on her friend until she was capable of standing on her own two feet as a translator, something that would take some time. For her part, Tamiko was very happy to be working with a friend.

After the divorce went through, Mineko lived in the apartment of another friend of hers in Kamata, until a couple of months ago when she moved to Kodenmacho near Nihonbashi. Tamiko still had no idea why she was so set on that particular neighborhood. Although Mineko claimed it was for "inspiration," Tamiko felt certain that there was something else behind her choice. Mineko's face always glowed when the move came up in conversation. There was obviously something about the area that excited her. Sure that Mineko would eventually confide in her, Tamiko never pressed for an answer.

Everything was going well until something unexpected occurred, something that threatened to undermine their friendship. This time it came not from Mineko's side but Tamiko's.

Tamiko had first met Koji Tachibana about a year ago. Along with some publishing friends of hers, she'd gone to look at the nighttime cherry blossoms near the Imperial Palace. An editor she knew had brought Koji along. He was single and three years younger than Tamiko. A videographer, he'd moved to Japan a couple of years ago.

The two of them had soon begun seeing a lot of each other, getting closer and closer. Neither of them had said anything about living together or getting married. They both enjoyed a similar lifestyle—working hard at home and only getting together when they wanted to relax.

Koji, though, had recently come out with an unexpected proposal: He planned to move back to London—and wanted Tamiko to come with him as his wife.

Puzzlement, dismay, and confusion characterized Tamiko's initial response, but as this welter of emotions receded, excitement and joy remained.

She had neither aging parents to care for nor long-term contracts to fulfill. She was free to drop everything and take off with Koji. Just one thing weighed on her mind: Mineko.

Mineko had embarked on her new life because of Tamiko's promise to take care of her until she was established as a translator. She couldn't *not* feel guilty about letting her friend down.

Still, it never occurred to Tamiko to turn Koji down. She couldn't imagine life without him.

After considerable soul-searching, Tamiko made up her mind to talk things through with her friend. She was certain that Mineko would see things from her point of view.

No such luck. The more Tamiko spoke, the tenser the expression on Mineko's face became.

"I can't believe it. I only got divorced because you said you'd help me out. . . . ," she said bitterly.

Tamiko sympathized. If someone had done the same thing to her, she'd have been indignant, too. Though perhaps insecurity was the problem, more than indignation.

The two women went their separate ways after this uncomfortable exchange. That was three weeks ago. And they were due to meet again for the first time on *that* day—June 10.

Tamiko had changed the original seven o'clock appointment after Koji had called her and insisted on seeing her right away. He was waiting in Ginza, he said.

When Tamiko got there, Koji had taken her straight to a jewelry shop. She was led to a seating area at the back, and a ring with the most brilliant diamond was produced for her inspection.

"Say you like it, and I'll sign for it," Koji said. Despite her age, Tamiko had burst into tears. She would have hugged Koji then and there, if there hadn't been other people around.

After they left the store, she had given the ring to Koji to take care of and had caught a taxi to Kodenmacho. This would be only her second visit to Mineko's apartment. *Probably better if I don't mention the ring*, she was thinking as she sat in the back of the taxi.

She had arrived at Mineko's apartment building at four or five minutes to eight. She took the elevator to the fourth floor and rang the doorbell. There had been no response. She pressed it a second time. Again, nothing. Thinking that was odd, she reached for the doorknob. The door had been unlocked.

The first thing she had seen in the apartment was Mineko sprawled on the floor. Was it a heart attack or a hemorrhage of some kind? As soon as she crouched down for a better look at Mineko's face, she spotted the livid marks around the neck.

With trembling fingers Tamiko had called the police on her cell phone. She couldn't remember what she'd said. After hanging up, she went and waited for the police in the hallway outside the apartment. The police must have told her to do so, she later thought.

The police came in no time. They led Tamiko out to a patrol car. She was expecting to be driven off somewhere, but instead a detective climbed in with her and asked her some questions. Initially, Tamiko couldn't string together an answer. The detective betrayed no signs of impatience, and she gradually started to calm down. The detective was him—*Kaga*.

Ironically, it was only after she had recovered her composure that she realized the awful thing she'd done: *Mineko wouldn't have been murdered if she hadn't postponed their appointment.*

She recalled the scene from earlier that evening: she'd been in heaven when Koji presented her with the ring. Completely swept up in her own happiness, she hadn't a thought to spare for anyone else. *And at that very moment, the murderer was strangling Mineko, putting her through hell.*

Sadness, regret, and self-reproach welled up inside her. With Detective Kaga looking on in amazement, she burst out: "The whole thing's my fault. If I hadn't rescheduled . . . It's because of me. If I hadn't been so self-absorbed. It's me. I . . . I'm the reason Mineko was murdered. It's all my fault."

3.

That night Koji phoned Tamiko to see if she felt like going out for dinner.

"I'm sorry. I don't feel up to it yet."

"Okay then, I'll pop around to your place. I'll pick up something en route. What do you feel like eating?"

Tamiko shook her head into the receiver.

"Let me take a rain check. My place is a mess, and I haven't done my makeup."

"So what? I'm worried about you. Are you eating properly?"

"Yes, I'm eating. You don't need to worry. I just need to be alone. That's all."

Noticing the edge in her voice, Koji went quiet.

"I'm sorry," Tamiko apologized. "I want to see you too, you know. There's nothing I'd like more than a nice little cuddle. Being with you would help I forget about this whole horrid business."

"Why not let me come around, then?"

"It doesn't feel right. Just think of what poor Mineko went through. It's not fair for me to run away from reality. No, spending time with you, feeling even a smidgen of happiness, forgetting about Mineko even for a very short time—that's the coward's choice."

Koji went quiet again. Tamiko guessed he was trying to process what she had said.

Although Tamiko meant every word that she said, she wasn't being completely candid. In her heart of hearts, she was convinced that if she and Koji hadn't met up that evening, Mineko wouldn't have been killed. She felt that if she saw him with that guilt stewing inside her, things between them would never be the same again, and all their lovely shared memories would become something painful.

She couldn't bring herself to tell Koji what was eating at her. If she did, she knew that he would start blaming himself. After all, he was the one who pressured Tamiko to change her schedule that day.

"Is there really nothing I can do?"

"I appreciate your being there for me."

At the other end of the line, Koji sighed.

"I hate the person who did this; hate them from the bottom of my heart. Murdering your friend is heinous enough, but the psychological pain they inflicted on you—that's unforgivable. I'd like to kill the person responsible."

Tamiko pressed her free hand to her temples.

"For God's sake, Koji, don't talk about killing people."

"I'm sorry."

"My pain is neither here nor there. What I want to know is why this happened. Mineko was such a lovely person. . . . The police asked me all sorts of questions, but I don't have any worthwhile information at all. I feel so useless."

"Don't torment yourself. No one can know what they don't know, right?"

"I was one of her best friends."

"Listen, I don't know everything about my close friends. That's just how life is."

Now it was Tamiko's turn to lapse into silence. She knew what Koji was trying to say, but the crisp certainty of his tone only saddened her.

"A detective came to see me today," said Koji. "A different one from last time. This one's name was Kaga."

"I know him. We've met a couple of times."

"Bit of an oddball. God knows why, but he gave me a present: rolled omelet."

"Rolled omelet?"

"'Because it's a traditional dish,' he said. Anyway, he hands me this thing then asks if I'm more of a knife-and-fork or chopstick kind of guy. Nuts! I told him that I was better than average at plying the old chopsticks."

"What did he say about the murder?"

"He started out by asking me if Mineko and I had met. I said yes, that the three of us had gone out for dinner a couple of times. Next it was, did I remember what we'd talked about? I told him I couldn't remember all the details, but that it was probably stuff like how you and I met. He's like, 'Why don't you tell me about that?'"

"About how *we* met? Why should he care?"

"Search me. He wouldn't give me a straight answer when I asked the same thing. Like I said, he's a funny one. Next thing it's do I have a cell phone? When I say I do, he asks me to show it to him."

Tamiko remembered what Kaga had told her when he had dropped in on her earlier.

"And did you?"

"Sure. Then he's like, 'How long have you had this phone?' What on earth was all that about?"

"Goodness only knows," said Tamiko, though she knew perfectly well what Kaga was after. Believing that it was the murderer who had called Mineko from a pay phone, he wanted to check whether or not Koji had lost his cell phone. Kaga, in other words, regarded Koji as a suspect.

What an idiot! Tamiko thought. She'd been with Koji right up until she had gone over to Mineko's apartment and found her dead. His alibi was rock solid. The police shouldn't have any trouble figuring that out.

Unless—

Unless Kaga didn't believe her. Or did he think that Koji somehow arrived at the apartment just before her and murdered her friend?

She'd told Kaga that her plan to move to London had sparked some friction between her and Mineko. Surely no sane person could see something that trivial as a motive for murder? Or did Kaga think Koji had some other motive?

Kaga had made a good first impression on Tamiko. He seemed sensitive, someone it was safe to trust. That's why she had been so frank and open with him right from the start. The trouble was that she had no way of knowing if he was being straight with her. Perhaps he was just pretending to be sympathetic.

"Hey, Tamiko, are you still there?" Koji said.

"Oh . . . uh, yeah. Go on, what else did Kaga ask you?"

"That's everything. He sort of popped up, asked a few questions, and then vanished in a puff of smoke. It was kind of creepy."

"There's no need to worry. He was probably just double-checking something."

"I thought so, too," said Koji breezily.

"Listen, I'm kind of tired. I think I'm going to call it a night."

"Right. Sorry to keep you on the phone. Sleep well, okay?"

"I'll try. Thanks. 'Night."

"Good night," said Koji.

Tamiko hung up and collapsed into bed.

She wondered what the future held for her. Would the sorrow gradually fade away so she could enjoy being with Koji again? How was she supposed to process what had happened to Mineko? Would she just forget about Mineko in the natural course of things?

Tamiko closed her eyes. She'd hoped to fall asleep right away, but it wasn't happening. Instead, her head felt thick and heavy.

"Is that your final decision?"

Suddenly, Tamiko heard Mineko's voice and, in her mind's eye, saw her face. There was a sharp furrow of anxiety between her eyebrows.

It was when Tamiko had told her about her plan to relocate to London with Koji.

"Yes. I think it's what I want to do," Tamiko had shyly replied.

"What about your work? What are you going to do with your translation business?"

"I . . . I'm going to finish off all the projects I'm currently working on and then get out of the business. Chances are that my work will dry up anyway after I move to London."

Mineko's eyes flitted restlessly about. Noticing her bewilderment, Tamiko had quickly added more.

"Of course, I'll do what I can for you. I can introduce you to a number of translation agencies, plus there are some people I know in publishing who can probably send some work your way, too. There's no need for you to worry."

Mineko had avoided looking her in the eye.

"I can't believe it. I only got divorced because you promised to help me. . . ."

Tamiko had been at a loss for words.

"I'm sorry," she said. "I never saw this coming, either."

Mineko had pressed a hand to her temple.

"I'm screwed," she had muttered, half to herself. "If I'd known things were going to turn out like this, I'd have held out for more money."

She was referring to her divorce settlement.

"Don't worry. You're an excellent translator. You'll get more than enough work to make a living."

Mineko had glared at her coldly.

"How do you know that? It won't be that easy."

"I meant what I said."

"I don't want to talk about it anymore. I'm not blaming you. Hey, the man you love asks you to marry him, and any promises you made to your friends go out the window. That's normal enough."

"It's not like that. I feel awful. Can't you at least believe that?"

"Well, if you really felt guilty about what you're doing . . ." Mineko had shaken her head. "Oh, what's the point? I should never have trusted anyone else. When it comes down to it, I'm the one who has to take care of myself."

"But Mineko . . . ," protested Tamiko.

Mineko had put the money for her drink on the table, stood up, and stalked out of the café.

Her back as she walked away—that was the last time Tamiko had seen Mineko alive.

She was tormented by remorse. *I shouldn't have let things end like that. I should have run after her and hashed things out. We could have reached an understanding.*

Instead, Tamiko had left things hanging for nearly two weeks. Mineko had every reason to see her as selfish and irresponsible. And when they were finally going to get together again, she'd called at the last minute to push the appointment back an hour. On the phone, Mineko had just said, "Okay, eight o'clock it is. See you later." Inside, though, she was probably seething. And that hour's delay had ended up costing Mineko her life.

"Forgive me, Mineko," murmured Tamiko. God only knows how many times she'd said those words since the murder. But in her heart, she knew that no matter how many times she said she was sorry, her friend would never hear.

4.

The humid air clung to her the moment she stepped through the sliding glass door. In an instant every single pore on her body seemed to ooze sweat. Ignoring the discomfort, Tamiko thrust her feet into her sandals. She was not yet ready to leave the building, but she was sick and tired of being stuck in her apartment. She needed to get some air in her lungs.

When had she last been out on the balcony? She'd actually rented this particular apartment because it overlooked a small park, but since moving in, she'd barely ventured outside to enjoy the view.

She was about to lean on the balcony railing when she suddenly noticed that it was black with grime.

She had gone back inside to fetch a rag when her cell phone pinged to indicate an incoming text. It was from Koji.

> I want to firm up our plans for moving back to the UK. What are your feelings about the move? Let me know.

Tamiko clapped the phone shut with a sigh. Koji was getting jittery. He couldn't plan his work without a clear date for his return to London. Tamiko guessed that he was probably more anxious than the text implied. It was typical of his good nature to be so tactful and avoid any high-pressure language.

Tamiko found a cloth and went back out onto the balcony. As she wiped the railing, she thought about Koji. It wasn't fair of her to take advantage of his kindness. Nothing was going to bring the dead back to life; at some point she would have to let go of Mineko. But could she really just pull up stakes and go to London? Wouldn't she hate herself for it?

The handrail now looked as bright and shiny as new. She let the air out of her lungs and looked at the street below. A figure was approaching. It was Detective Kaga, this time carrying a white plastic bag.

Abruptly, he raised his head and looked right up at her. Surely he hadn't sensed that she was staring at him? Kaga grinned cheerfully. She responded with a curt nod.

It's good timing in a way, she thought. *I can ask him what he was really after when he went to see Koji.*

A couple of minutes later, Kaga was standing outside the door of her apartment.

"I brought you some rice crackers this time instead of something sweet."

He held out the bag.

Tamiko gave a pained smile. "Do you always give presents to the people you question?"

"Huh? I don't think so. . . . Don't you like rice crackers?"

"I do. But getting all these presents from you just makes

me feel guilty." Tamiko took the bag. "Anyway, come on in. The place is a bomb site, as usual."

Kaga stayed where he was. His arms were crossed, and he had a thoughtful look on his face.

"What is it?"

"Can't you come out with me today?" Kaga said. "I want to take you somewhere. There's something I want you to see, rather."

Tamiko felt defensive. "Where are we going?"

"An area you know well. The Ningyocho district, less than ten minutes' walk from Mineko Mitsui's apartment."

"Why do we need to go there?"

"You'll see when we get there. I'll be waiting downstairs. There's no hurry. Take your time getting ready." Kaga spun on his heel and strode to the elevator before Tamiko could reply.

Where was he going to take her? What was he planning to show her? With no idea what he had in mind, Tamiko made herself up properly for the first time in ages.

When she came down to the street, Kaga hailed a cab.

"By the way, did you like it?" he asked, as the cab picked up speed. "That sweet almond pastry I brought over last time?"

"It was fabulous. You've got excellent taste, Detective Kaga," she replied. Tamiko wasn't being diplomatic; she meant every word.

"Oh, I don't know about that, but I'm pleased you liked it."

"I heard you gave my boyfriend rolled omelet."

"He told you? I wasn't quite sure what to get for someone raised in the UK. I ended up opting for omelet. Mr. Tachibana wasn't annoyed, was he?"

"Of course not. Though he did describe you as 'unusual.'"

"Wandering around Ningyocho, I come across all sorts of little shops. They're very much the sort of places that make you want to buy gifts for people. I suppose a detective turning up with rolled omelet might creep some people out. I should be more careful." Kaga gave a toothy grin.

Kaga got the driver to stop just after they had turned at the big Suitengumae intersection. They were on a broad one-way street lined with shops and restaurants of all different shapes and sizes.

They walked along the sidewalk until Kaga came to a halt in front of a china shop. The sign above the door said "Yanagisawa's."

"Hello?" called Kaga, as he stepped inside.

"Ye-es," called a woman, emerging from the back. She looked about twenty, had dyed brown hair and earrings. The jeans she had on were artfully ripped.

"Oh, you again, Detective Kaga?" The ingratiating smile vanished from her face.

"Sorry I'm not a proper customer."

"Doesn't matter. What do you want today?"

Kaga was clearly a frequent visitor here. Given the coldness of his welcome, Tamiko guessed that he was there to make inquiries rather than to buy anything.

"Do you still have those things you showed me the other day?" Kaga asked.

"Yes. You told us to hang on to them."

"Can you bring them out for a minute?"

"Sure."

Kaga waited for the woman to disappear into the back of the store, then turned to Tamiko.

"To be honest, there's something here that I'd like you to see. A few days before she was killed, Mineko Mitsui came here to look at their chopsticks. I'm guessing she planned to give them as a present to someone. What I want you to do is to try and think who that someone might be."

"Chopsticks? Now you mention it, I—"

Tamiko was interrupted by the return of the woman clerk, now carrying a long, thin box.

"You mean these?" she said, handing the box to Kaga.

Kaga opened the box and nodded. "Have a look," he urged Tamiko.

Tamiko peered inside. The box contained two sets of chopsticks: a long black pair and another slightly shorter, vermilion pair. It looked like a his-and-hers set.

"I can't tell anything just from looking at them," she said.

"Take them out and have a careful look. They've got a decorative pattern."

Tamiko duly extracted the black chopsticks. Kaga was right. She gave a start when she saw the decoration.

"What do you think?" asked Kaga. "That cherry blossom design is made of real mother-of-pearl. That's why it's that nice silvery color."

"What? Was Mineko planning to—?"

"You were out of this particular set the day Ms. Mitsui

came by, weren't you?" Kaga asked the shop clerk. "Could you tell us what happened?"

The young woman nodded and took a step forward.

"These chopsticks caught Ms. Mitsui's eye on a previous visit, so she came here specifically to buy them. She was disappointed that we were out of stock. She went home empty-handed, but I put in an order for a new set, which arrived the day before yesterday. . . ."

Even before the woman had reached the end of her account, Tamiko felt the hot rush of emotion. Her face became flushed, and the tears began to stream from her eyes.

"Seems you've figured out whom she was planning to give them to," said Kaga.

Tamiko's head jerked up and down, and she pressed her hand to her mouth.

"I . . . it was me. She was going to give them to me and my fiancé."

"Cherry blossoms have a special significance for you and Mr. Tachibana. You first met when you both went to enjoy the nighttime cherry blossoms."

"That's right. Koji had never seen so many cherry trees in his life. He loved it. Cherry blossoms became a symbol of our happiness."

"Which, I suppose, is why both your mobile phone straps have a cherry blossom motif? I noticed that Mr. Tachibana had one, too."

Tamiko's eyes widened.

"So that's why you got him to show you his cell phone."

Kaga nodded.

"It occurred to me when I saw the strap on your cell phone that maybe you were the person for whom Mineko Mitsui planned to buy the chopsticks. It was just a hunch, and I had no proof. If I got you to look at the chopsticks and I was wrong about them, I'd only cause you even more pain. That's why I went to see Mr. Tachibana first."

"I thought you were looking at him as a suspect."

"That the cops were 'hot on his tail,' eh? That's natural enough. Apologize to him from me, please."

Tamiko took another long look at the chopsticks. They meant that Mineko had forgiven her. She'd planned to give these chopsticks to Koji and her so they could enjoy the memory of the Tokyo cherry blossoms after moving to London.

"Those things I brought around to your place the other day—the passion fruit and sweet almond pastry—Mineko Mitsui tried to buy some just before she was killed," Kaga said. "I guess she planned to serve them to you at her place, but they were sold out too, unfortunately."

"Those pastries . . ."

"It was when the people at the pastry shop told me about her trying to buy them that I realized that Ms. Mitsui probably wanted to mend fences with you. That only made me more determined to pinpoint the person she wanted to give the chopsticks to."

Wiping the tears away with the back of her hand, Tamiko looked hard at the detective.

"Aren't you supposed to be investigating her murder, Detective?"

"Oh, I am investigating the murder; of course I am. But

my job as a detective should go beyond that. People who've been traumatized by a crime are victims, too. Finding ways to comfort them is also part of my job."

Tamiko lowered her eyes. A single tear dropped onto the hand in which she held the chopsticks.

A wind chime tinkled above her head.

7

THE PRESIDENT OF THE CLEANING COMPANY

Koki Kiyose was sitting in an easy chair with a pipe between his teeth and a thick file open on his knees when there was a knock on the door.

"Is that you, Marsh?" asked Koki, forcing himself to sound calm. "Come on in."

The door opened, and Ikuo Yamada came in, a gray wig on his head.

"I've completed the fifth volume of our memoirs, Wike." Yamada allowed his rich bass voice to resonate as he held out a bound volume.

"It's finally done, eh? So now we have it—*The Full Record of the Murder at the Evil Prince's Mansion*. I remember it so well: the tension and the intellectual excitement. All I regret is that I never got to meet the criminal mastermind, who had the pride of a true artist, and—"

"Stop," someone yelled. It was Shinozuka, the director of the theater company. Koki winced.

"What's wrong with you, Koki? Your performance is so one-note. Your speech should project the character's sense of self-worth, tinged with nostalgia for the old days and a soupçon of sadness as the cherry on the cake. I need you to give it more feeling." The expression on Shinozuka's face was stern.

"I'm sorry. Let me take another stab at it."

"No, we'll take a quick break. There's something I need to deal with. Okay, everybody," said Shinozuka to the rest of the staff. "Take ten."

The tension that had filled the cramped performance space suddenly lifted. Koki could feel himself being drawn back to reality from the make-believe world of the play.

Despite Shinozuka's having announced a ten-minute break, the rehearsal didn't resume after the allotted time was up. The director and the lead were in his office having a talk. Maybe *talk* was not the right word; it was more like a unilateral declaration: since Koki was clearly unable to concentrate on his performance, Shinozuka wanted him to step down.

Koki bowed his head apologetically. He knew the director was right.

"I'm sorry. I promise to do better. I'll improve my focus."

"Stop bowing. I don't want your apologies. I know why you're having trouble concentrating. For God's sake, your mother's been murdered, and the killer's still out there."

Koki raised his head and looked Shinozuka in the eye.

"I'll do it. I'll find a way to get my concentration back."

Shinozuka frowned.

"You're missing the point, Koki. If we could will ourselves to concentrate, then no one would ever be unhappy. I know you're doing your absolute best, and I have a great deal of respect for your talent. The state you're in now, though, leaves acting out of the question. That's my final decision as the director."

Koki lowered his head again. This time he was not apologizing; he was drooping with disappointment.

"There's nothing I can do to make you change your mind?"

"Not this time, I'm afraid," said Shinozuka gently. "The company will need your talents again in the future—of that I'm sure. Right now, it's impossible. When you're over what's happened and can focus on the performance without needing to force it, then I'd love for you to be in a play of mine. As the lead, of course."

Koki clenched his jaw and looked at Shinozuka.

The director responded with an encouraging nod. "Come back when this business with your mother has been sorted out."

"Fine," Koki snapped back.

When Koki spotted the nameplate for Takamachi Consulting Law Office, he wondered how much this was going to cost him. His image of lawyers was one of fat cats rolling in money.

The office was on the third floor. A young female receptionist sat behind a pair of glass doors. Koki timidly pushed his way in and gave her his name.

"I've got an appointment with Ms. Takamachi at four o'clock. Nothing to do with anything legal. Just need to ask her a couple of questions. . . ."

"Very good, sir. Please take a seat."

The receptionist picked up the phone and announced Koki's arrival. Then, replacing the receiver, she led him down a corridor and asked him to wait in a small meeting room.

The room was tiny, with only a table and a couple of folding metal chairs. Koki sat with his back toward the door. He felt slightly nervous.

He'd wondered what to do with himself after Shinozuka had made him step down. His mother's murder was weighing heavily on him, but it wasn't just that the case was unsolved. He'd done nothing for her before that, and now he was dogged by a sense of guilt.

Since leaving home, Koki had been so obsessed with acting that he'd barely given his parents a thought. He'd felt only indifference when they told him about their divorce. They were adults, free to do whatever they darn well wanted. If they'd decided to split up and go their own ways, then so be it. The fact that he was their son didn't give him the right to interfere. Basically, he just didn't care.

With Mineko, though, it was a different story. Newly divorced and forced to stand on her own two feet, she must have had to make serious decisions about her job and future. Nonetheless, she'd still been thinking about him, her only son.

She had a reason for moving to a neighborhood with which she had no connection—and it was an important one. It was close to the pastry shop where her son's girlfriend was working. When she discovered that the girlfriend was pregnant, she wanted to be nearby to keep a friendly eye on her.

She hadn't discussed the matter with anybody else; nor had she introduced herself to the girlfriend. She was probably worried that Koki would get annoyed, or maybe she was frightened that Naohiro would try to stick his oar in and influence things.

"Personally, I think that your mother enjoyed every minute of her new life in Kodenmacho. The pleasure of silently watching over someone, anticipating the future, probably meant a lot to her."

Those were the slightly cryptic words Detective Kaga had used. At the time, Koki didn't understand; now he understood so well that it almost caused him physical pain.

Kaga had given Koki the address of the pastry shop. The one his mother had mistaken for the café Ami worked at. He and Ami went there, and both broke down in tears at the sight of the pregnant clerk. Despite never having met Koki's mother, Ami wailed. "I wish it wasn't a case of mistaken identity. I wish I really *was* her. Wouldn't that have been lovely?"

Koki's chest hurt whenever he thought of Mineko. Finally realizing how precious a mother's love is, he now knew how foolish he was to have turned his back on it. He felt partly to blame for what had happened: if they had been in regular contact, maybe she wouldn't have been murdered.

Shinozuka was definitely right: Koki couldn't focus on acting now. Perhaps, though, there was something else he could do: find out about his mother.

The trouble was, he had no idea where to start. The police had cordoned off her Kodenmacho apartment, so, son or not, he had no hope of examining anything that might give him an insight into her new life.

Racking his brains, he remembered something Kaga said about his mother having hired a lawyer to negotiate her divorce and that the two women were still in contact. Maybe the lawyer would be able to tell him about her recent life.

The next question was how to locate the lawyer. Koki could think of only one way: it was the last thing he wanted to do, but he called up his father, Naohiro, and asked him for the lawyer's contact details.

"Why the hell do you want to know?" snarled Naohiro. "What business have you got with some damn lawyer?"

"Nothing to do with you. Just tell me."

"No way will I tell you. If you start dicking around and screw up the investigation, that'll be a huge problem."

"That's not going to happen. I just want to find out more about Mom."

"That's exactly what I mean by dicking around. The cops will get to the bottom of your mother's murder. Until then, sit tight and wait. You're an amateur, so butt out."

"You've got it all wrong. I'm not trying to solve the case. I just want to learn about Mom."

"Learn what, exactly?"

"Any damn thing. It's like I know nothing about her. And I bet you don't know the first thing about her either, do you, Dad? Do you know what was on her mind just before she was killed? Do you have any idea why she was renting an apartment near me? No, of course you don't."

A moment of silence.

"You're saying that you do?" Naohiro asked.

"Yeah, I do. But don't worry about it. It's got nothing to do with you, and it wouldn't mean anything to you. You'd probably just say Mom's an idiot. You're fine not knowing anything,

Dad, but me—me, I'm different. I want to know all about Mom. But I won't make trouble for you, I promise you that."

Koki delivered this rant without pausing for breath. Another silence followed. Finally, there was a heavy sigh, then Naohiro said, "Okay, just wait a minute."

Naohiro gave him the name and contact details of the lawyer, Shizuko Takamachi.

"There's probably not much point in telling you this now," continued Naohiro, "but our divorce was a mutual thing. Mineko was the one who initiated it; she said that she wanted to 'start a new life.' I thought she was being selfish, but I went along with it. The lawyer negotiated things between us, sure, but there weren't any ugly fights about dividing up our assets."

"Then why bother telling me? The lawyer will tell me the same thing—if it's true, of course."

"Everyone sees things differently. The lawyer will probably say that she did a good job working out the settlement. The truth is, we never needed a lawyer. There was no dispute. I just wanted to let you know."

"All that crap about 'settlements' and 'dividing up assets' means nothing to me. I couldn't care less about stuff like that."

Having got the lawyer's contact information, Koki had no further use for his father, and he hung up.

A plump woman with a round, amiable face, Shizuko Takamachi looked around forty. Koki imagined that clients like his mom would find her very reassuring.

Getting to his feet, he introduced himself and thanked her for seeing him. With a nod, Shizuko Takamachi gestured for him to sit back down.

"Please accept my condolences. It must have been a dreadful shock."

"Very much so," replied Koki.

"I was shocked, too. As you may be aware, your mother came to see me a number of times recently. I never picked up the slightest hint that she was in danger. If anything, she seemed happy to have regained her independence."

"You have no idea why she was murdered, then?"

"No. I can't think of anything significant enough to have any bearing on the crime."

"When did you and my mother first meet?"

"When your mother decided to file for divorce. A friend of hers introduced our practice to her, and she made an appointment with me."

"But the two of you stayed in touch even after the divorce was finalized. Were you friends?"

The lawyer frowned. Despite her rather ordinary, roly-poly appearance, she obviously picked her words with care.

"Friends? You could safely characterize it in those terms, yes. Ms. Mitsui sent along news via email, and I replied, when I had the time. That was our relationship. Life can be challenging for a newly divorced woman, so I was there for her, if she needed someone to talk to. It was like a follow-up service: if we ended up discussing legal matters, I could hardly do it free of charge, of course."

"Just now you said you couldn't think of anything significant enough to have any bearing on her murder. Can you think of anything less significant but that might still be relevant?"

A faint smile appeared on Shizuko Takamachi's lips.

"Your mother and I are both grown women. We didn't email about trivialities."

"What did you email about, then?"

"Things that I cannot reveal to you, even though you are her son. Lawyers have a duty of confidentiality toward their clients, and your late mother is still my client, as far as I am concerned."

The lawyer's voice was gentle, but Koki was intimidated by her crisp enunciation and the professional pride and strength of will it implied. *Bet she's good at playing mind games in court,* he thought.

Rather unexpectedly, the lawyer smiled.

"As I said, your mother seemed happy to me. That came through in her emails. She was considering a range of options with regard to her future, but I doubt that there was any link to her murder."

Koki again felt the heat of emotion in his chest. He knew that the optimistic tone the lawyer had detected in his mother's emails came from her excitement about the birth of her first grandchild.

Still, as the lawyer had said, they were both grown women, with no interest in exchanging frivolous emails. What *had* Mineko been consulting her about?

Koki realized that he wasn't going to get that information out of this lawyer. He wondered what to do.

At that moment, an image flashed into his mind's eye. *I'm sure he will know.*

"Are you all right?" the lawyer asked

"I'm fine. Thank you for your time. I know you must be very busy," said Koki as he rose to his feet.

2.

The intercom on the table buzzed. Naohiro, who was reading through a document, reached out and grabbed the receiver.

"Yes?"

"Mr. Kishida is here," said Yuri, in a husky voice. Naohiro loved her voice. The sound of it made him feel that all was right with the world.

"Show him in," he said.

The door opened, revealing the scrawny figure of Yosaku Kishida. He was so thin that he resembled a suit dangling from a hanger.

"Did you run the numbers?" Naohiro asked, moving over to an armchair in the meeting area of the room.

"Yes. I'll cut to the chase: they're not good at all."

Settling himself into the chair facing Naohiro, Kishida pulled a file out of his briefcase and plunked it on the table.

"What's the problem? Is it the cost of wages?"

"That's the one. Right now, we've got seventy-one part-time and temp employees. We need to get that number down to fifty if we want to see a light at the end of the tunnel."

"You want me to fire twenty people? That's crazy. The business will just grind to a halt."

"Okay then, make it ten. Minimum."

Naohiro was groaning when the door opened. "Excuse me," said Yuri, making her way into his office. She was carrying a tray with two teacups on it. She placed one cup in front of Naohiro and the other in front of Kishida. She was tall, with long legs, arms, and fingers. Her skirt ended well above the knee. She wore a silver ring—obviously handmade—on one of her pinkies. It was a present from Naohiro, as was the necklace with a small diamond that hung around her neck.

Her job done, Yuri bowed crisply and exited the room. Naohiro and Kishida hadn't said a word while she was there.

"Do I really have to fire ten people?" Naohiro muttered. "That's not something I enjoy doing."

"Recently, some companies have even been canceling job offers to new graduates before they start. That's the world we live in. We really don't have a choice. Ten temporary and part-time workers have got to go. While you're at it, why not throw in one more and make it eleven? You hardly need a full-time tea maker on the staff."

Removing the lid from his cup, Kishida took a sip of green tea.

"Here we go again." Naohiro lips were twisted in a sneer.

"How many years ago did you found this company?"

"Twenty-six."

"It was actually twenty-seven. When you set up this cleaning service company you were only thirty. I never expected you to get this big, and I thought I'd never earn more than pocket money from working with you. I'd only just started out as a licensed tax accountant myself, and I took you on because I hardly had any clients myself."

"Yeah, you never tired of telling me that you didn't think the business would succeed."

Naohiro pulled his teacup toward him.

Kishida had been a year below Naohiro at university. When Naohiro established his own company, he'd gone to Kishida for help. Kishida had handled all the company's finances since then. Those twenty-seven years had gone by in the blink of an eye.

"I respect your abilities as a businessman. I've always tried to keep my nose out of your business, but I've got to talk to you about that girl."

"Must we go through this again?"

"Yes, just one more time. If it's difficult for you to get rid of her because you hired her yourself, how about sending her to another department? Having her as your secretary is grossly indiscreet."

"What's indiscreet about it?"

Kishida sipped his tea.

"A detective came to see me at my office yesterday. He asked me a bunch of questions, but your secretary was the thing he was most interested in. *What's the nature of her relationship with Mr. Kiyose? When did they meet?* I couldn't very well tell him that; it made me nervous."

"Nothing to get nervous about. Just tell the guy what you know."

"What? Should I have said that she used to be a hostess at one of your favorite nightclubs?"

"What's the problem?"

"I couldn't do that. I just kept repeating that I didn't know anything about her. What else could I do?"

"Sounds like no big deal to me," snorted Naohiro.

"I don't mean to criticize, but you should know better than to bring your girlfriends into the workplace. You're a single man now, for goodness' sake. If you like her, go ahead and marry her. No one will complain about that."

Naohiro looked at Kishida's bony face.

"You're advising me to remarry immediately after the murder of my ex-wife? How d'you think that will look?"

"Okay, forget about getting married. How about living with her?"

"That would look worse. Look, just stop sticking your nose into my private life. I never asked you to manage *that* for me."

"I'm not trying to manage your life, I'm warning you—"

Naohiro picked up the file that was lying on the table. "I'll take a good look at these numbers of yours, and I'll be in touch when I've decided what to do."

Kishida sighed. He shook his head as he got to his feet.

"Your employees don't like this sort of thing, either. Of course they look askance when you suddenly bring in a young woman like that."

"They can gripe all they damn want. I couldn't care less. Everyone enjoys taking potshots at the boss."

"I'm worried that we're running out of time."

A moment or two after Kishida had left, there was a knock, and the door opened. Yuri came in, looking sheepish.

"Were you eavesdropping?" asked Naohiro.

"I couldn't help overhearing. I seem to be causing a lot of trouble."

"Don't worry about it. It's my company, after all."

"Yes, but . . . I was waylaid by a detective on my way home yesterday. A guy named Kaga."

Naohiro frowned.

"I know who you mean. He's from the local precinct. I met him when the cops took me around to Mineko's apartment. What business did he have with you?"

"I don't really know. He asked me a ton of questions that had nothing to do with the murder."

"Such as?"

"Such as, 'You're very tall, do you do any sports?' and 'What sort of accessories do you like?'"

"Accessories?"

"He noticed my ring. Said it was unusual." Yuri held out her left hand. "He got me to show it to him."

"Did you?"

"I couldn't think of any good reason not to."

"Can't be helped," sighed Naohiro.

"What should I do?"

"You don't need to *do* anything," Naohiro replied. "There's nothing to worry about. There's nothing that detective can do to us."

3.

They'd arranged to meet in an old-fashioned Japanese-style coffee shop with brick walls and wood-framed windows.

Above the red awning there was a sign reading "Founded in 1919" in bold lettering. The interior was simple, with square wooden tables and small stools.

The place was only about one third full. There were a few businesspeople, but the majority of the customers appeared to be elderly locals who were chatting away merrily. Koki had heard that neighborhood coffee shops were struggling, but this place seemed to be doing well.

"Did you notice how this place writes its name, Kissako, on the sign out front?" asked Kaga, nursing his coffee. "With the ideograms for *enjoy*, *tea*, and *go*?" As usual, the detective was casually dressed, with a white shirt on top of a T-shirt.

"I wondered about that. What does it mean?"

Kaga looked pleased to be asked.

"It's a phrase from Zen Buddhism. It means, 'Have a cup of tea.'"

"Really?"

"Originally, though, it had a slightly different nuance. It meant something like, 'Get a move on and go—drink your tea.' At some point, though, the meaning got reversed; it went from being a slightly hostile remark to something you said to welcome people and make them feel at home."

"Wow, you really know this neighborhood inside out."

Kaga smiled ironically.

"I only just got posted here, so I'm a newcomer. One of the regulars here told me all of this. This area's fascinating; wander down any random street, and you're sure to find something curious. Like, it's funny how the best-known dish at the yakitori grilled chicken restaurants around here is rolled omelet. Your mother used to go to Suitengu Shrine almost every day. I bet she enjoyed the walk."

Having started off talking about unrelated things, Kaga had nimbly segued to Koki's mother's murder, the topic they were there to discuss. Koki was impressed: clearly detectives had their own techniques for steering conversations.

"What is it you wanted to talk to me about?" said Kaga.

Koki swallowed a mouthful of iced coffee, then explained that he was keen to find out what the emails between Mineko and her lawyer were about. He was frank about Shizuko Takamachi having said little to him.

Kaga looked into his cup and listened in silence. When Koki finished, he raised his head and blinked a few times.

"That's not very flattering. Do I look like someone who's happy to spill the beans on an ongoing investigation? That wouldn't make me much of a cop."

"I didn't mean that. I'm anxious to find out more about my mother's recent life, and approaching you was the only way I could think of. . . . We'd already met, so I thought that might count for something. . . . I apologize." Koki clenched his fists on his thighs. His palms were damp with sweat.

Kaga put his coffee cup down. He was smiling benignly.

"Hey, I was just pulling your leg. No need to get wound up. I won't shoot my mouth off, but sharing confidential information can sometimes help drive an investigation forward."

Koki looked at the detective in surprise.

Kaga leaned forward, placing both elbows on the table.

"Before I tell you what you want to know, there's something I want to ask you. Why do you think your parents got divorced? Go on, speak frankly."

Koki was slightly taken aback.

"The reason for their divorce? The other detective asked me about that. My guess is that it was incompatibility, if that's the right word."

"What's your personal take? Did you think it was unavoidable?"

"When I got the news, I wasn't that put out. According to my dad, my mom was being selfish and demanding. On the other hand, my dad never cared much about either of us, so for my mom to fall out of love with him seemed natural."

"Okay."

"What's that got to do with anything?"

Kaga ignored the question. "Do you know what your mother's divorce settlement was?" he asked.

Koki leaned back a little in his chair.

"No idea."

"Oh, really?" Kaga looked thoughtful.

"Could I—?"

"Your mother," Kaga plowed on, "seems to have decided recently to ask your father for an additional lump sum payment. She'd already gotten the original settlement, but she no longer felt that was good enough, apparently. Two possible reasons occur to me. The first is that she was worrying about the viability of her translation work, because the friend who was intending to send work her way unexpectedly decided to move abroad. The second reason you can probably guess for yourself: Ms. Mitsui believed she was about to have a grandchild. What would be more natural than for her to want to help the young couple?"

A lightbulb seemed to go on in Koki's brain.

"Oh, I get it. My mom was discussing money matters with her lawyer."

Kaga reached for his cup.

"That is something I can neither confirm nor deny. Ms. Mitsui apparently wanted to reopen negotiations with the other party, Naohiro Kiyose, on the way the money had been split."

"That's pretty irresponsible of her." Koki scowled. "Even if my dad was in the wrong, she was the one who asked for the divorce, and they'd already reached an agreement—"

"Take it easy," said Kaga soothingly. "As I told you, there'd been some unexpected developments in Ms. Mitsui's life. She wasn't just reopening the negotiations on a whim. She also believed she had plausible grounds for what she was doing."

"Plausible grounds?"

"She'd uncovered a new reason why she couldn't have remained married. She believed that if she could pin responsibility on the other party, she could claim compensatory damages."

The detective's slightly convoluted statement confused Koki, but after running through it several times in his head, he grasped what Kaga was saying.

"You think my father had a bit on the side?"

Koki had raised his voice, and Kaga darted a nervous glance around the café before returning his gaze to him.

"Your reaction suggests that you didn't know."

Koki shook his head.

"How could I? I haven't seen my father for ages. I'd be the last one to know about something like that."

"What about before? Did your father always have an eye for the ladies? Did he and your mother ever fight about anything like that?"

"Not so far as I know. Dad neglected us, but that was because he was so focused on his work; he wasn't out living the playboy lifestyle. Frankly, I can't imagine him having an affair."

Kaga nodded, then, slightly hesitantly, pulled a cell phone from his pocket. He pressed a few buttons, then turned it around so Koki could see the screen.

"I'm breaking the rules. Don't tell anyone I showed you this."

It was a picture of a young woman in a suit, apparently unaware that she was being photographed.

"You snapped this secretly?" asked Koki.

"I told you it was against the rules, didn't I?" Kaga grinned. "Ever seen her before?"

"She's very pretty. I've never seen her, no."

"Look carefully. You're quite sure you don't recognize her?"

Koki took another careful look. Maybe Kaga was right. Koki had a vague sense of having seen the woman before, but it felt more like illusion than reality. He explained as much to Kaga.

"Is that right?" Kaga returned the cell phone to his pocket.

Koki decided to try his luck.

"Who is she?" he asked.

Kaga hesitated briefly, then said, "Someone currently in close proximity to Naohiro Kiyose. Don't go getting the wrong idea, though. We have no confirmation that they are lovers."

"But that's what you suspect, Detective Kaga. You think she's my father's mistress."

"*Mistress* is the wrong word. Mr. Kiyose is single. After the divorce, at least, he's free to go out with whomever he wants without his ex-wife having the right to claim damages."

Koki realized what Kaga was hinting at.

"Okay. So if my father had been seeing this woman *before* the divorce, my mother might have a claim."

"You're a sharp lad," said Kaga, with a smile.

"You wouldn't be taking photos of this woman unless you thought she had some connection to the murder, would you?" An idea came to Koki. "You think she was my father's lover prior to the divorce, and that my father killed my mother to stop her finding out? Or something like that?"

Kaga stared at Koki.

"Razor-sharp instincts *and* brilliant deductive powers."

"You're making fun of me now."

Kaga, his expression serious again, drank down the rest of his coffee.

"We like to explore all the possibilities. Part of our team is exploring that line of inquiry."

"But what about you, Detective Kaga? Do you suspect my father?"

"Me? Pffff. I don't really know. Besides, it hardly matters. The job of a precinct detective like me is to support the Metropolitan Police detectives." Kaga looked at his watch. "It's getting late. I'd like to stay longer, but I have another appointment. Sorry."

He picked up the bill and rose to his feet.

"I should pay for this," said Koki, reaching for the bill.

"You're still mastering your craft. You need to save your money." Clutching the bill, Kaga headed for the counter.

4.

Koki ducked his head when he saw Naohiro emerge from the building's lobby. Naohiro didn't so much as glance at the fast food joint on the far side of the street where Koki was sitting. He hailed a cab and was driven away, even though his normal routine was to take the train home.

A few minutes later, a young woman in a white blouse came out of the same building. This was who Koki had been waiting for. He sprang to his feet, smacking one of his shins hard against the leg of the table.

He left the restaurant and hurried after the woman. She appeared to be headed for the subway. *Thank goodness she's alone,* thought Koki.

Koki had known one of his father's employees since he was a boy. Koki had called the man last night and asked a few questions about what his father had been up to recently. His friend proved very cagey. In the end, Koki lost his temper and just asked straight out if it was true about his father having a mistress.

"No, that's not true. That's just gossip. The girl's young and pretty, so everyone makes her out to be his mistress as a joke. You shouldn't take it seriously."

Koki wasn't going to let his friend be so evasive.

"Tell me exactly what's going on. I'll decide if it's gossip or not," he declared.

After making Koki promise not to reveal where he'd gotten the information, his friend had told him that the woman's name was Yuri Miyamoto and that she'd been working as Naohiro's private secretary since April.

Yuri Miyamoto had to be the woman Kaga had shown him a photograph of. Koki was sure of it.

And now there she was—a tall woman with excellent posture, striding briskly down the street. She took such long strides that Koki had to break into a half run to catch up with her.

When he was right behind her, he brought his breathing under control, then called her name: "Miss Miyamoto?"

She stopped walking and spun around, one hand clutching the strap of her shoulder bag. Her eyes widened at the sight of Koki.

He bowed slightly.

"Sorry to surprise you like this. I'm the son of Naohiro Kiyose. My name's Koki."

She blinked a few times and said, "So?"

"I need to talk to you. It will only take ten minutes. Can you spare the time?"

Her uncertainty was obvious from the way her eyes darted from side to side. Getting flustered when someone you didn't know waylaid you was only natural. Koki waited for her to regain her composure.

She didn't need long.

"All right, let's go." She was looking right into his eyes.

"Mr. Kiyose," a voice called out from behind him just as he was turning down Amazake Alley. When Naohiro turned around, he saw Detective Kaga hurrying toward him.

"Fancy bumping into you. Or maybe it's not a coincidence after all?"

Kaga scratched his head and smiled wryly. "Your recent visits to Nihonbashi are the talk of the task force."

"Am I under surveillance?"

"Let's not get melodramatic. It's important for the investigation that we keep tabs on everybody."

Naohiro shrugged and stuck out his lower lip.

"What do you want with me, then?"

"I have a few questions. The first is, why do you keep coming to Nihonbashi like this?"

"Do I have to answer?"

"Is there a reason you don't want to tell me?" Kaga shot back with a smile.

Naohiro snorted, then said, "You okay to walk and talk?"

"Exactly what I hoped to do. This is a nice neighborhood for a walk."

The two men set off side by side. It was evening, and it

had cooled down a little. A wind chime tinkled somewhere in the distance.

Naohiro paused in front of the window of a shamisen shop.

"According to my son, Mineko had a special reason for living around here. I want to know what that reason was. That's why I keep coming here. I've got this notion that if I walk around enough, I might be able to figure out what it was. My son tells me it's none of my business, though."

Naohiro's face, which was reflected in the shop window, was etched with grief.

"Mr. Kiyose, why did you agree to divorce your wife?"

Naohiro tottered as if his knees had buckled.

"Do we have to discuss that?"

"It didn't have anything to do with Yuri Miyamoto, did it? She wasn't the reason you wanted a divorce. I'm right, aren't I?"

"What are you trying to say?"

"That now, when it's too late, you've realized how much you loved Mineko Mitsui . . . your wife. That's why you're doing everything you can to learn something about her life in this neighborhood. Am I right?"

Naohiro slowly shook his head.

"My feelings for Mineko never changed. There's nothing for me to 'realize' about them. Anyway, getting divorced was the right thing to do, the right choice for both of us. It's because I want to believe that, that I want to find out what Mineko had discovered here in Nihonbashi that made her want a divorce."

Kaga thought for a moment, then pulled a cell phone out of his pocket.

"Have you got any plans for tonight, Mr. Kiyose?"

"Tonight? No."

"Then why don't we grab something to eat? I'd like to talk to you about your wife."

Koki took Yuri Miyamoto to a café and steered her to a table in the back corner where no one could overhear them.

"I'll get right to the point," he said, keeping his voice low. "What's your relationship with my father?"

"I'm his secretary," said Yuri Miyamoto, staring into her latte.

"That's not what I'm talking about." Koki leaned over the table toward her. "I'm asking you whether you have a personal relationship with him."

Yuri Miyamoto looked up.

"That's private. I'm not obliged to tell you anything."

Koki wasn't expecting her to counterattack. He'd taken it for granted that she would tell him what he wanted to know.

"I'm his son. I think I have a right to know about his relationships with women."

"If that's what you think, perhaps you should ask him directly."

"He wouldn't tell me the truth. That's why I'm asking you."

"All the more reason for me not to talk to you. I'm sure

President Kiyose has his own perspective, and mine is in line with his."

Koki's left leg started jiggling beneath the table. It happened when he got annoyed. Yuri Miyamoto sat there, completely indifferent, drinking her latte with blank-faced detachment.

She's certainly a looker. . . . The thought pushed its way through Koki's resentment. Despite her self-possession, he could see that she was still young. *She's not even ten years older than me.*

"My father is a suspect. The police think he might have killed my mom. If you're his mistress and your relationship predated the divorce, my mother would have had the right to claim compensatory damages from my father. The police think he killed her to avoid having to pay."

Yuri Miyamoto's eyes widened.

"That's absurd. How can you suspect your own father?"

"It's the police who suspect him, not me."

She shook her head vigorously.

"The important thing is how *you* feel. If you really trusted your father, you wouldn't be so easily influenced by what other people say."

Was she telling him off? Koki angrily clenched his jaw.

"When you get down to it, I guess I don't trust him much at all."

Yuri Miyamoto's eyes took on a steely look. "You're shittin' me?"

"Oh, very street. I love it."

"Who cares how I speak? You're serious? You really don't trust your own father?"

"No, I don't. More to the point, I can't. He never paid any attention to his family; even his own wife filing for divorce didn't give him pause. Then, the minute he's divorced, he gets himself a woman like you. How can I trust a man like that? He didn't even bother coming to my mother's funeral."

Yuri Miyamoto was looking up at the ceiling and muttering something to herself.

"What's got into you?" asked Koki.

Ignoring him, she kept on muttering. Listening closely, he managed to make out what she was saying: *"I can't handle this anymore. I can't handle this anymore."*

Koki was about to say something, when she tilted her head back down. There was steel in her eyes.

"Koki, there's something I need to tell you."

"Huh?"

"I shouldn't be the one to do this, but I simply can't bear it anymore. I'm going to tell you the truth."

"The truth? What do you mean?"

"Just shut up and listen." As if to get her courage up, Yuri Miyamoto downed her latte in a single gulp.

5.

The restaurant to which Kaga took Naohiro was Matsuya. Since it described itself as a ryotei—an old-fashioned Japanese-style restaurant—on the sign outside, Naohiro was surprised when they were shown into a big room with Western furniture.

That was about as far as Naohiro's interest in the design of the place went. His whole focus switched to Kaga as soon as the detective opened his mouth. Kaga revealed Mineko's reasons for choosing to live in Kodenmacho—how she'd located her only son, discovered that his girlfriend was pregnant and then moved to be near them both, unaware that through a series of coincidences she'd gotten the wrong impression of what was really going on. Koki was right, thought Naohiro. None of it had anything to do with him. If Mineko hadn't been murdered, the whole thing would have been nothing more than a silly story for them to laugh about. Now, however, it was different: listening to Kaga, Naohiro felt a tightness in his chest.

"So what do you think?" concluded Kaga, as he reached for his beer.

Naohiro had ordered the same craft beer from Hida, and like Kaga, he'd yet to drink a drop.

"The whole thing's a big surprise. I'd never have guessed what was behind her move," stated Naohiro frankly.

"According to her lawyer, your wife had her doubts about your fidelity at the time of the divorce. She was pretty confident that a thorough investigation would turn something up. In the end, though, she opted for a friendly negotiation. Her priority was her independence. That she was prepared to go for compensatory damages at this late stage tends to suggest that she had a strong reason for doing so."

"Something to do with her thinking that our son was about to become a dad, you mean? That would make sense." Naohiro took a swig of beer. "But I wasn't unfaithful to her."

"I hear that the presence of a certain Yuri Miyamoto is setting tongues wagging at your firm. Those rumors could have found their way back to your wife. She might have regarded them as grounds to sue for damages."

Naohiro shook his head. "That's ridiculous."

"You may think so, but when you install an unknown young woman in your private office immediately after getting divorced, people are bound to speculate that there was a preexisting relationship. And the two of you did have a relationship, didn't you? The next question is, what kind of relationship was it? When a man and a woman are involved, people tend to jump to the same conclusion. . . . No one would ever think of a blood relationship."

Naohiro started and looked hard at Kaga. The Nihonbashi detective, apparently unaware of having said anything shocking, was coolly lifting an appetizer to his mouth.

Naohiro heaved a guttural sigh.

"Why am I not surprised? I thought you'd figured it out when Yuri said you'd spoken to her. You asked about her ring, didn't you?"

"The ring she had on her left pinkie was handmade. I don't want to be rude, but it was easy to see that it wasn't the work of a professional. As it wasn't in line with her overall look, I guessed that it was a gift from someone special. I'd seen similar rings before—fifty-yen coins hollowed out with a file."

Naohiro was scratching the corner of his eyebrow with a fingertip and smiling sheepishly.

"They were quite popular twenty-something years back.

Men who didn't have the money to buy a proper ring made them for their sweethearts. Nobody makes them these days—let alone a pinkie ring version."

"I gave that ring to her mother as a present."

"I guessed as much. The mother must have been petite, with delicate little hands and fingers, making the ring the right size for her ring finger."

"I was in my twenties and didn't have a penny to my name." Naohiro tipped a slug of beer down his throat.

It had happened back when people still went to bars to sing karaoke, rather than rent private rooms, Naohiro explained. Having graduated from college but having not yet found a full-time job, he was making ends meet by working at a little karaoke bar. The pay was atrocious, but he was young. The idea of saving anything had never crossed his mind.

A woman by the name of Tokiko worked at the same bar. She was the manager and was five years older than he. She'd already been married—and divorced.

One night, when Tokiko was drunk, Naohiro had taken her back to his place. They began sleeping together. Naohiro was head over heels in love with her and was convinced that she felt the same.

On Tokiko's birthday, after they had closed the bar, Naohiro gave her his present—a ring made from a hollowed-out fifty-yen piece. As he handed it to her, he proposed.

Overcome with emotion, Tokiko began to cry, repeating the words "thank you" over and over, and promising to treasure the ring all her life.

Naohiro hadn't gotten an answer to his marriage proposal that night.

"I'm heading back to my parents' place for three days tomorrow. I'll give you my answer after that. There's something I want to give you, too."

Tokiko was smiling though her eyes were puffy with tears.

Sure enough, Tokiko didn't come in to work for the next three days. But she didn't reappear on the fourth day, either. The bartender who was subbing for her told Naohiro that she'd quit.

Naohiro had rushed over to Tokiko's apartment. The place had been cleaned out. He was mystified. A few days later, he received a letter from her. There was no address on it.

Despite being deeply touched by his offer of marriage, Tokiko wrote, she was going to decline. It wasn't right for a person like her to hold back a young man like him who had so much going for him. She also gave him a scolding: his parents had paid for his college; the least he could do in return was find something worthwhile to do with his life.

Naohiro had felt as if a bucket of cold water had been poured over his head. It suddenly dawned on him just how much he had taken his parents' kindness for granted and how blind he'd been to the realities of life. Tokiko's letter was full of love, but he could also detect that she was aware of his immaturity.

From that day on, Naohiro had been a changed man. He quit his job in the bar and joined a support services company.

It was a decision that ultimately paid dividends. The knowledge he'd built up at that business served as the foundation for the cleaning company he started.

"I bumped into Yuri in a Ginza hostess club a couple of years ago. She was the spitting image of Tokiko. That was surprise enough, but what really blew my mind was the fact that she had that ring on."

"She was wearing it when you met her?" asked Kaga.

Naohiro nodded.

"'What's with the ring?' I asked her. I got a shock when she told me it was an heirloom from her mother, who had died three years earlier from pancreatic cancer. 'What's your mom's name?' The question was on the tip of my tongue, but I managed to stop myself. I needed to calm down and think things through first.

"After that, I paid repeated visits to the club. Every time I went there, I paid extra so that Yuri would sit with me. I did my best to get her to open up about herself. You never really know if those hostesses are telling you the truth, but she told me that she'd been raised by a single mother."

Eventually, Naohiro found out a decisive piece of information: Yuri's date of birth. She'd been conceived back when Naohiro and Tokiko were involved.

One night, Naohiro decided that it was time: he told Yuri that he needed to talk to her alone.

"There's something important I need to tell you. It's connected to your mother. I'm guessing her name was Tokiko. Am I right?"

Yuri's eyes widened with surprise. "How did you know?" she asked.

That was when he was sure it was true. The room seemed to spin around him. *Does this sort of thing really happen?* he was thinking.

When the club closed for the night, Naohiro took Yuri to one of his favorite Japanese restaurants. He picked it because it had private rooms. The moment they were alone together, Naohiro confessed to being her father. He spoke about everything that had happened between them—including that he had no idea about Tokiko being pregnant.

"I apologized for all the grief I'd put them through. It was pretty damn obvious that life hadn't been easy for them. Maybe I hadn't known anything about it, but the ultimate responsibility was still mine. After all, if I hadn't been such a poor excuse for a man, Tokiko might have agreed to marry me," said Naohiro.

"How did Ms. Miyamoto respond?" Kaga asked.

"With surprise, naturally enough. She had a hard time believing it was true, I think. Who could blame her? Still, she realized I wasn't just some old man with the hots for her. We didn't talk much that first evening, but Yuri got in touch a few days later to talk some more."

"Things seems to have settled down quite nicely now," said Kaga.

"As I already had a family, my plan was to help her out discreetly for the time being."

"Which is when your wife came out and asked for a divorce?"

Naohiro snorted with laughter.

"Ironic, isn't it? My experience with Tokiko had taught me that women liked men who worked hard. Now Mineko was telling me that hard work alone wasn't enough. Must be something wrong with me. I just can't seem to get the balance right."

"But losing Mineko enabled you to bring Yuri closer to you."

"I wanted to be a proper father to the girl. I certainly wasn't prepared to let her keep working as a hostess in a Ginza nightclub. I knew that hiring her would trigger all sorts of gossip, but I planned to reveal that she was my daughter when the time felt right. I wanted to tell Koki first, but Mineko's murder made that impossible. Koki seems to hate me more with every passing day."

Naohiro tipped what was left of his beer down his throat. He'd always dreamed of going out drinking like this with his son, listening to his troubles and dispensing fatherly advice. But the reality was that every single conversation they had ended in a fight.

"I wonder what good things you and your ex-wife got out of the divorce?"

Naohiro screwed up his face in distaste. "That's not a very nice thing to say."

"I'm not trying to be sarcastic. Ms. Mitsui, convinced that your son's girlfriend was pregnant, moved to live near him. The minute you were single again, you hired Yuri. In other words, you both wanted the same thing: family. The bonds of family are strong, Mr. Kiyose. You and Koki are family, you mustn't forget that."

Naohiro looked at Kaga. The detective smiled shyly and fiddled with his chopsticks on the table.

"I'm sorry. I shouldn't have said that. It was overstepping my bounds."

"No," murmured Naohiro. The cell phone in his jacket pocket pinged to announce an incoming text. "Excuse me a moment," he said and pulled it out.

It was from Yuri. The first word was "Urgent," so Naohiro read it right away.

I am with my little brother. Give me a call if you can join us.
Yuri.

Naohiro gasped and froze, staring at the screen.

"What's wrong?" Kaga asked.

Naohiro silently showed him the text. Kaga frowned briefly, then smiled.

"Looks like your new family is already coming together. Go on, go and join them."

"Thanks." Naohiro stood up. "Was the ring enough for you to work out that Yuri was my daughter?" he asked, still standing by the table.

That would be quite a feat of deduction, thought Kaga, grinning mischievously.

"It was a gut thing. I thought she might be, the minute I saw her."

"You're kidding?"

"They look very much alike, Yuri and Koki."

Naohiro just grunted.

"Koki said that her face looked familiar. I think he'd seen it in his mirror."

Naohiro stared at Kaga, shaking his head.

"One last question. What's your rank?"

"Sergeant."

"Well, they should promote you to lieutenant," declared Naohiro, and headed for the door.

8

THE CUSTOMER AT THE HANDICRAFTS SHOP

1.

Masayo Fujiyama was at the desk in the back of the store, working her way through a pile of payment slips, when the customer appeared. The hands of the clock indicated it was a little after six. On weekdays few, if any, customers came in this late, and Masayo was so focused on her work that it was a while before she realized anyone was there.

Of course, she didn't know whether this particular customer would actually buy anything. Maybe he was just browsing. Still, Masayo never neglected a prospect, so she got up and walked over to the entrance. The customer was male, probably in his late thirties, and wearing a blue short-sleeved shirt over a T-shirt.

It was the spinning tops that seemed to have caught his eye. The tops came in three sizes—small, medium, and large—and were decorated with concentric red, white, and green circles. Picking up one of the small ones, he held it in his hand.

"Good old throw tops, eh?" said Masayo. "You probably played with them as a child."

"Exactly what I was thinking." The man looked up and smiled. His face was lined and a little on the dark side. "This is typical of Ningyocho. I mean, you wouldn't find a shop stocking things like this anywhere else in Tokyo."

"We've got a good selection of old-fashioned toys, if they're something you're interested in." Masayo pointed to another display table. "Like these pellet drums and Jacob's ladders over here. Everything in the shop is handmade from exclusively Japanese materials."

"How so? Because they're traditional Japanese handicrafts?"

"That's part of it. It's also because I don't like to sell things without knowing exactly what's in them. Little children are always sticking toys into their mouths. These manufacturers are as careful about the pigments as they are about the materials, so the toys are totally child-safe."

"I see. That's great." The man ran his eye over the other toys on display, before his gaze returned to the top in his hand. He really seemed to have taken a fancy to it.

"That particular top is made in Gunma Prefecture. We buy it plain and decorate it here."

"How about the string? Is that made in Gunma, too?"

"We source that from somewhere else, but it is made of all-natural materials."

The man nodded, then held the top out to Masayo.

"I'll take this one."

"Thank you very much."

Taking the top and the money, Masayo walked to the back of the store. Talking to the man had clearly been the right thing to do. Her theory was that people who liked handmade products were generally sociable creatures.

Masayo had opened Hozukiya in Ningyocho some twenty-four years ago. Her family had a fabric store in Nihonbashi, and her business was an offshoot of the family's traditional business. She'd been interested in traditional Japanese handicrafts since childhood and started to collect them long before deciding to devote herself to the business. She visited the manufacturers to personally select the products in the store. Hozukiya also produced its own line of original products, many of which incorporated woven fabrics that she procured through the main family business.

Masayo wrapped up the top and got the change out of the cash register. When she looked up, the customer was standing nearby, examining a shelf of tote bags.

"Those are all made of specially selected new fabrics," Masayo explained. "We don't just cobble them together out of remnants. We never use odds and ends here."

The man smiled.

"You're very particular about the materials you use."

"Absolutely. These are things that people handle."

Masayo handed over the top and the change.

The man stuffed the change into his pocket and looked around the store.

"How late are you open?"

"What time do we close? It varies, but normally sometime after seven."

"What's your busiest time?"

Masayo gave a rueful smile.

"We get slightly more customers on weekends and holidays, but even then the place isn't exactly busy. I run the shop half as a hobby."

The man looked down at the wrapped-up top in his hand.

"Right. Are these tops big sellers?"

"Big? No. They sell from time to time. The buyers tend to be middle-aged or older, and generally they buy them as presents for their kids or grandkids. Computer games may be all the rage, but toys like this have a certain human quality."

"I couldn't agree more. Has anyone bought one recently?"

"A top? Let me think . . ."

Masayo was puzzled. *Why was the man asking so many questions? Why did he care whether other people were buying spinning tops?*

Her doubt must have been written all over her face.

The man gave a sheepish grin. "I'm sorry. All these questions must be making you nervous. Here's why I'm asking."

He pulled out a dark brown wallet, tilted it sideways, and flipped it open. There was an ID card and a badge inside.

"Oh, you're a policeman. . . ."

"Yes, from the Nihonbashi precinct. I wanted to keep our chat nice and casual. That's why I didn't say anything."

Masayo reassessed his appearance now that she knew he was a cop. She thought she could detect a steely determination behind his mild, amiable expression.

"Is there a problem with my spinning tops?" Masayo inquired nervously.

"No, no, no." Kaga waved away her concerns. "It's not the tops that are important. I'm looking for someone who bought a top. Very recently, indeed."

"What exactly are you investigating?"

"I'm afraid I can't tell you. All I can say is that it has nothing to do with your shop."

"Well, one can't help wondering. I mean, one of my customers is involved, aren't they?"

"We haven't established that, so you're better off not asking. The more you know, the less natural your behavior will be, should that person come in again."

"Oh, maybe you're right."

"So can you recall any customer who bought a top recently?" said Kaga, repeating his question.

"Give me a moment."

Masayo rifled through the payment slips she'd been working on earlier. They would give her an idea of what she'd sold and when.

A minute before, she'd told Kaga that her customers bought tops from time to time. That was overstating the case. She had no recollection of having sold even one recently.

"Aah," she exclaimed, looking at a payment slip.

"Have you found a sale?"

"We sold one on June the twelfth. The same size that you just bought, Detective."

"How about before that?"

"Before that? . . . There's a gap of a whole month."

"Good. Now, do you recall anything about the person who made this purchase on the twelfth?"

"I'm afraid I wasn't working that day. It was sold by Misaki, our part-time worker."

"Oh yes? When will she be coming in next?"

"Tomorrow."

"Would it be all right for me to drop by and have a word?"

"No problem. Can I tell her it's about the person who bought the top?"

"Be my guest. See you tomorrow."

The man who'd introduced himself as Detective Kaga left the shop, clutching his spinning top.

"I wonder if it's got anything to do with that murder over in Kodenmacho," said Misaki Sugawara, tying on her apron.

"There was a murder in Kodenmacho?" Masayo was shocked. It was the first she'd heard of it.

"Sure. Didn't you know? The police were over at Naho's place, asking questions."

Omakara, the rice cracker shop, was on the same side of the street as Hozukiya. Naho was the only daughter of the family who ran it. She and Misaki were roughly the same age, and the two young women were friends.

"What are the police doing at a rice cracker store, for God's sake?"

Misaki cocked her head.

"Search me. Naho didn't go into much detail."

"The whole thing freaks me out a little. It would be too awful if there was a link between one of our spinning tops and the murder, like if it were an important piece of evidence, or something."

"You know what they say: no such thing as bad publicity."

"Thanks but no thanks. It wouldn't be good for our image."

"I wonder . . ." Misaki inspected the calendar on the accounts desk. "Anyway, we sold that top on the twelfth, and I'm pretty sure the murder took place before then. I doubt it would be evidence of anything much."

"You really think so?"

"Yes. Maybe it's not significant after all," declared Misaki breezily, bringing the discussion to an end.

Kaga appeared just after lunch. Masayo listened in on the exchange between Misaki and the detective from the accounts desk at the back.

"Around what time on the twelfth was the top purchased?"

"Just after six, I'd guess. It was just starting to get dark."

"Do you remember anything about the person who bought it?"

"It was a middle-aged man, not especially tall, and he was wearing a suit. Looked to me like he was on his way home from the office." Misaki reeled off her answer smoothly thanks to the heads-up she'd got from Masayo.

"If you saw a photo, do you think you could identify him?"

"Oh, I doubt it. I hardly look at the customers' faces at all. I tend to see more of their backs and their hands."

I need to have a word with the girl, thought Masayo, when she overheard Misaki's answer. *How can she figure out what the customers are looking for without at least a discreet peek at their faces?*

"Did anything about him stick in your mind? Anything. It doesn't matter how trivial."

Misaki tilted her head quizzically. "I can't really think of anything. . . ."

"The top comes in three sizes: small, medium, and large. Did he go right for the small size?"

"Hmmm. I was busy serving another customer, so I can't really be sure. I think he spent a while standing looking at the tops." Once again, Misaki's response was less than scintillating.

"Interesting." Kaga nodded, then turned to Masayo. "And you've not sold any other tops since the twelfth, right?"

"Except the one you bought yesterday, Detective."

"Right. Okay then, give me all the tops you have on display outside. I'll pay for them, of course."

"All of them?"

"Yes, the whole lot. There's no need to wrap them up. How much is it?" Kaga pulled out his wallet.

"Excuse me, Detective?" said Masayo, seizing the moment. "Is there any link between our tops and the Kodenmacho murder? Are they going to end up being used as evidence of something?"

Kaga's hands froze on his wallet and his eyes widened. The question had obviously caught him off guard. He blinked as he looked first at Masayo, then at Misaki, then gave a small, self-deprecating smile.

"In this neighborhood, everyone knows everyone else. Rumors travel fast."

"Is that a yes?"

Kaga paused a moment, before shaking his head slowly and seriously.

"Your tops have no link to the case. And the fact that they have no link is what makes them important."

Masayo frowned. "What that supposed to mean?"

"I'll be able to explain one of these days. You'll just have to be patient for now, though. Could I get a receipt, please?" he said, as he extracted a ten-thousand-yen note from his wallet.

2.

Reiko Kishida was looking over the pizza menu when her cell phone started vibrating on the table. Reiko's mouth turned down at the corners when she saw the name on the screen. Her father-in-law was calling, but she didn't want to pick up. She knew what he wanted. She stared at her phone a moment more, then picked it up.

"Hi, this is Reiko."

"Hello, it's me. Katsuya told me the police were at your place?"

"That's right. They came by the day before yesterday."

"Yeah? I'm actually in the neighborhood. Do you mind if I swing by your place?"

"Right now? You can if you want, but Katsuya isn't back yet. He's going to be out late tonight." Reiko tried to sound as unenthusiastic as possible. She didn't want her father-in-law coming around, and she didn't care if he knew it. In fact, all the better if he did know.

His reaction was not what she'd hoped for.

"Is he? Well, no matter. You're the one I want to talk to. You were the one who talked to the police."

"Yes, but—"

"I just want you to tell me what happened. I'll be there in ten minutes or so. Sorry to barge in on you."

The phone went dead.

If you're really so darn sorry, then maybe try not coming? Reiko glared at her cell phone. She was kicking herself for picking up. Her father-in-law, who lived alone, was a master at cooking up reasons for dropping in on them. How many times had he done so this month already?

Reiko looked around the living room. Not even the most charitable person could describe it as tidy. Shota's toys and women's magazines littered the floor, and the sofa was buried under clothes that people had flung onto it.

What a pain in the ass, she thought, getting to her feet. She decided to hide the pizza delivery menu as well as tidy up. She didn't want to be criticized for failing to cook a proper meal again tonight.

She was busy tidying when Shota, who was supposed to be asleep in the next room, ambled in.

"What are you doing, Mom?"

"Cleaning up a bit. Grandpa will be here any minute."

"Grandpa's coming?" The eyes of her five-year-old son lit up.

"I don't think he'll stay long. You know Grandpa: always busy."

Reiko hoped that would be a self-fulfilling prophecy.

A few minutes later, the front door intercom buzzed.

It was Yosaku Kishida, her father-in-law. He had brought along some cream puffs. Shota was crazy about the things.

"Sorry to barge in at dinnertime. Are you busy cooking?"

Yosaku looked toward the kitchen as he settled himself in an armchair.

"Actually, I only got back a few minutes ago. I was about to get started on the dinner," Reiko said, handing her father-in-law a glass of barley tea. She glanced down at Shota, who was trying to pry open his grandfather's briefcase. "Shota, stop it."

"I'm sorry. Bad timing." Yosaku pulled his briefcase toward him and took a swig of barley tea. "I'll be as quick as I can. What did the police want to know?"

"It was no big deal. They just wanted to know what time you dropped by the evening of the tenth, stuff like that."

"Tell me more."

"More?" Reiko looked down at the table.

There had been two of them, a Detective Uesugi of the Tokyo Metropolitan Police and a Detective Kaga from the Nihonbashi precinct. Reiko had never met real-life detectives before.

Uesugi had done most of the talking. They were cross-checking statements from different people connected to an ongoing investigation, he explained. He started out by asking whether Yosaku had visited on the evening of June 10. When Reiko confirmed that he had, Uesugi requested specifics. She told him exactly what had happened in detail; namely, that her father-in-law arrived at around eight o'clock and stayed for roughly one hour.

"Then he wanted to know what we'd talked about. I said that we discussed the preparations for Granny's death anniversary."

That was the truth. Reiko had gotten a call from Yosaku at lunchtime that day to say that he was going to come to discuss the arrangements. Reiko remembered how relieved she'd been when he said he'd be there after dinner.

"Did they ask you anything else?" Yosaku was staring at her with a searching look in his eyes. It made Reiko uncomfortable.

"Anything else . . ."

While Reiko was trying to remember, Shota, who had been playing happily by himself, came up to them.

"Grandpa, will you spin this for me?" he said, holding out a spinning top and a length of string.

"Oh, yeah. Later, okay?" Yosaku patted his grandson's head.

"That reminds me. They did ask about the top."

"What!" Yosaku looked alarmed. "Did you show it to them?"

"No, I didn't. The policemen came, and Shota was over there. Then—"

Kaga was the one who'd brought it up. "That's an unusual toy to get for your boy. Very old-fashioned. Where did you get it?" he'd asked.

"I told him that I didn't know. That I hadn't bought it, rather you'd been given it and brought it around for Shota. Kaga then asked me when that was."

"What did you say?" Yosaku asked.

"I said the twelfth," said Reiko. "That you'd gone out of your way to bring it around on the twelfth. Did I say something wrong?"

"No, no . . . that's fine. Did they say anything else about the top?"

"No, that's everything. The two detectives didn't stay long. They were very nice and polite, I must say."

"Oh, really?" sighed Yosaku, winding the string around the top.

"Do you know what the police are investigating? Are you involved in something?"

"It's nothing serious. There's been a minor fraud at a corporate client of mine. The police are looking into that. And they're investigating me, as they think I could be in on it."

"Gosh, how awful!"

Yosaku owned his own tax accounting business. Most of his clients were small and medium-sized businesses, and with the recent recession, things were probably rocky for some of them, Reiko guessed.

Yosaku flung the top on the floor in front of Shota. It started spinning, but soon toppled over. Shota was nonetheless delighted.

"I seem to have lost the knack. I was quite a spin master back in the day." Yosaku picked the top up off the floor.

It was after ten o'clock by the time Katsuya Kishida came home. His face was flushed, and Reiko wondered if he had been drinking. Loosening his tie as he entered the apartment, he went straight to the kitchen for a drink of water.

"Pizza again tonight? What the hell!" he commented. He must have noticed the empty box.

"What's it to you? You were out having some fancy dinner."

"I don't go out for fun, you know. It's called relationship building. It's the nutrition aspect that worries me. It's not good for a growing boy to eat nothing but this crap day in, day out."

"He doesn't eat 'nothing but crap.' You know I cook plenty of proper meals."

"Not sure I'd describe frozen food and boil-in-the-bag meals as proper myself—" retorted Katsuya, opening the refrigerator. He stopped mid-harangue. "Oh, was someone here today?"

He must have spotted the box of cream puffs.

"Yosaku dropped by."

"My old man? *Again?* What did he want this time?" Katsuya undid the top few buttons of his shirt, pulled it open, and flung himself onto the sofa.

"He was asking about that business with the police the day before yesterday. You told him they'd come by."

"That? What did my old man have to say about it?"

Reiko recounted her conversation with Yosaku. Katsuya's brow furrowed.

"Dirty dealings at a client company, eh? Doesn't sound like good news for him."

Katsuya picked up the string for the top from the table. Shota was already asleep.

"Is your father's firm all right? You don't think it's going to collapse because of this?"

"No chance. I'm sure he'll be fine." Winding the string around the top, Katsuya threw it vigorously across the floor. Failing to spin, it bounced a few times before crashing into the skirting board.

"Don't go making dents in the walls."

"That's funny." Katsuya cocked his head as he got to his feet and went to retrieve the top. "I used to be pretty good."

"Oh, I've just remembered. The credit card company called today."

Katsuya froze in his tracks.

"What did they want?"

"Something about payment. They asked me to give them your mobile number, so they'll probably contact you tomorrow. Don't tell me you're back doing that again?"

"Doing what again?"

"Getting behind on the payments. You can get in serious trouble."

"There's nothing to worry about."

"Really? I wouldn't know."

"What's with the attitude? I'm not the only one who

spends money around here. You don't exactly take it easy with the family credit card."

"My card's got a very low limit. One or two stores, and I'm maxed out."

"You're still spending money." Katsuya smacked the top back on the table, grabbed his jacket, and left the room.

Reiko sighed and switched on the TV. It was a fifty-inch flat-screen, which she'd just bought earlier this year. After shopping, watching her favorite movies was what she liked to do best.

Despite Katsuya's insisting that there was nothing to worry about, Reiko suspected that he'd fallen behind again. It had happened once before, and Yosaku had to bail him out.

Reiko and Katsuya had gotten married six years ago. They'd been in the same high school class and dated for more than five years. Katsuya wasn't interested in getting married straight out of college. He claimed that, what with this being his first job, he needed more time to get his feet under him. Reiko knew what he really meant: that he wanted to play the field a bit more before making a commitment. The last thing she wanted was for him to keep her dangling, only to dump her. She'd been so sure that they were going to get married that she'd never bothered to look for a job.

She decided to trick Katsuya into marrying her. It was hardly rocket science. All she needed to do was to get pregnant. Since Katsuya always left Reiko to take the necessary precautions, he didn't suspect a thing when she assured him that "today was a safe day." Sure enough, Reiko conceived. Initially, Katsuya wasn't thrilled, but when the parents on both sides welcomed the news, he decided that getting married was a pretty good idea after all.

Reiko had no major complaints about married life. Looking after her boy was quite demanding, but her mother, who was still on the young side, lent a helping hand, meaning she could do what she had to without stressing out. Since her parents lived nearby, she could leave Shota with them whenever she wanted to go out with her college friends. Not having to worry about money was the thing she liked best. Reiko had no idea what Katsuya's salary was or how much he had in the way of savings. Within the bounds of common sense, she bought whatever she wanted and ate whatever she was in the mood for.

She had a vague notion that the two of them lived luxuriously compared to other young couples, but Katsuya never really demanded that she cut back, and she took that as a sign that everything was okay.

Besides, thought Reiko, even if their bank account dried up, they'd be fine. They could always fall back on Yosaku. If Katsuya was behind on his credit card payments, Yosaku would be happy to bail him out again.

3.

"Hello," said someone. Masayo looked up. Detective Kaga was standing in the doorway.

"Oh, hi there, Mr. Detective. What are you after today?" Masayo took off her reading glasses.

"I wouldn't really say that I'm *after* anything. I just came by to say thank you." Kaga held out a white shopping bag as he strolled over to her desk. There was a white box inside. "This is for your help with the investigation. These are fruit pastries and sweet almond jellies. I hope you like them."

"Oh, you shouldn't have." Masayo took the bag.

Kaga had come by three days ago. Wondering if he'd made any progress, Masayo just came out and asked.

Kaga nodded. "Thanks to you, we found a clue that should help us unravel the case. It won't be long now."

"That's good news," Masayo said. A second later, she shot a suspicious look Kaga's way.

"Is something wrong?" he asked.

"You said, 'thanks to me.' That must mean that our spinning tops *did* play a part in the murder."

"No, that's not the case." Kaga made an apologetic gesture.

"Well then, please tell me what the case is. Be straight with me. After you were here, I read up on the Kodenmacho murder. The papers said that the woman was strangled. That's when I realized why you were so keen to find out who'd been buying tops here."

"Oh, and why might that be?" Kaga was looking grave.

"Because of the string, of course. The top was neither here nor there; the important thing was the string, wasn't it? You can strangle someone with string." Masayo was jabbing her finger at Kaga's chest.

It wasn't actually Masayo who had come up with the idea. Misaki, the part-time clerk, suggested it.

Kaga recoiled slightly, a manufactured expression of surprise on his face.

"Darn it, how did you figure that one out?"

"You hardly need to be a genius to do so. Now, since one of our tops played a part in a murder case—"

"You're wrong there, quite wrong. You sold your top on the twelfth, right? The murder, however, took place on the tenth. I'm afraid your theory doesn't pan out."

Masayo gurgled something incoherent.

Misaki had actually pointed out the same thing. Despite the police's interest in the store's spinning tops, the time frame meant that it couldn't have been used as the murder weapon.

"Using forensic science, we can identify the exact kind of string used to commit the murder. The various tops on the market each have different types of string. And it turns out there's a lot of different types of string out there."

At that point, Kaga caught Masayo's eye. He shot a sheepish grin in her direction. "Anyway, what am I doing lecturing you about string? Talk about preaching to the choir."

"With traditional string, there's braided, woven, twisted, and knitted string, and then there's . . . let me see . . ." Half talking to herself, Masayo counted out the different types on her fingers.

"The string on the spinning tops you sell is the braided variety, right?"

"Right. It's made by braiding multiple fibers together. It's actually made by machine rather than handmade, but they're very fussy about the materials used and whether they're a good match with the top itself. It's not like any old string will do, you know."

"I'm sure it won't," Kaga agreed. "Anyway, braided string was not used to commit the murder."

"No? Then I really don't understand what's going on. If you knew that, then why bother investigating our tops in the first place? Or didn't you know what kind of string had been used when you were here last?"

"No, I already knew it wasn't braided string."

"More and more mysterious. Well, why, then?" Masayo gave Kaga a hard stare.

Kaga smiled and looked around the shop.

"I was actually transferred here quite recently. I'm a newcomer, still familiarizing myself with the neighborhood."

"Oh?" Masayo was confused.

"I'm looking around, visiting all sorts of places, trying to get to know the neighborhood as fast as I can. I've discovered that a lot of premodern Tokyo culture still survives here; maybe 'Japanese culture' is a better word. I imagine you picked this area for your store here because of that?"

"You're right. I chose this neighborhood because of its special character."

"This is probably the only district in Tokyo where you can get wooden spinning tops outside of the New Year's holidays. Your store's not the only place, either. I found another shop that sells tops: a toy shop on Ningyocho Boulevard."

"I know the place you mean. They'd be sure to have them."

"They sell a different line of tops with a different variety of string. The tops there all come with twisted string."

"Twisted string. Really?"

Masayo called up a mental picture of string with multiple strands twisted together like rope.

"Are you telling me it was twisted string that was used in the murder?"

Kaga didn't reply. He just smiled evasively and shrugged his shoulders.

"Top string exists for the purpose of spinning tops, not to kill people with. Anyway, I've got to be going."

Kaga spun on his heel and strode briskly out of the shop.

4.

When Reiko got back to the apartment, she dumped her shopping bags onto the sofa. Before doing anything else, she opened one of them and pulled out a dark blue box. She took the lid off the box and tore off the white tissue paper wrapping to reveal a new handbag. She took it out of the box and headed for the bathroom. She had already spent ages looking at herself holding the thing in the mirror at the store, but she wanted just one more look.

Standing in front of the bathroom mirror, she experimented with different ways of holding the bag and different poses. Which one made her look the best, and would make other women jealous?

Katsuya hadn't said anything more about the late credit card payment, so she assumed he'd sorted it all out. To her, that was reason enough to go on a spree. She bought a dress and a load of cosmetics in addition to the bag. She knew that she'd probably spent more than she should, but everything would be fine.

Satisfied that the bag was up to its task, she went back to the living room. She was just about to try on the dress when the doorbell rang.

Probably a delivery, she thought. It was a little after six p.m. Her parents had taken Shota to the zoo, and Reiko was supposed to pick him up from their place at seven.

She lifted the intercom receiver.

"Yes?"

"Sorry to come by unannounced. It's Detective Kaga. We met a few days ago."

"I'm sorry?"

"I was here with another detective, Detective Uesugi."

"Oh yes."

"Do you have a moment? I'm sorry, but there's something I need to ask you."

"Right now?"

"Yes, it's nothing terribly major. It won't take long. Five minutes should be more than enough."

Reiko gave an irritated sigh. He was a detective, so she couldn't very well send him packing. She wondered what sort of mess Yosaku had gone and got mixed up in.

"Okay then, come on up," she said.

The doorbell rang while she was still busy hiding the evidence of her shopping spree.

When she opened the door, Kaga was standing there, holding out a white plastic bag.

"They're ningyo-yaki, half of them with sweet bean paste, half without. The pastry shop where I got them has a very good reputation."

"Thank you very much."

Reiko's parents both had a sweet tooth. The cakes would make the perfect present for them.

She led Kaga into the living room, then slipped into the kitchen. Taking a big plastic bottle of oolong tea out of the refrigerator, she poured out a couple of glasses.

"Where's your little boy today?" Kaga asked.

"At the zoo with my mom and dad."

"Sounds nice."

When she came out of the kitchen carrying the glasses on a tray, she found Kaga standing in the living room, with the top spinning furiously at his feet.

"Wow, that's amazing," Reiko said. "Detective Kaga, you really know what you're doing."

Kaga turned and smiled. "Oh, hardly."

"Come off it. It's spinning perfectly. Neither my husband nor my father-in-law could get the thing to work well. They were hopeless. With my husband, the thing never even got going; it just toppled right over."

As Reiko put the tray down on the table, something white caught her eye. It was the string for the top. What was it doing on the table? How had Kaga managed to spin the top without it?

Kaga bent down and plucked the still-spinning top off the floor.

"You were out?" he asked, strolling back to the sofa and putting the top back on the table. He wasn't holding string.

"Yes, seeing a friend. I haven't yet had time to change. I only just got back."

"Really? You did your shopping after seeing your friend, then?'

"Huh?"

"I saw you with a whole armful of shopping bags."

Kaga sat down and picked up his glass of tea.

So the detective hadn't just happened to drop by. He'd been lurking nearby, waiting for her to return. He'd said it was "nothing terribly major." But was he telling the truth? Reiko felt herself growing tense.

"Where did you go shopping?"

"Ginza."

"Do you ever go to Nihonbashi?"

"Occasionally. Mitsubishi Department Store is around there."

"How long does it take to get there by taxi?"

"Nihonbashi? Probably about . . . uhm . . . fifteen minutes."

"Gosh, this is such a convenient place to live."

Although the apartment wasn't all that close to the local subway station, you could get to Ginza or Nihonbashi in no time by cab. That was the reason Reiko had chosen this particular neighborhood.

"Excuse me, Detective, but why are you here today?"

Kaga put down his tea and sat upright on the sofa.

"I want to ask you about June the tenth. Can you talk me through the whole thing again?"

"The whole thing? I don't think there's anything more I can tell you."

"Yosaku Kishida, your father-in-law, came by to discuss

the arrangements for the anniversary of his wife's death. Was that an urgent matter?"

Reiko tilted her head to one side and exhaled through her teeth. "I'm probably not the best person to ask about that. The anniversary is still two months away, so my husband was pretty relaxed about it. My father-in-law seemed to be taking it more seriously."

Reiko herself couldn't have cared less.

"So they discussed that. Then what?"

"I wouldn't say they discussed it. It was more like they agreed to start thinking about what to do."

"Is that all? Hardly seems worth getting together in the first place."

"I suppose not," murmured Reiko.

She frowned and peered at the detective.

"Anyway, why are you asking me about this? Does it really matter what they discussed? Is it a problem?"

"No, it's not."

"What the heck are you investigating here anyway? How is my father-in-law involved? Come on, tell me. I won't say another word until you do. I'm under no obligation to talk to you."

There was an edge to Reiko's voice. If it came to a shouting match, she was confident of winning.

Kaga scowled, then gave an emphatic nod.

"I guess you're right. The least I can do is to tell you the nature of the crime we're investigating."

"It's some sort of corporate accounting fraud, right?"

"Wrong. This is a murder inquiry."

"What!"

Reiko's eyebrows shot up. That was the last thing she'd expected to hear.

"On the evening of June the tenth, a murder was committed. We haven't yet identified the perpetrator. We are currently checking the alibis of everyone associated with the case. Yosaku Kishida is one of those people. When we interviewed him, he told us that he was here that night. I'm here to confirm that."

Reiko had been holding her breath. Her heart was still pounding like a jackhammer even after she released the air from her lungs.

"Is that what this is all about? My father-in-law didn't say anything about a—"

"He probably didn't want you to worry. You'd be alarmed if you heard that he was involved in a murder case. And naturally so."

"You're not kidding. My heart's racing." Reiko looked at the detective.

"Anyway, if that's what this is really about, let me make myself as clear as possible. My father-in-law came here. He arrived at about eight and left a little after half past nine. I've no idea what he did after that, though. . . ."

Kaga smiled.

"Mr. Kishida told us that, after leaving here, he went to a bar in Shinbashi and drank there until late that night. We've confirmed that."

"I'm glad to hear it. So his alibi holds up." Reiko felt a sudden twinge of doubt in her chest, and her face clouded over. "But I've watched my fair share of crime shows on TV. No one ever believes the family members."

"I wouldn't say no one believes them," replied Kaga, with a rueful grin. "More that as evidence, it carries somewhat less weight. There's always a chance that family members are covering for one another."

Reiko now understood why Kaga was being so persistent in his questions about June the tenth. He thought she might be lying. If she and her father-in-law were coordinating their stories, then the more questions he asked, the more likely she was to slip up.

"Trust me, Detective Kaga. My father-in-law was here in this apartment on that night. That's the God's own truth."

Reiko spoke passionately. What would the neighbors think if they heard that her father-in-law was a suspect in a murder? Would little Shota get bullied at school?

"The best thing would be if you could somehow prove that to me," said Kaga.

"Prove it?" Reiko cast her mind back to the evening of June the tenth. There had to be a way of proving that Yosaku really had been here.

"You told me that Mr. Kishida brought this with him on the twelfth?" said Kaga. He was holding up the top, which was decorated with a pattern of green and yellow circles. "What I can't figure out is why he didn't bring it on the tenth, if he came then anyway."

The question seemed reasonable enough. It would be a disaster if the top ended up serving as proof that Yosaku hadn't been there on the tenth. Reiko could feel the panic mounting.

"No. You're right. He actually did bring it with him on the tenth."

"On the tenth? But you said the twelfth the other day."

Reiko shook her head.

"No, he brought it with him on the tenth. The thing was, he'd forgotten the string."

"He forgot the string?"

"Because he'd left the string behind, at first my father-in-law didn't mention that he had the top with him. Then Shota—my son—opened up his granddad's briefcase and found it there. When I asked my father-in-law what on earth he was doing with a spinning top, he explained that he'd been given it by a friend."

"And he brought it here, intending to give it to his grandson as a present, until he realized he'd mislaid the string—is that it?"

"Yes, that's right. He thought he'd left it on his office desk. He took the top with him, promising to bring it back with the string as soon as he could."

"So he brought the top back with him—this time with the string—on the twelfth of June?"

"Precisely. Shota was really excited about his new toy, so I pestered my father-in-law to bring it back soon."

"I see," Kaga agreed. "I think I understand."

"Detective Kaga, you've got to believe me. My father-in-law was here with us on the evening of the tenth."

Reiko was looking at the detective with desperation in

her eyes. Why anyone would suspect her father-in-law she didn't know, but he had a proper alibi, and she was determined to get that point across.

Kaga smiled gently.

"I believe that you're telling the truth. Your account is extremely convincing. In fact, thanks to you, everything now fits into place."

"Really?" Amid her relief, Reiko felt a slight shadow of anxiety. What exactly had she said that had been so "convincing"? What exactly "now fit into place"?

Kaga got to his feet and thanked her for her help.

He slipped his shoes back on just inside the front door then put a hand into his pocket.

"I forgot this. Give it to your son. He'll be better off with this."

Kaga was holding out a length of string. A little thinner than the string her father-in-law given them, it was twisted like rope.

"Tops need the right kind of string to work properly. You'll have much better luck with your top if you use this string."

Kaga opened the door, stepped into the hallway, then turned back to Reiko.

"There's one thing I forgot to mention: the place and time that the murder was committed. The place was Kodenmacho in Nihonbashi, and we estimate the time as sometime between seven and eight that evening."

"Nihonbashi between seven and eight?" Reiko repeated quietly to herself, then started. So her testimony about her father-in-law visiting them here at eight o'clock wasn't an alibi after all.

What, then, had Kaga really come to check up on? She tried to ask him, but he said goodbye and pulled the door shut behind him.

5.

It began drizzling. It was the kind of rain that soaks you through before you know it—and a sure sign that the rainy season was just around the corner. Tooru Sagawa stepped outside and pulled the awning out farther before pushing the articles on the display a little closer to the front of the shop. The items were mostly old-fashioned wooden toys: building blocks, cup-and-ball games, and stacked Daruma dolls. As the shop was quite close to the Suitengu Shrine, many parents of newborn babies walked this way. Sagawa made a point of displaying things outside that would appeal to them. At the same time, he never put things that might appeal to elementary and middle school children in the street, as they would just steal anything that caught their eye. He once put a line of cute toy sets out in the street, only to have the damn kids steal the most popular ones and leave him with lots of incomplete sets. It wasn't a happy memory.

Sagawa was checking out the overcast sky, when he noticed someone approaching. It was a man in a white shirt. Sagawa had met him once before. The man's name was Kaga, and he was a detective who'd recently been transferred to Nihonbashi Precinct.

"It's started raining," said Kaga, holding his hand out palm-upward.

"The rainy season will be upon us any day now. It's a bad time for business; still, I suppose it brings us a step closer to the busiest season."

These days you barely saw any children in Ningyocho. Once the schools broke up for summer vacation, however, children would pour in from somewhere and cluster outside Sagawa's shop. He needed to get a move on and order fireworks in time for the summer rush. He'd been running his toy shop for twenty years, give or take, and had a pretty good idea of what sold when.

Kaga was examining the wooden toys. A group of spinning tops decorated with concentric green and yellow circles seemed to have caught his attention.

"That reminds me, did you sort out that business of the spinning tops you asked me about the other day?" inquired Sagawa.

Kaga smiled and nodded.

"I think I'm about to. You were right: they had tops at Hozukiya, too."

"What did I tell you? Everything there is of very high quality. I pop around from time to time just to take a look."

The last time Kaga came by, he'd asked Sagawa about his spinning tops. His first question: had he had sold any recently?

"Sold any? No. Lost any to pilfering? Yes," Sagawa had replied. That aroused the detective's interest. He asked when the shoplifting had occurred.

June tenth, Sagawa told him. Sagawa inventoried all the items in his shop on a daily basis. That's how he knew that one of the tops outside the store had been lifted.

The detective had then bought a top and unwound the string from it right in front of him. After taking a good hard look, he'd muttered something about it being the twisted variety of string. Few people knew the terminology, so Sagawa was surprised.

Kaga then asked him if he knew any other local shops that sold wooden tops. The only place that occurred to him was Hozukiya. Kaga must have gone straight there after Sagawa told him about it.

"How come you don't ask me any questions?"

"Questions about what?"

"About the investigation I'm working on," Kaga replied. "It's usually the first thing people ask me when I make inquiries. 'What's happened? What are you investigating?'"

Sagawa chuckled.

"What good would it do anyone to tell an amateur like me? If a detective's on the case, something nasty must have happened. Learning more about it will just make me depressed."

"I wish more people felt like you," said Kaga.

Sagawa picked up a spinning top.

"A toy store is in the business of selling dreams, so I need to maintain a positive, fun frame of mind. I go out of my way not to hear any negative news. Still, I would like to ask you one thing. What connects the top that was stolen from here to your case? I'm not asking you to go into detail. Did it play a positive part in the case or not—that's all I want to know."

Kaga lapsed into a brief, thoughtful silence, then shook his head.

"Let's not go there. It's confidential."

"Okay. No big surprise. Forget about it, then. Good luck with the case."

"I'll be seeing you," said the detective as he wandered off into the rain.

9

THE DETECTIVE OF NIHONBASHI

1.

From his very first glimpse of the crime scene, Hiroshi Uesugi knew that this case wasn't going to be easy. There was no specific reason for him to feel that way; if he'd had to put it into words, he'd have said something about the killer having luck on his side.

At eight p.m. on June 10 a woman's body was found in a Kodenmacho apartment. The person who discovered it was a friend who'd dropped by for a visit.

Based on the state of the body, death was estimated to have occurred within the last two hours. The friend had originally planned to get there one hour earlier, at seven. Had she not rescheduled at the last minute, she might have walked in when the crime was under way, or at least caught sight of the perpetrator. That was what made Uesugi feel that the murderer was lucky.

An investigation task force was set up in Nihonbashi Precinct, in whose jurisdiction the murder had been committed. It was there that Uesugi met the detective who'd been first on the scene. His name was Kaga, and he'd just been transferred to Nihonbashi.

Uesugi was familiar with the name. Stories were making the rounds about the various homicides Kaga had solved. Rumor had it that he was also a onetime all-Japan kendo champion.

Something of the athlete was still visible in Kaga's lean, hard physique, but the laid-back expression on his face hardly radiated professional competence. Uesugi also took an instant aversion to his sloppy way of dressing: a short-sleeved shirt worn over a T-shirt.

"Hey, Kaga, you always dress like that on the job?" was the first thing Uesugi said to him.

"Not always, but most of the time," Kaga breezily replied. "Lately it's been so damn hot."

The guy's a jerk, Uesugi thought. It was a letdown after all the stories he'd heard about Kaga and his razor-sharp mind and bloodhound nature. When had he lost it? Perhaps the rumors had exaggerated his skills out of all proportion. When you got down to it, if the guy was that good, the Tokyo Metropolitan Police would have plucked him out of a precinct posting long ago.

It didn't take long to build a profile of the murder victim. Her name was Mineko Mitsui. Divorced about six months ago, she lived alone and worked as a translator. The friend who found her was in the same business.

The day after the body was found, the captain ordered Uesugi to take a junior TMPD detective with him and go to see the ex-husband of the victim, a Mr. Naohiro Kiyose.

When they broke the news of his former wife's death to Kiyose, he seemed unable to process it. He just sat there with a bewildered look, providing only the most mechanical responses to Uesugi's questions. It took a while for the news to sink in.

"Is it really true?" he suddenly muttered in an interval between questions. "The poor thing was murdered. . . . ? Why her, of all people . . . ?"

Kiyose's reaction struck Uesugi as too genuine to be faked.

Naohiro Kiyose was cooperative but had no information likely to help solve the case. It was understandable; the man hadn't seen his wife for over half a year. He claimed to have been having dinner with a client in Ginza when the crime was thought to have occurred, and it didn't take long to confirm his alibi.

The next person whom Uesugi and his partner from the Homicide Division of TMPD spoke to was Koki Kiyose, Mineko Mitsui's only son. He was an actor with a small theatrical company.

Like his father, the young man appeared to have no idea why anyone would want to kill his mother. For his part, he hadn't been in touch with her for nearly two years. He seemed to have no interest in his parents' divorce and claimed to know nothing about why they'd split up.

"These days, plenty of people get divorced when they're older," was his blasé comment. "I was like, hey, if that's what you want, go for it."

Typical stupid kid, thought Uesugi to himself. *They're always so sure that they've grown up under their own steam, without their parents' support or protection counting for anything.* After dropping out of college, Koki Kiyose was trying to launch a career as an actor. Of course, the boy was too blind to realize that he'd only been able to develop an interest in something so flaky because of the freedom and privilege he'd enjoyed as a college student.

He's still a child, was Uesugi's take on Koki. He was still immature; his parents would have to keep an eye on him to make sure he stayed on track. His parents would need to make sure he was making the transition from boyhood to manhood. That was something only parents could do.

Koki was living with a waitress by the name of Ami Aoyama. The apartment they shared was registered in her name.

Why am I not surprised? thought Uesugi, sneeringly. *Like I thought, this kid can't stand on his own two feet. He just went and found someone else to mother him. If I were his dad, I'd grab him by the scruff of the neck and drag him home kicking and screaming.*

Uesugi and his partner failed to get any meaningful leads out of the victim's son or ex-husband; nor did the other investigators have better luck. The only witness testimony they had was from someone who'd seen an insurance salesman leaving the victim's apartment at 5:30 p.m. on the day of the murder. When the salesman's statement was found to contain inconsistencies, they thought they might be on to something, but his alibi was corroborated not long after. (Uesugi didn't know how this had been done.)

Although the task force held a big daily meeting attended by all the investigators, even drawing up a basic list of suspects proved a struggle. Mineko Mitsui, the victim, didn't have a wide circle of friends. Everyone who knew her was adamant that she was the last person on earth to have enemies. The police, meanwhile, hadn't managed to find anyone who stood to gain from her murder. From the crime scene, it was clear that the perpetrator had neither robbery nor rape in mind.

The only progress the police could claim to be making was in clearing up a number of little mysteries that had initially appeared hard to explain. These were things like why one of the little cakes at the crime scene had wasabi in it, and why the victim had a brand-new pair of kitchen scissors, despite already having a perfectly good pair. At the daily meeting, the top brass would simply announce that they had "established that such-and-such a detail was irrelevant to the case." Uesugi had no idea who had solved these mysteries, or how.

On the sixth day after the murder, they finally came across something that deserved to be called a lead. Someone had called Mineko Mitsui's cell phone a matter of minutes before her murder. Now they managed to establish where she was when she took the call: a clerk at a pastry shop not far from her apartment had overheard snatches of the conversation. The gist of it was:

"Hello, yes? . . . Oh, it's you. But why are you calling from a pay phone? . . . Oh, poor you. Okay, just hang on a second."

The most striking thing was the complete absence of formality. It was reasonable to assume that Mineko Mitsui was talking to a member of her immediate family, a relative, or a close friend.

Although it was far from certain that the caller was the perpetrator, the chances were that he or she had some kind of connection to the murder. A decision was made to take another look at all the victim's acquaintances from the present to her previous life as a housewife, and, even before that, when she was a student. A thorough investigation was launched to see if any old acquaintances had recently contacted the victim.

Uesugi was one of the detectives assigned to this task. One thing, however, bugged him. Who'd found out that Mineko Mitsui was in the pastry shop in the first place? No one saw fit to explain that to the investigating team.

Uesugi had a vague sense that there was something not quite right about the whole investigation.

2.

While the testimony of the pastry shop clerk was something of a morale boost for the investigative team, neither the relatives nor the friends of the victim could provide them with anything useful. Only one new piece of information came to light—that Mineko Mitsui was consulting about money matters with the same lawyer she'd used for her divorce. Although the division of the assets was over and done with, Mineko Mitsui was hoping to reopen negotiations with her ex-husband. Clearly she'd realized that supporting herself was going to be harder than she thought.

It was thought that Mineko Mitsui could have been planning to sue for compensatory damages based on Naohiro Kiyose having been unfaithful during their marriage. Mineko Mitsui had discussed it with her lawyer only on a hypothetical level. That was why Shizuko Takamachi, the victim's lawyer, hadn't seen fit to bring this to the attention of the police earlier.

They immediately started looking into Naohiro Kiyose, and it didn't take long to unearth someone who looked like mistress material. Kiyose had hired a woman by the name of Yuri Miyamoto as his personal secretary right after the divorce. Rumor inside the company had it that the two were lovers.

If she could prove that the relationship predated her divorce, Mineko Mitsui stood a decent chance of winning compensatory damages. Now, finally, they'd found someone who would profit from her murder.

Naohiro Kiyose had an alibi for the day. But that didn't mean he hadn't hired someone to do it. Hiring contract killers off the deep Web was becoming more common. Uesugi was put in charge of investigating Kiyose's relationship with Yuri Miyamoto.

"Go around to this guy's place and question him," the captain said, handing Uesugi the name and address of Yosaku Kishida.

"Kishida? I've seen that name somewhere before."

"He's an accountant. His company handles the finances of Naohiro Kiyose's firm. He's known Kiyose for thirty years, apparently. Whenever anyone asked Kiyose's employees about Yuri Miyamoto, they all said the same thing: 'If you want the low-down on the boss's private life, Mr. Kishida's your man.'"

"I remember where I came across the name. His company was on the list of incoming calls to Mineko Mitsui's cell phone, wasn't it?"

"That's right. Kishida says she had some questions for him about her tax return."

"Think that's all it was?"

"Search me. Ask him that along with everything else."

"Got you."

Uesugi slipped the piece of paper into his back pocket.

"Shall I assign one of the young guys to go with you?"

"I'm fine. Something like this, I can handle on my own."

Uesugi had just walked out of the police station, when someone called after him. When he turned around, Detective Kaga was hurrying toward him.

"Would it be all right for me to come along?"

"You know where I'm heading?"

"To Kishida Tax Accountancy's offices. I heard you discussing it with the chief," Kaga replied nonchalantly.

"Why so keen to go along? Think you'll get an arrest out of it?"

Kaga smiled. "If it comes to that, you're welcome to the credit. I've reasons of my own for being interested in Kishida Accountancy."

"Your own reasons? Meaning?"

"Tell you later. You're cool with me tagging along?"

Uesugi snorted. "I won't stop you, if that's what you mean."

Kishida's office was on the second floor of a six-story building. Behind the glass doors at the entrance was a reception desk. Behind the receptionist was a scrawny man in his late fifties, busily typing on a laptop.

Uesugi went in, introduced himself, and asked for Yosaku Kishida.

The man inside the office got to his feet. It was Kishida. Looking slightly rattled, he steered the two detectives over to a meeting area with armchairs.

Kishida presented them with his business card. As he examined the card, Uesugi got things going by asking Kishida about his relationship with Naohiro Kiyose. Kishida hemmed and hawed, but confirmed that the two men had known each other for a very long time.

"What about Kiyose's family? Were you friends with the late Mineko Mitsui?"

Kishida cocked his head ambivalently.

"Kiyose's wife and I were not that close. I almost never went to their house."

"You received a phone call from Ms. Mitsui on June the second. What was it about?"

"I believe I've already told you."

"I'm sorry to ask you to repeat yourself, but kindly talk us through it again. In detail." Uesugi took out his notebook.

Kishida sighed softly.

"She wanted to know how much we would charge for doing her tax return. Since I knew nothing about the scale of her income or her expenses, I couldn't give her a quote off the cuff. All I could do was promise that if she brought the job to us, we'd take care of it as reasonably as possible."

"Did you talk about anything else?"

"No, that was it. We didn't talk long."

"What do you know about the reasons behind the Kiyoses' divorce?"

Kishida thought for a moment.

"I know that Mineko was the one who wanted it. And that's about it. It's something that the two of them thrashed out between them; it wasn't my place to stick my nose in."

"You don't think that Mr. Kiyose had reasons of his own? Another woman on the side, something like that?"

Kishida's eyes widened. He shook his head vehemently from side to side.

"I really don't think so. President Kiyose's not smooth enough to pull something like that off."

Uesugi decided to get to the point.

"He recently hired a new personal secretary, a woman by the name of Yuri Miyamoto. What do you know about her? Were strings pulled to get her the job?"

"No . . . uhm . . . that," Kishida spluttered, his face the picture of dismay. "I'm just the accountant. As an outsider, I really don't know much about HR issues at my clients' companies. I heard that President Kiyose was acquainted with Ms. Miyamoto prior to giving her the job, but that's all I know."

"They were 'acquainted'? What exactly was the nature of this 'acquaintance'?"

"I really don't know. That's what I've been trying to say," Kishida said, with obvious irritation.

The man's frightened Naohiro Kiyose will put him through the wringer if he shoots his mouth off, thought Uesugi.

Uesugi decided to ease off. The guy didn't look like he could give them much more. Uesugi snapped his notebook shut.

"You're a busy man, Mr. Kishida. Thanks for your time."

"Could I just ask one thing?" broke in Kaga, as Uesugi was getting to his feet. "Mr. Kishida, where were you on the evening of June tenth?"

Kishida stared at Kaga with a look of incredulity. Uesugi, too, was taken aback. While it was standard practice to check the alibis of everyone closely associated with the victim, there was no reason to treat Kishida as a suspect. If Kaga pressed Kishida too hard for an alibi now, it might backfire and gum up the investigation later.

"What? Am I a suspect?" Sure enough, Kishida's face was taut with anger.

"You must understand that this is purely a matter of procedure. We ask everyone the same thing," replied Kaga serenely.

When Kishida shot an anxious, searching look at Uesugi, he smiled and gave him an encouraging nod.

"I'm sorry, sir. Red tape. You know how it is."

Kishida's expression relaxed a little. He retreated to the back of the office, muttering peevishly to himself. When he returned, he was carrying a diary.

"On June the tenth, I went around to my son's place after work," Kishida announced, as he leafed through the diary.

"About what time did you leave here?"

"Sometime after six thirty. I can't be more precise than that, I'm afraid."

Kishida went on to explain that, after leaving the office, he spent a while in a bookstore and reached the apartment of his son and daughter-in-law around eight. Sometime after nine he set off from there to a Shinbashi bar that was a regular hangout of his, before finally making it home sometime after midnight.

Kaga asked Kishida to provide him with the addresses for his son and daughter-in-law, and for the bar in Shinbashi. "That's everything from my side," he announced, bringing the interview to a close.

Uesugi laid into Kaga the minute they were back out on the street.

"That wasn't the time and place to start pressuring the man about his alibi. Stop playing the loose cannon. I don't like it."

"You can't deny I was right to ask, though. Kishida has no alibi for the time between seven and eight o'clock."

"What's the big deal about that? There are always more people without alibis than with alibis. Besides, we've got no reason to suspect Kishida."

Kaga stopped and turned to look at the traffic whizzing up and down the boulevard.

"Have you met Koki Kiyose?" he eventually asked, his eyes fixed on the road. "The victim's only son?"

"Yeah, I went to see him the day after the murder," Uesugi replied. "The kid's a spoiled brat. Wet behind the ears."

Kaga shrugged. "That's rather harsh."

"Kids like him piss me off. Think they're God's gift to the world when they can't do a damn thing for themselves. I blame the parents. Kids only turn out like that if they're not raised right. Some parents are so terrified of their children hating them that they don't discipline them. That's a surefire way to turn kids into arrogant little shits."

It was only after Uesugi had come to the end of his rant that he realized he'd overstepped. He cleared his throat. "What's that fool of a boy done anyway?" he asked.

"I tried asking him about his mother's way of speaking: you know, who she was formal with, who she was more casual with."

Uesugi was surprised to discover that Kaga was trying to work out who had called Mineko Mitsui from the pay phone. He couldn't help being interested. "Oh?"

"Basically, he thought that his mother was the same as most people. If she was talking to someone she knew well, then she would be very relaxed and informal. Conversely, if she was dealing with someone she didn't know well, she could be very proper and polite."

"Talk about useless. Hardly worth asking the question, if that's all the answer you're going to get."

"I followed that up by asking him to provide me with a list of everyone Mineko Mitsui spoke to without bothering with all the formalities and niceties—everyone he could think of, at least. He hadn't seen his mother for two years, so chances are he forgot a lot of people. Still, he did his best and came up with quite a few names. Can you guess who was on his list?" Kaga paused for dramatic effect. "Yosaku Kishida, the accountant."

"What!" Uesugi's eyes were like saucers. "You're kidding me?"

"Apparently, our accountant friend regularly dropped by the Kiyose home. Koki often heard his mother chatting with him in the most casual manner. Of course, given Kishida's long relationship with her husband, there's nothing extraordinary about that. Nonetheless, Ms. Mitsui apparently was informal only with people she knew well."

A groan burst from Uesugi's lips. "And Kishida just told us that he barely went to the Kiyoses' house and didn't know the victim particularly well."

"Smelling a bit fishy, eh?" Kaga grinned merrily.

Curling his lip, Uesugi looked Kaga in the eye.

"Now I know why you were so eager to come with me. I wonder if that discrepancy is enough to make Kishida a suspect, though? The guy has no motive for killing Mineko Mitsui."

"Maybe we just haven't found it yet."

"Knock it off, will you? If you look at it that way, there will be no end of suspects." Uesugi turned his back on Kaga and walked off. After a few steps, he paused and spun on his heel. "If you're desperate to make an arrest, you'd better find another partner. I just do what the higher-ups tell me—no more, no less. My retirement's just around the corner."

Kaga merely grinned. Uesugi couldn't tell whether he'd taken his words to heart.

3.

An enormous truck roared past. Beside it, in the outer lane, a red sedan was accelerating fast. An SUV was approaching rapidly from behind.

Out of nowhere, a motorbike appeared. It shot past the SUV and threaded its way between the truck and the red sedan at breakneck speed.

A can of coffee in his hand, Uesugi watched the motorbike until it was out of sight. Then he sighed and took a swig of his drink. He wondered if his body temperature had affected the coffee, making it go from piping hot to lukewarm.

Uesugi was on his way back to the police station after a before-hours visit to a nightclub. Since Yuri Miyamoto used to work as a hostess, it made sense to make inquiries at her old workplace. They needed to pin down the nature of her relationship with Naohiro Kiyose and then, if the relationship was a sexual one, to find out when it had started.

He spoke to several people, all of whom had the same disappointing answer: there was nothing going on between Naohiro Kiyose and Yuri Miyamoto.

"If you saw them together, you'd know what I'm talking about," declared a grizzled male employee of the club in a black suit. "Yuri was Mr. Kiyose's favorite girl—no doubt about that—but I don't think he had designs on her. He enjoyed talking to her. How can I put it? He behaved more like a dad with his daughter."

Maybe I'm wasting my time here, thought Uesugi. *Maybe we're just overcomplicating things*. What if Kiyose had simply decided to offer an office job to his favorite hostess—and that was all there was to it? In that case, Mineko Mitsui would have no grounds to sue Kiyose for damages, and Kiyose would have no motive for murdering her.

Uesugi had just gulped down the dregs of his lukewarm coffee, when he heard a voice to one side of him. "Thought I might find you here." Kaga was walking toward him.

"How'd you know I'd be here?" Uesugi asked.

"One of your colleagues told me you'd gone to make inquiries in Ginza. He thought you'd probably walk back this way."

Uesugi crushed the empty can in his fist.

"Some people would do well to keep their stupid mouths shut."

If his colleague had told Kaga about this place, he'd probably filled Kaga in on the background. Uesugi couldn't bring himself to look the other detective in the eye.

"What do you want?" asked Uesugi, his eyes averted.

"I want your opinion on something. Will you come to the apartment of the son of the accountant with me?"

"The damn accountant again? You just don't know when to let things go, do you."

"It wasn't about tax returns."

"What are you going on about now?"

"The reason why Ms. Mitsui called the Kishida Tax Accountancy office. He said she asked him about her tax returns. I don't think that's true."

"What was the call about, then?"

"I'm guessing that she called Kishida to sound him out

about the relationship between her ex-husband and Yuri Miyamoto. Was it sexual? When had it started? She may have mentioned something about a tax return, but just as a pretext for the call."

Uesugi was quiet for a while. Kaga's theory sounded plausible. The quickest way for Mineko to get the dirt on her ex-husband's love life was to ask his friends. And if that person was someone she knew, so much the better.

"Why didn't you mention that when we went to see Kishida?"

"At the time, I thought he knew that Naohiro Kiyose and Yuri Miyamoto were in a relationship and that he was concealing it from us. We now know that's not the case. There is no special relationship between Mr. Kiyose and Ms. Miyamoto—or nothing romantic, at least. I imagine that you learned the same thing from your inquiries in Ginza, Detective Uesugi?"

Uesugi glared at Kaga.

"How did you find that out?"

"I'll get to that later. Anyway, given that there was no untoward relationship between Mr. Kiyose and Ms. Miyamoto, then Mr. Kishida had nothing to hide from us. Does that mean Ms. Mitsui didn't ask him anything substantial on the phone? No matter how you cut it, that just doesn't seem likely." Kaga swiveled around and looked Uesugi in the face. "You've got to admit that Yosaku Kishida is worth investigating?"

Uesugi snorted contemptuously.

"If you want to do that, then go talk to my captain. He

can assign you another partner better suited to the job. The two of you can make your sensational little arrest together."

"Except that you're the detective in charge of investigating Kishida. From here we can get to his son's apartment in fifteen minutes by car."

"Yes, but—"

Ignoring Uesugi, Kaga raised his hand and hailed a passing taxi. Holding the door open with one hand, he motioned Uesugi in with the other.

Uesugi clambered in, a sour look on his face.

As the taxi sped toward the apartment, Kaga briefed Uesugi on the son and his wife. Katsuya Kishida worked for a construction consulting company; he and his wife were both twenty-nine years old; they had one child, a five-year-old boy.

"If you know that much already, why not go ahead and finish without me? I won't get pissed off or anything."

Kaga didn't reply. "There it is. It's that building there," he exclaimed, pointing with his finger. Apparently he'd scoped out the location in advance as well.

Katsuya Kishida was not yet back. According to his wife, he did a lot of corporate entertaining and was back late most nights.

Without mentioning anything about a homicide investigation, Uesugi asked the wife to confirm that Yosaku Kishida had dropped by on the evening of June 10. Reiko stated that he had indeed come by at eight o'clock. Apparently he'd called earlier that day to say that he'd be coming around that night to discuss the ceremony for his wife's death anniversary. When Uesugi inquired about Kishida's appearance, Reiko insisted that he was very much his usual self. She didn't seem to be taking the interview too seriously.

Unable to think of any more questions, Uesugi let his eye drift around the living room. A number of things immediately caught his eye: the oversized TV; the bottles of expensive liquor on the sideboard; a glossy handbag—stamped with a logo that even he recognized—tossed carelessly onto the sofa.

The five-year-old son was playing with a spinning top on the floor. Kaga seemed interested and asked the mother where she'd bought it. Her answer was that Yosaku Kishida, her father-in-law, had brought it with him on the evening of June 12.

"You're quite sure it was the twelfth?"

"Sure I'm sure. Why should you care, anyway?"

"Oh, no particular reason," murmured Kaga indifferently. Uesugi, however, detected a sharp new gleam in his eye.

"Well, that was a total waste of time," declared Uesugi as soon as they were outside the building. "I think she's telling the truth about Kishida arriving at eight. Nonetheless, that doesn't provide him a full alibi. I wonder why he made a point of coming here that night?"

"We don't yet know. But did you see how that young couple lives? Didn't that bother you?" Kaga asked.

"They're certainly living large, but I wouldn't say it bothered me. Bad times or good, people with money always have money!"

"That's what I mean. The woman said that her husband was out wining and dining clients every night. But I called the company to check. Katsuya Kishida is in the accounts payable department. Correct me if I'm wrong, but normally accountants don't do a whole lot of corporate entertaining."

Uesugi stopped midstride and turned to Kaga.

"What are you getting at?"

"I don't really know myself yet," said Kaga, raising his arm. A taxi pulled up to the curb beside them.

4.

Uesugi spent the next day making inquiries on a completely different case. When he got back to the task force headquarters, the captain called him over. As Uesugi walked across the room, the captain glanced around suspiciously, then extracted something from inside his desk. Uesugi caught his breath when he saw what it was.

"Ha. So you have seen it before, then?" The captain peered up at him.

He was holding a top: a wooden top decorated with concentric green and yellow lines. The same top that Katsuya Kishida's son had been playing with.

"What's that thing doing here?" asked Uesugi weakly.

"Kaga came across it in a toy shop in Ningyocho. This top is sold together with a length of string. He sent the string down to forensics. They're comparing it against the ligature marks."

Ligature marks? That meant the strangulation marks on the victim's neck.

The murder weapon had yet to be discovered. Despite knowing that twisted string with a diameter of three to four millimeters had been used to commit the crime, they hadn't yet found an object that matched the description.

"Oh, and he asked me to give this to you."

The captain handed Uesugi a handwritten note.

The hastily scribbled note read: "A top like this one was stolen from a toy shop in Ningyocho on the evening of June 10. Kaga."

Stolen on the day of the murder!

"Kaga wanted you to fill me in on this spinning top. What's the man talking about?" The irritation was audible in the captain's voice.

Uesugi simply ignored the question. "What did forensics have to say?" he asked.

The captain must have sensed that Uesugi wasn't in the mood to play games. He picked up a document from the corner of his desk.

"The string's thickness and the width of the fibers were a perfect match for the strangulation marks on the neck."

Uesugi inhaled noisily. The blood was pumping furiously through his veins.

The captain started to ask a question. Uesugi raised a hand to cut him off.

"Where's Kaga?"

"No idea. Gone out somewhere. Said he needed to make some follow-up inquiries on this."

"Okay. I'll give you my report after I've spoken to him. You're going to have to wait."

"What the hell?"

In response to the captain's sour glare, Uesugi bowed and walked away. When he consulted his watch, it was a little after seven.

It was nearly eight by the time Kaga returned. Uesugi grabbed him by the arm and dragged him out into the passageway.

"What the hell's going on? You want to play to the crowd, be my guest. But don't try and suck me into it."

Kaga gently prized Uesugi's hand off.

"Precinct detectives never get to solve cases all on their lonesome. The important thing is the news about the top. Did you hear?"

"Yeah, the captain filled me in. Why'd you zero in on it?"

"I don't know, really. Tops are more of a New Year's present, so it seemed funny for the kid to have gotten one at this time of year. Plus it's not like there's a whole load of shops that stock them. Who sells the things? I could only think of one place."

"That Ningyocho toy shop? Well remembered."

Kaga gave a nod.

"I've been walking around the precinct pretty much every day since I got posted here. I've got a pretty good idea of what's sold where."

"Don't imagine the shopkeepers are too thrilled to have a cop swinging by all the time."

"I thought so, too. That's why I do my best not to look like one," said Kaga, giving his shirt a discreet tug forward.

So that's it! Uesugi suddenly understood why Kaga had been dressing like a slob.

"You said the top was stolen?"

"On the evening of June tenth. Just before the murder."

"Procuring the murder weapon from a shop along the way to the crime scene? Would anyone actually do that?"

"God knows. Takes all sorts to make a world."

"The string matches the strangulation marks, but we can't definitively prove that that particular string was used in the murder."

"I know. What we can be sure of is that Yosaku Kishida disposed of the string from that top."

Uesugi frowned. He didn't understand what Kaga was getting at.

"Kishida gave his grandson a spinning top and a length of string. The string, though, wasn't the original string that came with the top. It was braided, rather than twisted string. Kishida must have picked up a second length of string somewhere else and put it together with the original top."

"You think he threw away the original twisted string after the murder?"

"That seems a reasonable assumption, yes."

"Which means . . ." Uesugi thought a moment. "That things would get really interesting if we could locate the shop where Kishida got the braided string."

"That's why I've been trying to find the place," rejoined Kaga.

"Did you succeed?"

"Perhaps." Kaga nodded a couple of times. "We should know for sure in two or three days."

5.

The hands of the clock stood at half past six.

Uesugi and several other investigators were sitting in a car parked at the curb, keeping an eye on the lobby of the building next to them. Kishida's office was in the building, and Kishida was inside. Another team had the back door under surveillance.

An arrest warrant for Kishida hadn't yet been issued. The plan today was to bring him in for voluntary questioning. Once in custody, Uesugi was convinced, it would only be a matter of time before the man confessed.

Kaga had come across a new batch of tops in Ningyocho. They came in three sizes: small, medium, and large, and he'd brought the shop's whole stock, boxes and all. He found them on display in the street outside a traditional Japanese handicrafts store. All the tops at this shop had braided string.

"Finding just the string for a top isn't easy. My guess was that Kishida bought a brand-new top just for the string that came with it. Since he'd be reluctant to buy a second top from the shop where he stole the first one, I tried hunting down another place that sold wooden spinning tops."

As the string that came with each size of top was different, Kaga speculated that Kishida must have examined a number of them in an effort to find the one with the best string to go with his original top.

Kaga's hunch was right. When forensics checked the

boxes, they found fingerprints that matched the prints that had been lifted from Kishida's business card on many of them.

The last question that needed to be cleared up was why Kishida felt compelled to give the top to his grandson and had gone to such lengths to do so. Kaga had a theory about that, too.

"Something must have happened involving the top when Kishida went over to his son and daughter-in-law's place on June tenth. He would never have gone to such lengths otherwise."

But what could that "something" be? Kaga was currently at Katsuya Kishida's apartment doing his best to get an answer. He was pretty confident that he'd be able to extract the necessary information from the wife, Reiko.

A call came in to Uesugi's cell phone at 6:30 on the dot.

"Uesugi here," Uesugi said.

"Hi, this is Kaga. I've just left Katsuya Kishida's apartment."

"Did the wife tell you what you needed to know?"

"Sure did. I was right. Yosaku Kishida had a spinning top in his briefcase on the evening of the tenth, the same kind of top that was shoplifted. His grandson found it when he was digging around inside."

Although Kaga delivered this explanation at breakneck speed, Uesugi managed to follow.

"Okay. So he was forced into a corner: he *had* to give the top to his grandson."

"I discreetly let Reiko Kishida know that the string was different and Kishida's alibi meaningless. I'm prepared to bet that she's on the phone right now, either to her father-in-law or her husband."

"Got it. Leave the rest to me."

Uesugi hung up.

It was about ten minutes later that Yosaku Kishida emerged from the building. He was looking tense. The shadows cast by the low evening sun only deepened the lines on his face.

Uesugi signaled to his crew. All the detectives got out of the car and marched over to Kishida.

He did not respond when they blocked his way. He glanced up at Uesugi vaguely, as if his mind was somewhere else. Eventually the detective's presence registered: Kishida's eyes widened, but he still said nothing.

"Mr. Kishida?" said Uesugi. "We'd like to ask you a few questions. Could you come with us, please?"

Kishida's jaw fell, and his eyes goggled. With his haggard, sunken cheeks, he looked more like a death's-head than a human being.

A moment later his whole body sagged. He buckled at the knees and crashed wordlessly to the ground.

6.

The Statement of Yosaku Kishida

It was twenty-seven years ago that Naohiro Kiyose first contacted me. We'd gone to college together, though he was in the year before me. He was setting up a cleaning company and wanted my help. I had only just started my own accounting practice; as business was still in short supply, I accepted his offer without a second thought. Knowing his character and his abilities, I was pretty confident that any business Kiyose launched was likely to succeed.

His business did succeed and on a scale beyond my wildest dreams. I hadn't realized how much demand there was for a cleaning service. His company expanded very rapidly.

Soon after Kiyose's marriage, we decided to set up a second company, a dummy company, as a tax shelter. He appointed Mineko, his wife, as nominal CEO of this new entity. She had to be paid a salary, of course. I opened a special bank account: it was in her name, but I was the one who managed it. The plan was to keep it as a source of emergency funds.

Twenty years passed. The Kiyoses and I remained on friendly terms. If there was any change, it was on their side. As you are aware, the Kiyoses ended up getting divorced. I don't know much about the reasons. After the divorce, Kiyose hired a former bar hostess called Yuri Miyamoto as his personal secretary, but I'm pretty sure that she wasn't what caused the divorce.

The two of them got divorced by mutual consent. Mineko hired a lawyer and demanded a fair settlement of assets. Both sides provided the details of their various personal bank accounts for the negotiations. I was there, of course, but largely kept quiet.

I believe that Mineko got a fair settlement. There was no evidence of Mr. Kiyose making any unaccounted-for withdrawals, and Mineko accepted the proposed settlement. So, as far as possible, their divorce was easy. I thought that it was all over and done with, at least as far as money matters were concerned.

I was wrong. Early this month, Mineko called my office. She wanted to get me to check up on something for her. She was adamant that I had to keep it a secret from Kiyose. I had no idea what the whole thing was about.

We met in a café close to Tokyo Station. Mineko seemed lively, far more animated than when she'd been married. It was nice to think that she was finally getting what she wanted out of life.

After a bit of a small talk, Mineko broached the topic she wanted to discuss. It was Yuri Miyamoto. She'd heard rumors about the president's new secretary and the kind of woman she was. She asked if I thought she was Kiyose's lover. Earlier I said I didn't think Yuri Miyamoto was the reason they got divorced. That was because of this conversation: obviously, at the time of the divorce Mineko was unaware of Yuri Miyamoto's existence.

I said that I didn't know if they were lovers. And that's God's own truth. I still don't know. With her background as the boss's favorite hostess, chances are that something was going on, but Kiyose himself never said anything about it to me.

Mineko wasn't worried about Yuri Miyamoto being her ex-husband's lover; all she cared about was *when* their relationship had started. That was when I realized that she planned to sue for compensatory damages if Kiyose had been unfaithful during their marriage.

I reiterated that I knew nothing about Kiyose and Yuri

Miyamoto's relationship. Mineko proposed that we examine the movement of money in his accounts. If the two of them were lovers, she guessed that he'd have been giving her cash and buying her all sorts of expensive things.

I explained that payments to and from his accounts had been reviewed as part of the original divorce settlement. Mineko's answer was to suggest that perhaps Kiyose was using company money. It would be simple enough for him, as company president, to set up an account for her under a plausible-sounding name and direct money to it. That was totally out of the question, I countered. If he were doing anything like that, I'd be the first to know. I was the person who had to sign off on the accounts.

But Mineko wouldn't listen. I was a friend of her ex-husband, she argued, so maybe I was covering for him? She wanted the company's books to be audited. My guess is that she planned to hire another accountant to do the audit.

I started to get a bad feeling: it looked like things were heading south fast.

Sure enough, my worst fears came true when Mineko started talking about the shell company we had set up twenty-some years ago. She wanted someone to investigate its accounts for her. When the Kiyoses negotiated their divorce settlement, the shell company had been classified as a "tangible asset belonging to the main company." As such, it was off the table.

I managed to keep a calm exterior, but inside I was in a state of complete panic. Things were going on with that shell company that I didn't want anyone else finding out about.

I'd been helping myself to money from the CEO account—the one in Mineko's name—for several years. But that wasn't the half of it. Kiyose had signed over control of all the shell company's accounts to me. Taking advantage of that, I'd diverted monies way in excess of what he owed me for handling his taxes to my own company's account. It was probably around thirty million yen, all told.

All the money I embezzled went to pay off my debts. Not only was my accounting business doing poorly, I'd also dug myself into a major hole with my gambling habit. I always hoped I could repay the money before anyone noticed it was gone. I couldn't, though.

Anyway, Mineko and I went our separate ways, after arranging to meet at the same café in a week's time. I was insane with worry. I'd advised her not to mention her plans to anyone for the time being, but I knew that if I didn't take action, she would eventually get herself a lawyer and approach Kiyose directly. I knew him. Since he had nothing to hide, he would be quite happy to let her poke around all she wanted. That would mean exposure and ruin for me.

The week went by, and I still had no idea what I was going to do. As agreed, Mineko and I met for a second time. She was getting impatient. It was obvious that if I didn't help her, she'd get in touch with Kiyose herself. Panicking, I promised to have a report ready for her within the next couple of days. In fact, I had no idea what I was really going to do.

I couldn't catch a wink of sleep that night. I was obsessing over how to deal with Mineko, but still I couldn't come up with a plan. Time seemed to pass much faster than normal.

I don't know when the solution came to me. All I can say is that by the time I left my office the next day, I knew exactly what I had to do. The fact that I called my son's place to say I'd be there at eight is proof of that. I wanted to be sure I had an alibi. Yes, that's right. The solution that had come to me was that Mineko had to die. It was evil, I know, but what other option did I have?

I set out for Kodenmacho, briefcase in hand. I was already on the subway when I realized my mistake. *I didn't have anything to kill her with.* Maybe a strong man can throttle someone bare-handed, but me? No way. I couldn't expect to chance upon the perfect murder weapon in her apartment, either.

I got off the train and began wandering around looking for a knife. There were all sorts of shops. After a few minutes, I stopped outside a place called Kisamiya. It's a cutlery shop that's been in business since the Edo period. They had all these handmade carving knives on display.

The things in Kisamiya were all so sinister and menacing. They freaked me out. There were these monstrous shears that doubled as a sashimi knife. The sight of them made me physically flinch.

I realized that I could never do it with a knife. I needed to kill her quickly, so she wouldn't be able to run away. Even if I managed to do that with a knife, blood spatter would be a big risk. Disposing of the weapon wouldn't be easy, either.

Above all, buying a knife in a place like that would probably come out during the police investigation.

If knives were out, what weapon should I look for? Strangling seemed like the best option; it would prevent her from crying out and eliminate the risk of blood spatter. I started looking for string. I didn't want to use my own necktie. I was worried that it might leave fibers on the neck that the police could trace back to me.

String is something you can buy anywhere. I went into a convenience store to buy a roll, but changed my mind when I saw the CCTV cameras. The police were sure to send someone around there when they figured out what kind of string had been used. Quantity was another problem. I needed a meter at most; how was I supposed to get rid of all the string I *didn't* use?

Leaving the convenience store, I resumed my wandering, looking for a place that sold string more suited to my purpose. I came across a fabric store that had a wide selection of string and cord. Still, a man like me buying a length of cord and nothing else at a shop was sure to strike people as odd. The clerk would definitely remember me. I went into a few places that sold belts and ties, but my nerve failed. I was convinced that the store clerks would remember me, no matter what I bought or where I bought it.

That was when the tops caught my eye. There was this shop—I didn't notice its name—with all these wooden toys displayed outside. The tops were there along with everything else.

I was lucky. There was no one near me in the street and

no one in the shop, as far as I could tell. I grabbed one of the tops, shoved it into my suit pocket, and hightailed it out of the area. I'd never stolen anything from a shop in my life, and my heart was pounding away for quite a while after.

Once I'd put some distance between myself and the shop, I pulled the string off the top and put the top into my briefcase. The string felt strong enough to strangle someone with. I put it in my pocket and went over to a nearby pay phone. I didn't use my cell, in order to avoid my number coming up on Mineko's phone.

Mineko picked up fast. When she expressed surprise about my calling from a pay phone, I lied and told her my cell phone was broken.

She'd been out, she explained, but would be back home in a minute or two.

I asked her if we could meet up at her place. That would be fine, she said, provided we finish up by eight, when a friend of hers was coming over. I assured her that I was already close by and that our business wouldn't take long at all.

It was probably a little past seven when, doing my best not to be noticed, I slipped into her building, walked up to her apartment, and rang her doorbell. By this point, I'd taken the string out of my pocket and was holding it bunched up in my right hand.

Mineko didn't suspect a thing. She invited me in. It was just the two of us.

The minute she turned her back on me, I threw the string over her head and pulled it tight, crossing my hands at the back of her neck.

Mineko had no idea what hit her. She hardly even fought back. It must have been a good ten seconds before she began thrashing with her arms and legs. She really struggled, flinging herself this way and that, jerking her head around. She never made so much as a peep, though; perhaps she couldn't.

Eventually, she just sort of crumpled and collapsed and stopped moving entirely. Doing my best not to look at the body, I unwound the string from around her throat. I opened the front door a crack and peeped into the hallway. There was nobody there, so I slipped out. Using my handkerchief, I wiped my fingerprints off the doorknob and the doorbell.

Once I was out of her building, I walked a couple of blocks and caught a taxi to my son and daughter-in-law's place. I must have got there slightly before eight. We were supposed to be discussing the arrangements for the anniversary ceremony of my wife's death, but I was so tense that even small talk was a struggle.

It was then that my five-year-old grandson discovered the top in my briefcase. My daughter-in-law asked me why I was carrying something like that around with me. Unable to improvise anything clever on the spot, I made up some lame story about having been given it by a friend and left the string for it at the office. In fact, the string was right there, burning a hole in my trouser pocket. It was just that I couldn't bear the thought of my grandson playing with a piece of string that I had killed somebody with. I retrieved the top from him and promised to bring it back, along with the string, the next time I was there. I planned to pick up a suitable piece of string from somewhere.

I left my son and daughter-in-law's place and headed for Shinbashi. I drank a few whiskies at a bar, one of my regular haunts. In part, that was to give myself an alibi. Since the body had already been discovered by then, it was useless in that regard. I didn't know; I just imagined that I'd be better off being with other people than by myself. I got home late and burned the string.

The murder was big news the next day. Word of it even came to my office. I couldn't face the idea of going looking for new string for the top. I wasn't up to it; I spent the day cowering in terror, expecting a detective to show up with an arrest warrant at any moment.

The police contacted me for the first time on June the twelfth. They telephoned to say that they'd found my company's number in Mineko's list of recent incoming calls. They were nice enough and asked me what we had talked about.

I cooked up some story about her consulting me about her tax returns. Given Mineko's postdivorce plans to work as a freelance translator, she'd need to start filing a tax return of her own. The detective I spoke to seemed to swallow my story.

The fact that the police seemed to buy my story gave my confidence a boost. That evening I went out looking for a string for the spinning top. I hadn't the faintest idea where I could find one. Despite only needing the string, I figured I'd have to buy another top. Unable to think of any other neighborhoods likely to have shops selling old-fashioned spinning tops, I set off for Ningyocho again.

I didn't feel comfortable going back to the shop where

I'd stolen the top, so I walked around until I came across a shop that specialized in traditional handicrafts. It had these wooden spinning tops outside. There were three sizes: small, medium, and large. I had to look at all of them to see how they compared to the top I'd stolen, and eventually I settled on the small one. After leaving the shop, I pulled off the string and dumped the top in the trash outside a convenience store. I then went straight to my son and daughter-in-law's place and presented my grandson with the old top and the new string that I'd just bought. I thought I had successfully covered all my traces.

In fact, I hadn't shaken off the police. Far from it. I could sense their suspicions intensifying with every day that passed. The news that a detective had been around to my son and daughter-in-law's place really frightened me. *My time's up*, I thought.

It was when my daughter-in-law told me about a detective named Kaga giving her the right string for the top I'd given my grandson that I knew for sure that I wasn't going to get away with it.

What I did to Mineko is unpardonable. I wasn't myself when I did it. I should have come clean about embezzling the money and paid the price. Instead, in a misguided attempt to protect my good name, I killed an innocent woman. I am ready to take my punishment, no matter how harsh.

7.

There were no major inconsistencies in Yosaku Kishida's confession. The police, who used it as the basis for a reenactment of his movements at and in the environs of the crime scene, concluded that he could plausibly have done everything that he claimed to. Sure enough, when they investigated the accounts of Naohiro Kiyose's shell company, they found thirty million yen missing and unaccounted for. On top of that, almost twenty million yen had been withdrawn from the account in the name of CEO Mineko Kiyose. Naohiro Kiyose himself was quite unaware that money was being siphoned off in this way. He had complete faith in his accountant, who had been his friend for thirty or so years.

Despite getting off to a slow start, it looked as though the Kodenmacho murder case was going to be neatly tied up. You could see the satisfaction in the faces of the captain and the other higher-ups in charge of the case.

Did they have all the backup proof they needed? Not quite. The single biggest issue that still needed to be resolved was what Kishida had done with the money he'd embezzled. In his statement, he claimed it had gone to paying off the debts of his business and large gambling losses. As far as the police could tell from going over its books, his company wasn't actually doing that badly. Also, none of the people who knew Kishida well knew anything about his being a gambler.

Although the police pressed him repeatedly on this point, Kishida held to his story. If his company appeared to be in relatively good financial health, his cooking of the books explained that. As for the gambling, he'd been careful to indulge his habit only where he wouldn't be seen by people who knew him.

As the days passed, the higher-ups began grumbling that enough was enough. The perpetrator of a homicide had provided them with a confession, and they had everything that they needed to indict him. Knowing where the embezzled money had gone was neither here nor there.

Although Uesugi had been leading the questioning when Kishida provided his confession, he took a step back from the case. He wasn't the one who had cracked it; it was a local precinct detective who actually figured the whole thing out. Since openly admitting that would entail a division-wide loss of face for Tokyo Metropolitan Police Department's Homicide Division, Uesugi decided that staying away from the task force HQ was the best course.

A persistent, gentle rain was falling. Uesugi was walking down Amazake Alley, umbrella in hand, when his cell phone buzzed. He checked to see who was calling: it was Kaga.

"What d'you want?" he asked.

"Where are you?"

"Out. Taking a stroll."

"If you're anywhere near Ningyocho, could we get together briefly?"

"What the hell is it now?"

"I'll tell you when I see you. I'll be waiting by the subway station," said Kaga tersely, then rang off.

When Uesugi got there, Kaga waved extravagantly to catch his eye. He then hailed a cab and ordered it to go to Asakusabashi.

"Where the hell are you taking me?"

"I want it to be a surprise. You'll enjoy it more that way," declared Kaga earnestly.

Uesugi guessed their destination just before they got there. He'd been there before: it was the performance space of the theater company that Koki Kiyose belonged to.

"What'd you bring me here for?"

"You might as well go inside."

The actors were busy rehearsing in the cramped space. Several people turned to look at the two men as they walked in. Kaga nodded hello and, losing interest, the actors turned back to what they were doing.

Kaga pulled up a couple of folding chairs and set them side by side. Uesugi took the hint and sat down. Kaga did the same.

The play continued up on the stage. From the well-finished stage sets and props, it looked as though opening night was just around the corner.

In between scenes, the stagehands changed the sets. They performed their task fast and efficiently. It occurred to Uesugi that the actors weren't the only ones who needed practice to get their jobs right.

Uesugi recognized one of the people busily moving things around: it was Koki Kiyose. He had a towel wrapped around his head and was wearing a sleeveless running shirt. His bare shoulders glistened with sweat.

"Isn't that fellow in the play?" muttered Uesugi. Kaga put his finger to his lips to shush him.

The play was set in England a long time ago. It had a relatively small cast, and the main character was an old man.

He, it turned out, was a celebrated detective, now retired, who was recalling his past cases as he looked back over his life.

The two detectives ended up watching the play all the way through. Despite having arrived when it was about halfway through, Uesugi enjoyed it. It was poignant and touching.

"Not bad, eh?" commented Kaga.

"S'pose not," Uesugi rejoined, although he had actually liked it a lot better than that.

What bothered him was the fact that Koki Kiyose came out for a bow only at the final curtain. In this play, the kid was a full-time stagehand rather than an actor, Uesugi realized.

Just then, Koki Kiyose ran over to them shouting a greeting. He unwound the towel from his head, revealing hair sodden with sweat. He bowed deeply to Kaga.

"Thank you for everything you've done for us, Detective. I say that on behalf of my mother, too."

"Don't mention it. We're just doing our jobs, right?"

Kaga turned to Uesugi for confirmation. Uesugi nodded.

"I'm sure things will be tough, but good luck to you."

"Thank you."

"You weren't acting today?"

"No. I won't be performing for a while yet," Koki replied crisply. There was a determined look in his eyes.

"Because of what happened?" Uesugi asked, with a touch of hesitancy.

"My mother's murder was the trigger. I had to step down from the lead role because I couldn't concentrate. I think it was all for the best, in a way; I wasn't ready. I plan to resume acting when I've done some work on myself, built up my confidence.

"I've got to get back to work. I'll say good-bye," Koki said, returning backstage.

"Shall we go?" Kaga suggested.

"You brought me all the way here just to meet that spoiled brat?"

Kaga blinked with surprise. "Did he look like a spoiled brat to you?"

"I guess not." Uesugi rubbed his chin. "There was something different about him."

"You bet there was."

"How comc?"

"I'll tell you later. Bear with me a bit. It won't take long."

The next place Kaga took Uesugi was a pastry shop in Kodenmacho. It had a café area at the back, where the two men sat down. Although the place was clearly proud of its cakes, Uesugi, like Kaga, ordered a simple iced coffee.

"Surely this place is—"

"That's right. Mineko Mitsui was here just before she was murdered." Kaga directed a meaningful glance toward the counter. "You see the sales clerk there? She's the one who told us about the phone call Ms. Mitsui got."

"So it was you who located this place? No wonder my bosses didn't say anything about it. How on earth did you do it?"

"There's something else I want to tell you first. Let me take things in the proper order." Kaga took a long swig of his iced coffee, as if getting ready for a long speech.

He began with something that had happened at a rice cracker shop. It involved an insurance salesman who became a suspect when he concocted a fake alibi for the police.

The next episode, which was about an old-style ryotei restaurant, was connected to the single wasabi-spiked snack cake discovered in Mineko Mitsui's apartment. That was followed by stories involving a china shop Mineko Mitsui frequented; the proprietor of a clock shop whom she knew only by sight; then a friend of hers who was a translator. Although none of the individual stories had a direct link to the murder, Uesugi was kicking himself as he listened to Kaga. The precinct detective had looked into things that the rest of them had all dismissed as insignificant, keeping at it until he got to the truth, regardless of whether there was a connection to the murder or not.

Kaga finally got around to the pastry shop they were in. Uesugi was startled when the name of Koki Kiyose came up in this context. Kaga explained how Mineko Mitsui had made the mistake of assuming that the pregnant girl who worked there was the girlfriend of her son.

"That's the girl there," said Kaga, rolling his eyes at the girl behind the counter. Sure enough, her belly was somewhat swollen.

"Let me guess how this particular story goes: Ms. Mitsui was so thrilled that her son was about to become a father that she moved to be closer to him. Since, however, he was an aspiring actor, her precious boy didn't have a proper full-time job or salary to go with it. The idea of claiming compensation from her ex-husband came out of her desire to help him out?" Uesugi sighed. "No wonder he seemed different today."

"That's not the only thing that affected him."

Kaga then launched into another story—the most surprising one so far, thought Uesugi. Yuri Miyamoto, who was widely believed to be Naohiro Kiyose's mistress, was in fact his daughter.

"Keep that under your hat, please. The two of them haven't gone public yet about their relationship," Kaga said.

Uesugi was shaking his head in amazement.

"I can't believe that so many other things were going on in the background of this case. Anyway, if that's not enough to inspire the son to get serious about life, nothing will. He must have learned not to take his parents for granted."

"You've put your finger on it, Uesugi." Kaga leaned toward him. "Doing this job, this is something I think about a lot. When a terrible crime like murder is committed, of course we need to catch the person who did it. But we also need to follow through until we've figured out why the crime happened in the first place. Unless we can identify the cause, there's nothing to stop someone else from making the same mistake. Learning the truth can teach us all sorts of valuable lessons. Look at Koki Kiyose: he learned his lesson, and he changed as a result. Can you think of anyone else who would be better off changing?"

Uesugi was using his straw to stir his iced coffee. His hand came to a complete stop. He looked Kaga in the eye.

"What are you trying to say?"

"I think you know what I'm getting at. Kishida is hiding something from us. Why aren't you working harder to get him to come clean?"

Uesugi looked down at his hands. "I still don't get what you're saying."

"Maybe you sympathize with Kishida? But are you satisfied with the way things are now? Seriously, are you?"

"You listen to me." Leaning forward slightly, Uesugi glared at Kaga. "If there's something you want to say, why don't you just come out and say it."

"Okay then, here goes." Kaga's face darkened, and his eyes gleamed with an intensity Uesugi had not seen before. "You're the only person who's capable of getting Kishida to open up. So why don't you? Make him tell us the truth."

The bastard! Uesugi realized that Kaga must know all about him. He wouldn't be speaking to him like this unless he knew about the unspeakably foolish mistake he had made three years before.

"I'm not interested in standing out," said Uesugi softly. "I'm a scumbag. I don't deserve to be in the police. I applied for early retirement back then, but I let myself be talked out of it. I regret changing my mind. I wish I'd just walked away."

"Why don't you share your regrets with the suspect and see what happens?"

Reaching for his iced coffee, Uesugi shook the glass. The ice cubes clinked and rattled.

"That's just bullshit," he muttered.

8.

Yosaku Kishida was even thinner than the last time Uesugi had seen him. His cheeks had hollowed out further, and his eyes sunk even deeper into his skull. His shoulder blades protruded through the fabric of his jacket. He was like a skeleton in a suit.

Kishida was not looking at Uesugi. *Are those eyes actually seeing anything?* Uesugi wondered. They were unfocused, staring off into the middle distance.

"There's this one rather bossy detective in this precinct," Uesugi began. "He insists that I'm the only person who can do this. That's why I'm here to interview you again. To be honest, I have no idea whether I'll succeed in getting you to speak. I'm not confident in my chances. Still, at least do me the favor of hearing me out. I can't do more than that."

Uesugi sipped some tea from his cup.

"I'm going to be fifty-five this year. I've been married twenty-one years. I was keen to have kids from the get-go, but we had trouble conceiving. It took my wife three years to get pregnant. When she had a baby boy the next year, I was jumping up and down for joy."

Although Kishida didn't seem to be listening, a subtle change came over his expression, and his eyebrows were twitching.

"Maybe it was because I was already middle-aged by the time he came along, but I adored the boy; I was infatuated. Even when I was on stakeouts, I'd call the house when the other guys were out of earshot so I could listen to my son saying words he'd just learned in that sweet little voice of his. I was the original doting dad. I knew I was being ridiculous, but I felt more proud than ashamed."

Again Kishida's expression seemed to change. From staring vacantly at the table in front of him, his eyes swam into focus, as if he was making an effort to see something.

"I adored my son. No one can deny that—but adoring someone and taking proper care of them are two very different things. If you want to take proper care of your child, you make the choices that will give them the best possible future. I couldn't do that. I was happy floating on cloud nine, thrilled to have someone to pour my love into."

Uesugi took another swig of his tea.

"Then, miracle of miracles, my little boy started growing up. Kids can't stay adorable bundles of cuteness forever. They start causing all sorts of problems. Most dads react by running away, taking refuge behind that convenient old pretext of 'being busy with work.' I know I did. When my wife tried to talk to me about our boy, I'd just blow up at her. I never made a serious effort to discuss his problems with her. If she criticized my parenting, I trotted out the line about 'already having one full-time job' and deftly shunted all the family's difficulties onto her shoulders. I wasn't overly concerned when she warned me that our son was hanging out with a bad crowd. 'It's just a phase that any normal, healthy kid goes through,' I told her. I was determined to look on the bright side. I was deceiving myself."

Kishida shot a glance at Uesugi. The instant their eyes met, the older man looked away.

"It happened three years ago. I was on standby at Metropolitan Police HQ in central Tokyo when a call came for me. It was a local cop. We'd worked a case together one time. Anyway, this guy says he'd picked up a kid who was just about to ride off on a motorbike without a helmet on, and that the kid was making a big song and dance about his dad being 'Detective Uesugi of TMPD Homicide.' The cop was calling to confirm that he was my kid. He gave me the details, and I confirmed that yes, the kid was my son. I was pretty shocked: riding without a helmet was bad, but worse still was that my son didn't have a driver's license to begin with. The cop asked me what he should do. I said I was really sorry, but could he see his way to turning a blind eye just this once?"

Uesugi's voice was getting croaky. He reached for his teacup, but his hand stopped in midair when he realized that the cup was empty.

"The cop did as I asked. Since he'd not actually caught my son *riding* the bike, he was able to send him home with just a warning. It was a huge relief. The boy had just got into a good high school and could have been expelled. It was only later that I realized what a disastrous judgment call I'd made. I should have been tough. I should have asked the cop to follow the rules and come down on him like a ton of bricks. Perhaps then . . ."

Uesugi's voice caught in his throat. He sucked in a couple of deep breaths.

"Of course, I gave the boy a good telling-off myself. I don't think that anything I said really registered with him. He could probably tell that I didn't really mean it. It was a week later that I got the news: my son had been killed in an accident on the expressway. He took a sharp curve at eighty miles per hour, lost control, and smashed into a wall. He still didn't have his license, of course. The bike was borrowed from a friend; it was the same one he'd been caught trying to ride without a helmet the week before. I later discovered that he'd been bragging to all his friends that he could get away with anything by throwing around the name of his 'big-shot detective' father."

Pulling himself upright in his chair, Uesugi looked at Kishida, who was half hunched over the table.

"My son did something wrong, and I tried to protect him. In fact, all I succeeded in doing was pushing him even farther down the wrong path. I failed both as a parent and as a cop. Parents have a duty to set their kids on the right path, even if being loathed is the only reward they get. If parents don't do it, who will? You committed murder, Mr. Kishida, and you're going to pay for your crime. But do you want to pay that price without even confronting the truth? Chances are that will only lead to more disasters down the road. Well?"

Kishida was trembling all over. As the trembling slowly increased in intensity, a groan burst from his lips. When he finally lifted his head, his eyes were red with tears.

"Tell me the truth," commanded Uesugi.

9.

For the first time in several weeks, the sky was a cloudless expanse of blue. As if the clear weather came with a penalty clause, though, the sidewalk radiated heat. By the time Uesugi reached the coffee shop, his back was drenched with sweat.

Detective Kaga was sitting at a table that overlooked the street. He was busy jotting something down on a napkin. He grunted hello as Uesugi came up.

"What are you adding up there?" asked Uesugi, sitting down opposite him. The napkin was covered in pen strokes.

"What this?" Kaga screwed the napkin into a ball with his fist. "It's the number of men going by with and without jackets. The number of people with jackets on has gone down."

Uesugi called the waitress and ordered an iced coffee.

"We've verified how much Katsuya Kishida stole from his employer. It was close to fifty million yen."

"Wow, definitely not peanuts," Kaga replied, looking rather bored.

It turned out that Yosaku Kishida hadn't been siphoning money to cover debts of his own. He had started embezzling money—reluctantly—when Katsuya, his son, came begging for his help. Katsuya had been embezzling money himself from the construction company where he worked and, with an audit imminent, was about to be found out.

"The incredible thing was that Katsuya had absolutely no idea how his father got his hands on all that money. He just thought that his dad had the money on hand. Astonishingly obtuse! Katsuya's wife was equally oblivious about her husband's embezzling. She seemed barely aware that their lifestyle was more lavish than normal."

Kaga said nothing. He was staring at the street beyond

the window. Uesugi followed his gaze to the signboard of a rice cracker shop on the far side of the street.

Uesugi's iced coffee arrived. He tossed it down without bothering to use the straw.

"There's something I've been wanting to ask you. When did you first zero in on Kishida's son?"

Kaga tilted his head quizzically.

"I never really 'zeroed in on him.'"

"You sure? I think you figured out early on that he was involved and deliberately chose me as your partner."

Kaga's head tilted even further over, to signal complete incomprehension.

"When a detective's as sharp as you, you can partner with anybody; it doesn't matter. You chose me, and I know why. You'd heard about what happened to my son, and you thought I'd be the perfect person to get Yosaku Kishida to open up. Am I right?"

That was certainly the way things had turned out. Uesugi was convinced that this precinct cop had stage-managed the whole saga from start to finish.

Kaga smiled amiably and gave a little shake of his head.

"You're giving me way too much credit."

"Why did you choose me, then?"

"Two reasons." Kaga held up a couple of fingers. "The first is that you were responsible for investigating Yosaku Kishida. If someone else had been in charge, I'd probably have worked with them instead. What I knew about your son was the second reason. I heard that you very nearly quit the force because of what happened to him. It was a terrible experience, but the more terrible the experiences we go through, the more we should try to apply them to the work we do as detectives. That's why I chose you as my partner."

Kaga looked at Uesugi with cool, detached eyes. Uesugi looked away, wiping the moisture drops off his glass with a fingertip.

"You talk like you know all about me. How much do you really know?"

"You know that I was right about you."

"Were you?" murmured Uesugi. He was tempted to fight back. *I know all about you*, he wanted to say. He still recalled the story he'd heard just before he was assigned to this task force.

Kaga had once been in the Tokyo Metropolitan Police Department's Homicide Division. He'd been demoted back to a precinct detective after being summoned to appear in court as a circumstantial witness in a murder case. The victim's family had made a formal complaint about the "investigator's inappropriate emotional involvement" having delayed the resolution of the case. (As a matter of fact, Kaga's efforts had made a decisive contribution to unraveling what was a very difficult case.)

In the end, though, Uesugi kept his mouth shut. Detective Kaga probably wasn't the kind of person to waste time wallowing in regret.

"Yosaku Kishida's trial will be starting any day now. It was all too brief, but thanks for everything." Uesugi stood up, putting the money for his coffee on the table.

"Let's do it again sometime. I can show you around the neighborhood."

"Maybe next time we can choose a cooler time of year?" replied Uesugi, as he headed for the exit.

Just then, a young girl came in from the street. She wore jeans and a T-shirt, and her hair was dyed brown and symmetrically cut. She made a beeline for Kaga.

"Goofing off again, Detective Kaga?"

"Absolutely not. I'm on patrol."

"Pull the other one. You'll never get promoted at this rate."

Kaga chuckled merrily.

"Want a banana juice? My treat."

"No thanks. I've got to come up with some new hairstyling ideas. I'll be seeing you."

The girl left the café, crossed the street, and went into the rice cracker shop.

"She's the daughter of the family that runs that place," said Kaga. "She's studying hairdressing."

Uesugi walked back to the table. "May I ask you one last question, Detective Kaga? What kind of man are you?"

Picking up a fan that was lying on the table, Kaga flicked it open and began fanning himself.

"Me? Nobody special. In this neighborhood, I'm just a newcomer."

Keigo Higashino is the bestselling and most widely read novelist in Japan. Several of his works have appeared in English translations, including *Malice* and *The Devotion of Suspect X,* which was a finalist for the Edgar Award and the Barry Award. He lives in Tokyo, Japan.